THE SUFFERING

DAVID SODERGREN

Cover art by Maciej Kamuda

Paperback ISBN: 978-1-917910-09-5

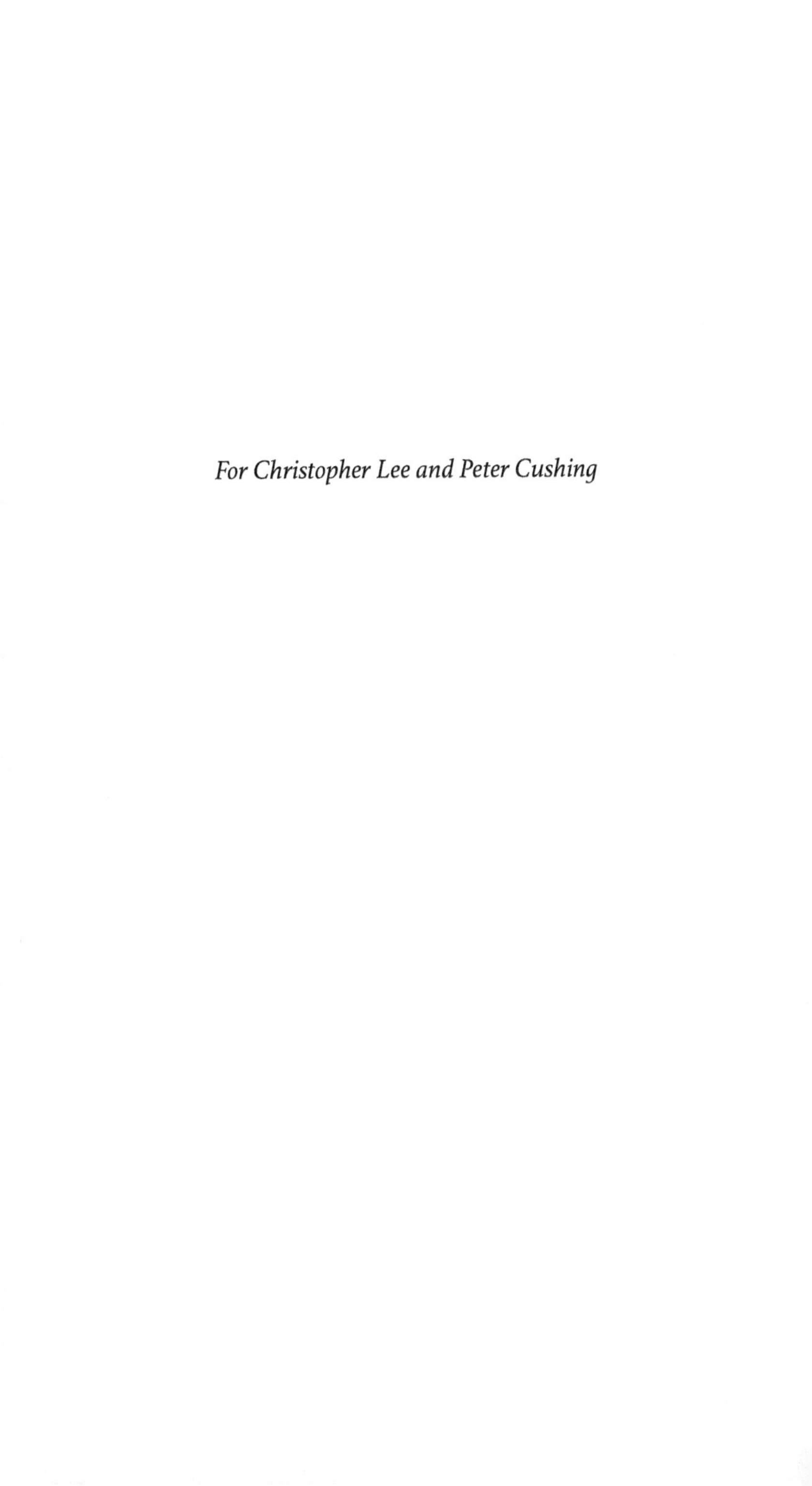

For Christopher Lee and Peter Cushing

"What cannot be cured by medicine is cured by the knife. What the knife cannot cure is cured with fire. And whatever this cannot cure must be considered incurable."

Hippocrates II

"Praised be You, my Lord, through our Sister Bodily Death, from whom no living man can escape."

Canticle of the Creatures
St Francis of Assisi

PART I

1

———

THE SANT'ARCANGEL CONVENT WAS ONE YEAR SHY OF ITS three-hundredth birthday when death came calling on a frigid November evening in 1896. Tucked away high atop a cliffside in Northern Italy's Apennine mountains, the sisters who dwelled there kept to themselves so devoutly that some residents of Cerbesca, the nearest village, were unaware even of the convent's existence.

To the godly sisters of Sant'Arcangel, this was ideal. Though they would never claim to pride themselves on their self-sufficiency — pride was, after all, a sin — most were content cloistered away far from the temptations of modern civilisation.

Most... but not all.

For the crumbling fortification housed women from all walks of life. From those who had chosen to devote their lives to God, to women who were there because they had no other choice. Some had been sold by desperate parents and relatives, while others had retreated there due to circumstances outwith their control. The convent was a refuge that offered solace, three meals a day, and a bed to sleep in, and for a woman with nowhere left to turn, that was sufficient.

In fact, with their differing ages and backgrounds, and varying degrees of faith, it was fair to say only one truth united the nuns of Sant'Arcangel.

The women may not all have been *born* within its hallowed walls... but all were expected to die there.

~

And so it was that on a crisp winter's day, with its chilly air and brittle grass and low, weak sun, Sister Ursula found herself deep in thought in the convent gardens, perched atop a rock in a manner unbefitting that of a nun.

Like a bird of prey, she gazed out over the untamed landscape. The sky was darkening, but if she squinted hard enough, she could make out the wisps of smoke from Cerbesca's chimneys, the village nestled snugly in the valley far below.

It was a six-hour horse ride down the rugged mountain track through forests and fields, a lengthy journey she had undertaken only once, and in reverse, on the day her father had dropped her off at the convent and bid a gruff farewell. She had been seven years old then, and was now, she thought, twenty-two. Time was difficult to keep track of in a place where, outside of the day-to-day rituals, time itself held little meaning.

As she often did on those long winter evenings, Ursula allowed her mind to wander unbidden, pondering the direction her life could have taken had she been offered the chance at a secular existence. Her fantasies were ill-defined though, for Ursula's understanding of the world outside of Sant'Arcangel was based entirely on two diverse sources; the books in the convent library, and hearsay from her notoriously unreliable friend Sister Isabelle.

"What's it like down there?" Ursula asked, shielding her eyes from the dying rays of the sun with blackberry-stained fingers.

Sister Isabelle popped a fresh berry into her mouth and chewed thoughtfully. For every one of the sweet fruits she plucked from the hedge and placed in her basket, another ended up in her tummy, which explained why Ursula's basket was overflowing while Isabelle's was barely half-full.

"Sister Ursula, anyone would think you were *born* in Sant'Arcangel."

Ursula giggled and clambered higher, using the worn grooves in the rock as foot-holds. "I may as well have been," she said, as she stood upright, battling a gale that billowed her tunic around her knees, exposing her long woollen socks.

A storm brewed on the horizon. The worst of winter was fast approaching, and with it would come the snow and the rain and the miserable, freezing fog, cutting off the convent from the outside world for four months of hardship endurable only through constant communion with God.

At least, that's what the Mother Superior insisted.

Ursula was not so sure. The older she got, the more she found the barren winters and extreme isolation tested her faith in her vocation. She loved God, naturally, and wished to praise him... but sometimes she wondered if there were other, more immediate ways to help people. Inspired by the infrequent visits of Cerbesca's resident doctor, an Englishman by the name of Dr Joseph Franco, along with her close perusal of the library's medical texts, she often wiled away the hours dreaming of caring for the sick and tending to those who were physically ailing rather than spiritually bereft. What good were the sisters of Sant'Arcangel actually doing sequestered up in the mountains? Surely devoting her life to God didn't mean hiding away from—

A berry pinged off her nose, and she glanced down to meet Sister Isabelle's keen gaze.

"Have you *really* never left the convent?" the woman asked, as if she hadn't just thrown fruit at Ursula's face.

"Never. And please don't waste the berries."

"I won't," said Isabelle, and ate another.

"Stop!" laughed Ursula. "They're supposed to last us all season!"

"And they will. We have enough berries and potatoes and cabbage in the storeroom to last a hundred winters, especially with Sister Giovanna's measly portions." Isabelle peered into her nearly empty basket. "You should give me some of your berries," she frowned. "Mother Superior will think I've been eating all mine."

"And she would be correct."

Isabelle's melodic laughter lilted across the valley. "Well, that's between you, me, and God, isn't it?" She placed another berry on her tongue. "And I know *he's* not going to tell."

"That's blasphemy," said Ursula, though she was used to such antics. Taking the Lord's name in vain was the least of her friend's sins. "You're incorrigible, Sister Isabelle, and I beg you not to take that as a compliment. Now kindly help me down, or I'll be stuck on this rock all winter."

Isabelle offered her hand. "Wouldn't that be delightful?" she mused as she helped Ursula onto the grass. "In the spring, when the snow thaws, we'll find you here frozen like a statue of the Virgin Mary, and we shall fall to our knees in honour of Ursula, patron saint of standing on boulders and freezing to death."

"You and your fanciful notions," smiled Ursula, playfully swatting her whimsical companion on the arm. They stood together in silent admiration of the view as the wind howled across the mountain. High above, black clouds amassed, and Ursula knew in her heart that today would be the last time she saw the village this year. She supposed she shouldn't complain. Her quarters were located at the rear of the convent, which meant her window overlooked the mountains in all their majesty.

Regardless of the season, that view always refreshed her soul. During the summer, she watched the grass grow tall and green, while eagles soared above serene lakes and ibexes defied gravity by scaling the sheer cliff-faces. And over the winter months, purest white snow blanketed the mountains, their peaks lost in the low cloud, the sun occasionally muscling through to sparkle off the glistening, frosted rocks.

Ursula liked to imagine the vista was a teasing glimpse of the bounteous glories awaiting her — she hoped and prayed — in heaven.

Still, she had been gazing at that same view most of her life. Wouldn't it be nice to experience something different, even for a short while? Buildings that weren't convents, and people who weren't nuns. It was hard to believe such people even existed! And what about men? In all her time here, she had seen precisely four of them.

Other than Dr Franco and his assistant Henrik, who visited twice a year, there had been a lost traveller seeking shelter and a lusty shepherd whom the Mother Superior had chased away with a broom when she caught him lurking in the convent washroom.

Ursula sighed.

There *had* to be more to life than this.

"I really would love to visit Cerbesca someday," she said, her smile at odds with her melancholy heart.

"You, my beloved sister," said Isabelle, "would have palpitations the moment you set foot in Cerbesca."

"Whatever do you mean?"

Isabelle sauntered around her in a wide circle, swinging her basket and causing the few berries she had picked to tumble out and roll across the grass. "It's not like Sant'Arcangel down there, my dear, *sweet* Sister Ursula. In Cerbesca, godless men roam the streets with lustful eyes and fire blazing in their loins."

Ursula was not to be dissuaded. "Licentious behaviour is to be expected of uncivilised men, from what you've told me."

"And what of the uncivilised women?" Isabelle smiled slyly. "When it comes to drinking and smoking and blasphemy, they're as bad as the men!"

Ursula gasped. "Speak not such falsehoods!"

Resuming her slow circling, Isabelle deliberately bumped her shoulder against Ursula. She lowered her voice. "And in the tavern, late at night, the barmaids flaunt their chests in dresses cut down to their *nipples.*"

Ursula's cheeks flushed with embarrassment. She loved her sister in Christ, but Isabelle always knew how to make her squirm. "You shouldn't speak of such prurient matters."

"We've all got nipples, Sister Ursula." Isabelle raised her eyebrows. "Even you, I should imagine."

"I... well, that's hardly the point. There are some subjects a woman of God should never discuss."

"Like nipples?"

"Indeed. From now on, nipples are forbidden as a topic of conversation."

"Well, I'm glad I know," Isabelle said, then muttered, "But clearly no one told the barmaids of Cerbesca."

Ursula resumed her berry-picking. "May we speak of more pleasant affairs?"

"You asked what it was like out there, and I'm only telling you."

"Yes, but I didn't ask about," — she glanced left and right to make sure nobody was listening nearby — *"nipples*. I wished to hear stories of the people. What they look like, what they do, what they wear."

Isabelle took a handful of berries from Ursula's basket and placed them in her own. "Oh, the women in the cities wear the most *splendid* garments! Frocks made from flowing satin and delicate lace, in hues of green and red and blue."

"Sinful colours," chided Ursula.

"Yes, so *wonderfully* sinful!" Isabelle stared off into the distance. "I think that's what I miss most about the real world. Not the food, or the people, or even the freedom." She smiled wistfully. "All the beautiful dresses I used to wear."

"I'm surprised. I thought the thing you missed most would be..."

"What?" asked Isabelle, adopting a guileless tone that did not suit her.

"I know you understand me."

"Not at all, Ursula. Pray tell, what is it you think I miss the most from my time before the convent?"

Ursula's cheeks burned red. "The... oh please, Sister Isabelle, don't force me to say it out loud!"

"There's no one around, Sister Ursula. I'm sure you can speak the word without bursting into hellfire."

Ursula glanced over the hedge at the well-trodden pathway towards the convent. The rundown stone walls cast a long shadow over the distant figure of Sister Giulia, who was chopping wood by the gardener's cottage, far out of earshot.

She leaned closer to Isabelle, and whispered, "The *s-e-x*."

Isabelle smiled maternally. "Oh innocent one, I still get plenty of *that* in the convent."

"Sister Isabelle, please!" Ursula shook her head. "You know very well that the s-e-x is a sin for a nun."

"I do." Isabelle plucked a ripe berry from her basket and raised it to Ursula's mouth, sliding the small fruit inside and letting her fingers linger on Ursula's plump lips. "But sinning is such fun. You really must try it sometime." Then she giggled and spun and looked to the sky. As she did so, Ursula removed the berry from her mouth and placed it back in the basket where it belonged.

"You're going straight to hell," she said with a wry smile.

"Perhaps," said Isabelle. "But don't you find it so boring here? Get up, pray, go to mass, pray, clean the floors and peel the potatoes until supper, pray... I know that's why we're here, but I think a little sin is good for the soul. It gives you something to atone for." She faced Ursula, her eyes gleaming. "And anyway, I'm not the *only* one who indulges in carnality every now and again."

"I know. It takes two people to sin the way *you* like to. Luckily, what yourself and Sister Maria get up to behind closed doors is none of my business."

"It's not just us!" insisted Isabelle. "What about Sister Gertrude? Nobody's seen *her* since Dr Franco arrived yesterday, because, from what I hear, his handsome young assistant has been examining her in *great* detail."

Ursula crossed herself. "Sister Gertrude doesn't even believe in God, and it's only a matter of time before the Mother Superior finds out what she and Henrik are up to and banishes her." She gave Isabelle her solemnest stare. "You and Maria should be careful too."

Isabelle shrugged. "I think I'm too sociable to be a nun. I used to throw the most wicked parties back when..." She trailed off, a yearning sadness dawning across her soft features. The expression made her look younger. She looked anxiously at the angry clouds, and said, "We should finish up. That storm is not getting any further away."

Ursula nodded, disappointed that Isabelle had halted her nostalgic reverie. She knew little of her fellow sister, other than that the woman had fled to the convent in exile from a wealthy family, and enjoyed spending her evenings in the affectionate company of Sister Maria. But she rarely spoke of her past, and Ursula preferred not to pry, so the mystery of Isabelle's background would have to, for now, remain unsolved.

With a pregnant silence in the air, they resumed their fruit picking, wandering amongst the hedges and filling their baskets — and in Isabelle's case, her belly — with the delicious berries. The vegetable patches and medicinal herb gardens had been thoroughly raided over the previous couple of days, and all that remained to be picked were the mushrooms that grew near the cliffs.

By the end of the day, none would remain, for once the snow started to fall, the gardens would become inaccessible. Oftentimes, large snowdrifts blocked the front door for weeks on end, and lay as high as the lower-level windows. Ursula shivered at the memory of winters past, so cold and so desolate. Inevitably, her thoughts turned to fond fantasies of living in Cerbesca and helping the venerable Dr Franco heal the sick. She had wished for a private communion with the doctor to discuss the possibility of leaving the monastic life to assist him, but he had been so busy since his arrival that she hadn't found an opportune moment.

Should she visit him in the old gardener's cottage where he and Henrik were staying? It hardly felt appropriate, and yet the prospect of another long winter here in the mountains—

"Ow!"

Ursula turned sharply towards Sister Isabelle.

The woman cradled her hand, wearing an expression of profound confusion. "I cut myself."

"On a thorn?"

"I... I don't know. I don't think so."

The wind picked up, rustling the hedges around them. Over yonder, the thin trees at the edge of the forest blew at an angle.

Clutching her basket, Ursula jogged to her sister. "Here, let me see."

Always keen to test her medical knowledge, she inspected Isabelle's hand. The skin on her fingers and palm was reddish-purple from all the squashed fruit, and dark blood oozed from a cut on her index finger. "It's nothing serious," said Ursula. "But we'll let Dr Franco have a look to be certain."

The minor cut was unworthy of attention, but Ursula knew this might be her only chance to speak to the doctor, and she had to take it.

A hedge trembled nearby. Then another, closer this time.

Ursula stole a wary glance. Wolves were known to roam the mountains, and though they seldom ventured beyond the forest barrier, caution was always advisable.

Isabelle, unaware of any impending danger, sucked the blood from her finger. "It's barely a scratch."

"Let's go anyway," said Ursula. The rustling hedges were making her nervous. "Dr Franco will be leaving soon, and he may have some salve for you."

"I shan't bother him over such a trifling injury."

Ursula swore she heard footsteps on the frozen grass.

"Do you hear that?" she asked quietly.

"Hear what?"

She laid her basket down. "It sounds like—"

Then the hedges parted, and before Ursula had a chance even to scream, a hand, caked with blood and grime, clamped shut on her arm. A young girl emerged, clad only in a white tunic, the fabric ragged and torn and marked with bloodstains of the deepest red. Choking, the girl opened her mouth and expelled a clod of crumbling earth, before collapsing against Ursula and sliding through her grasp like a sack of rags.

The heavens opened, and the first snowfall of the year began in earnest. Great white flakes swirled through the air, dissolving on the prone body of the unmoving, blood-soaked girl.

Winter, it seemed, had chosen the perfect fleeting moment of unexpected terror to arrive at Sant'Arcangel.

2

———

Sister Ursula blinked the snowflakes from her eyes and knelt by the crumpled girl, pressing two fingers to her neck. The flesh was cold and hard, but as she slid her fingers lower, she located a pulse, like the faint tremors of a fish thrashing beneath an icy pond.

"She's breathing."

Ursula's initial shock seemed to be wearing off, and in its place arose a queasy mixture of excitement and dread, the latter of which stemmed from the grisly wound on the girl's back. Something had torn her open. An animal? No, there were no teeth or claw marks. Only a single straight line where the flesh had parted under duress.

This was not the work of wolves, or a bear, or anything natural. The girl had been attacked with a bladed weapon.

Only a human could have done this.

Ursula rolled the girl over and hooked her arms under the shoulders. "Quick, help me get her inside."

Isabelle responded without hesitation. She looped her arms around the girl's ankles, and together the nuns raised her off the ground. She sagged between them, surprisingly heavy for such a slight thing. However, a lifetime spent sweeping floors and chopping firewood and peeling potatoes had strengthened both women's muscles, and they hoisted the unconscious girl into a comfortable position and carried her along the muddy, snow-speckled track towards Sant'Arcangel.

Ursula peered through the snowfall, seeking Sister Giulia. Her gaze found only the abandoned axe embedded in the wood-chopping stump. There was no one around to help them, and the convent had never looked further away. And yet, a small glimmer of hope presented itself as they trudged past the stables. She heard the neighing of horses from within, and saw Dr Franco's coach waiting outside the gardener's cottage. The doctor had not yet left for Cerbesca.

"Thank you, God," she whispered.

A strong gust thudded between her shoulder blades, knocking her off-balance. She stumbled, but did not release the girl. It struck again, this time bringing her to her knees.

"What's wrong?" asked Isabelle, her voice fraught with tension.

"Nothing." Ursula struggled to her feet. "Keep going, we're almost there." They resumed their walk, though Ursula was unable to resist a look over her shoulder. It was impossible, she knew, but she could have sworn that two very real hands had physically shoved her.

The idea frightened her, but she dug the heels of her sandals into the crispy ground and kept going, travelling as fast as possible while bearing in mind that Sister Isabelle was making the perilous journey backwards.

Wind whipped Ursula's skull. Once more she glanced back, and saw nothing but the silhouetted hedges swaying within the whiteout.

"Her legs," said Isabelle.

Ursula turned to her. The colour had drained from Isabelle's face.

"Look at her *legs*."

The hem of the girl's tunic had slipped to her waist, revealing a deep gash in her bare, pink thigh, just below her—

Ursula averted her gaze, focusing on the wound. The lesion was encrusted with coagulated blood, which surprised her. These injuries were anything but fresh. How long had the poor soul wandered the barren mountain before stumbling upon the convent? What torment she must have faced! And yet, guided by God's benevolent hand, she had found her way to a holy sanctuary, where she would receive aid and compassion. If greater proof existed of the Lord's miraculous nature, then Ursula had yet to see it.

"Hurry," she said. Already, soft snow coated the ground. The bitter flakes nipped cruelly at her exposed skin like so many insect bites, and when she glanced to her right, a rolling grey mist obscured Cerbesca.

They passed the axe in the tree stump, the handle sheathed in frost, and stepped into the shadow of the two-storey convent.

"Watch your feet," said Ursula as they approached the stairs that led to the solid oak door.

Isabelle checked her bearings, shuffling awkwardly up the three steps and pushing the heavy door with her bottom. It swung open on ancient hinges, and for the last time, a powerful blast of wind slammed heavily into Ursula's back with the force of a punch. She yelped in pain, and then, mercifully, they were in the entrance hall.

"Put her down there," she instructed, motioning to the threadbare rug in the centre of the room, upon which countless nuns had wiped their dirty sandals over the centuries. It wasn't exactly sanitary, but it was preferable to the cold stone floor.

Gently, they laid the motionless figure on the rug.

Ursula closed the door as Isabelle tugged the girl's tunic over her thighs to preserve her modesty, inadvertently laying bare the full extent of her injuries. In addition to the wounds on her back and leg, a deep cut had been hacked into her stomach, visible through the wide, bloody tear in her clothing.

"Fetch Dr Franco," said Ursula. When her friend didn't move, she shouted, *"Now!"*

Isabelle struggled unsteadily to her feet and scurried from the room, her sandals slapping rhythmically against the hard floor. The sound faded, leaving in its wake the whispered crackle of flickering candles.

Ursula checked the girl's pulse again. Faint, but present. Her pink legs were raw from the cold, the soles of her feet scratched and torn and, unlike the rest of her wounds, coated in a layer of fresh, wet blood.

Ursula held the girl's freezing hand and rubbed it. As she waited for Isabelle to return with Dr Franco, she glanced around the entrance hall. With its tall, arched ceiling and tasteful paintings, it was one of the more attractive rooms in the convent, designed to create a good first impression in the unlikely event of an unannounced visit from the Pope. Despite this, Ursula had never felt comfortable in the hall thanks to the imposing presence of a life-size wooden Jesus attached to a huge cross with real nails. He dominated the room, and the light from the wrought-iron candelabras in all four corners played across his impassive face, making the carving seem alive.

Ursula stood. At her feet, the trembling girl shivered, and a small plume of steam escaped her cracked blue lips.

"I'll be right back," said Ursula. "I shan't leave the room, I promise."

She walked to the doorway and peered into the darkness, glancing both ways down the lower-level corridor. Unlike in the entrance hall, the evening candles had not yet been lit, and it was painfully dark.

"Isabelle?" she called into the void. *"Dr Franco?"*

No response. Where were they? Tapping her foot nervously, Ursula looked back at the girl, then to the open front door.

How curious.

She was convinced she'd closed it.

Through the doorway, the snow swirled, spilling over the threshold and into the hall. Ursula crossed the room, and as she reached for the door handle, a sudden rush of air stole her breath and forced her back several steps. The door burst fully open, slamming against the interior wall with an ear-splitting crash as a gust of wind swept around the entrance hall like a cyclone, extinguishing each candle one-by-one. The wooden Jesus rocked violently back and forth, and a painting of the Virgin Mary dropped from its hanging and landed face down, cracking the frame.

On the rug, the girl's shabby tunic billowed. Ursula tried to fight her way across the room, but the wind resisted, forcing her back against the wall and pinning her to the freezing stone. A phantom gale battered her face, knocking her head left and right and not allowing her to scream. All she could do was watch helplessly as the girl's tunic rose, revealing blood-caked wounds and the dark patch of hair between her legs. She moaned, she whimpered, she kicked out, the tunic shifting abnormally... and then, all at once, the wind died down to nothing. The clothing draped back into place across the girl's thighs, the door swung shut, and all was quiet once more.

Ursula slid down the wall, frightened and confused. Unable to stand, she crawled on her hands and knees to the girl, certain that any moment now, Isabelle and Dr Franco would enter, bringing with them a welcoming sense of normality. But as she listened, she heard no shouts or frantic footsteps. Nothing but the dying strains of the wind and the anguished thump of her own heart.

"The doctor will be here soon," she said, her voice quivering as she discretely flattened the girl's tunic, unable to forget the wholly unnatural way it had risen and bulged, almost as if some invisible force had been under there with her.

No.

She wouldn't even *think* such a thing. The very idea was preposterous. They were alone in the room, and had been since Isabelle left. Fear and confusion were responsible for the uneasy sensation in her gut, not some wraith or apparition. It was all in her mind.

Wasn't it?

Ursula gripped the girl's hand and started to cry.

She couldn't help herself. The tears had to come out.

Because no matter how hard she tried to convince herself that everything was normal, and that her sense of foreboding was ill-placed, she could not shake the feeling that some sinister entity had followed them inside the convent... and decided to stay.

3

———

Dr Henrik Persson was not a religious man.

Raised as a Pietist by his Swedish parents, he had abandoned religion the day he turned eighteen, turning his attention instead to his own personal holy trinity: medicine, gymnastics, and women, though not necessarily in that order.

These passions he had pursued with an unwavering enthusiasm, throwing himself into gymnastic training while poring over medical textbooks. He studied the art of healing under some of the finest minds in Europe, and the art of love-making under, on top of, and behind some of the continent's most beautiful women.

At age twenty, his promising gymnastic career was cut short due to a back injury obtained while overindulging in his fondness for the opposite sex, when the bed containing all three energetic participants had broken, and Henrik had ended up at the bottom of the pile. Luckily, he was a man who saw the best in everything, and losing one love enabled him to focus on — and excel at — the field of medicine.

All of which is a long-winded way of saying that, as

someone with no deity to answer to, Henrik was utterly unashamed to be lying naked in a nun's bed, while the equally undressed nun rested her delicate head upon his chest.

The sweat on their bodies had cooled, and as the snow pattered against the windowpane, he longed for the warmth of a stiff drink. In previous years, he had managed to smuggle Sister Gertrude out her window and into the gardener's cottage, where he and Franco stayed on their twice-yearly visits. There, while Franco slumbered in his coach wrapped in sheepskin blankets, he and Gertrude whiled away the evenings making love while a fire roared in the hearth.

But not this time.

The Mother Superior, he feared, had grown suspicious of their liaisons. Wherever he went, watchful eyes gazed mistrustfully at him from the most unexpected places. Only Dr Franco's sudden decision to hold a seminar on basic first aid had allowed Henrik and Gertrude to steal some time together. He was eternally grateful to his mentor for the favour, and would make it up to him by paying for dinner once they returned to Cerbesca.

Speaking of which...

"I ought to get dressed," he said, stroking his lover's flaxen hair.

Gertrude opened her eyes with a restless flutter. "So soon? Please don't leave me with all these miserable nuns."

"I have no choice in the matter. The storm has begun, and if Franco and I don't go now, we risk being trapped up here all winter with your so-called *miserable nuns.*"

"I dream of such happenings. Of you, my Henrik, confined to the convent 'til spring and spending your every waking moment here in my bed." She laughed. "I even prayed for it to happen."

"A nun *praying?*" he grinned. "How novel."

"It was the first honest prayer I ever spoke."

"And if it were to come true, would you then believe in the existence of an almighty being?"

"No. Never." She caressed his firm stomach. "But I'd make love to you every night, and it would be wonderful."

He stretched, watching the snowflakes dot the window-pane and turn to criss-crossing dribbles of water. "Sadly, it is with a heavy heart that I must return to Cerbesca, where I shall spend my days assisting Franco, and my nights pining for you, my beloved."

She sighed, her breath pleasingly warm on his chest. "And there's nothing I can do to make you stay?"

"If only. Alas, I regret... *oh.*"

Gertrude's hand brushed his thigh, sliding between his legs. "Pardon me, Doctor. Did I interrupt you?"

Words momentarily deserted Henrik. He closed his eyes as his penis hardened at her exquisite touch. "You," he said, "are a terrible, *terrible* nun."

"The worst in Sant'Arcangel." She took him fully in her hand. "Some might even call me the worst nun in all the world."

"Such wisdom cannot be... mmmhhh... argued with."

Gertrude shifted onto her knees, positioning her legs on either side of Henrik. She arched her back and guided him inside her. "Then won't you stay? Just one more night?"

He wanted to. Good grief, he wanted to. But if the storm outside was any indication, the window for safe passage down the mountain grew ever-narrower. Regardless of how teasingly erotic the idea of being trapped with Gertrude until springtime was, the villagers of Cerbesca needed them.

Winter in the mountains was harsh and unforgiving, and as dearly as he loved Gertrude, he could not forsake those who relied on him.

And so he decided, as Gertrude leaned over and kissed him, her nipples trailing across his chest, that he had better make this last time count.

He rolled the nun onto her back, pinning her arms above her head the way she liked. They locked eyes.

"I love you," said Gertrude. "My handsome doctor."

"And I love you, my awful nun."

They made love as quietly as their untamed passions would allow, then lay in each other's arms for what would be the final time that year. Henrik would not return with Dr Franco until March of 1897, when they would collect the bodies of those nuns who failed to make it through the winter. Rare was the season with no casualties, and it tortured Henrik to imagine his beloved might one day number amongst the fallen. More than anything, he wished for her hand in marriage. But would she leave the convent for him? He was too afraid to ask. What if she rejected him? She spoke of love, but what if she only saw his occasional visits as brief distractions to stave off the monotony of convent life?

It would break his heart.

For Sister Gertrude had, in the finest possible manner, ruined him. Since the day they met, no other had mattered, and for the first time in his life, Henrik had remained effortlessly faithful to one woman.

What a damnable pity she was a nun.

"You will return in the spring?" Gertrude whispered as he reluctantly slid from her grasp and swung his legs out of the bed.

"As surely as the thaw follows the snowfall."

He dressed quickly, for the cold seemed to infest the convent walls, then watched as Gertrude stepped into her chunky thigh-high socks and fastened her underskirt. He couldn't help imagining her in those frilly undergarments he had seen in a Parisian shopfront a few years prior.

"I wish I could stay," he said. "You do know that, don't you?"

She turned to him, gauging his sincerity. "I know."

"And I shall return as hastily as the elements permit."

"That, I also know."

She affixed her scapular and wimple and placed a small wooden cross around her neck. Once she was ready, he took her in his arms for one last kiss. She tasted as sweet as she looked, and when they parted, he saw she was crying.

"I'll count the days," she said. "I'll count the minutes, too. Even the—"

"Dr Franco! Dr Persson!"

Together, they looked to the door. Whoever was calling was making their way down the hallway, their panicked cries increasing in volume. Henrik removed the wooden chair he had used to prop the door shut, straightened his tie, and stepped into the corridor.

A young nun — Sister Elisabeth, he thought — was running as fast as her short legs would carry her.

"I'm here, child," called Henrik. "Pray tell, what is the emergency?"

Sister Elisabeth skidded to a stop, then doubled over with her hands on her knees, panting. Henrik didn't think he'd ever seen a nun run before.

"A body," she said between stolen gasps. "They found... a body... outside."

"Who did?"

"I don't... know."

"And where is the body now? Are they still alive? Answer me, dammit!"

The nun looked up at him, her cheeks red from exertion. "Entrance hall," she said, and leaned against the wall to catch her breath.

Henrik nodded. "I'll be right there," he said, and ducked back into Gertrude's quarters to fetch his coat. He felt her hand grip his shoulder.

"It appears your prayer worked," he said grimly, and looked into her eyes. "Perhaps I'll be staying a little longer after all."

4

———

WHEN HENRIK ARRIVED IN THE ENTRANCE HALL, DR FRANCO was already present. He could not *see* his colleague thanks to the crowd of nuns encircling him, but the older man's shouted instructions boomed through the convent like thunderclaps.

"Ladies," Franco entreated, "I am not *asking* you to leave the room. I am *telling* you. Begone, please! I need to work, and this girl needs space to breathe."

The nuns, unused to the raised baritone voices of men, grudgingly shuffled backwards, then began to disperse.

Henrik struggled through the sea of bodies, fighting against the tide.

"The Mother Superior will hear about this," one woman grumbled as she sailed past him and out of the room, wringing her hands.

He caught sight of Franco kneeling by a fragile young thing in a blood-stained white dress. Two nuns had stayed behind on Franco's orders, and Henrik recognised them as Sisters Ursula and Isabelle.

He rushed to the doctor's side. "What's happening?"

"This girl was found outside," said Franco. "She's breathing, but unresponsive. There's a lot of blood, yet I wonder; does anything strike you as odd?"

Typical Franco, turning a potentially life-or-death situation into part of Henrik's unending education. He had been like this ever since the pair had met in a tavern in Frankfurt twelve years ago, a chance meeting that had resulted in Franco taking Henrik under his wing. From there, they had travelled across Europe, eventually settling in Cerbesca so that Franco could indulge his love of hillwalking between saving people's lives.

Henrik examined the girl, parting the gap in her clothing and inspecting the gash in her stomach. "It's not a fresh wound." He looked closer. "Far from it, in fact."

"Indeed. The patient was injured some time ago. What else can you tell me?"

Sister Ursula spoke up. "She's had no treatment."

"Go on," said Franco, shifting his gaze to the young nun.

Ursula nervously clutched the wooden cross around her neck. "The... the wounds appear infected."

"Very good," Franco said. He looked at Henrik. "Try to keep up, dear boy."

Henrik scratched behind his ear. A thin sheen of post-coital perspiration clung to him, and he happily let Ursula take the lead while his mind was elsewhere.

"And look at her feet," the nun continued. "They're cracked and bleeding. I think she's been running for some time with these injuries."

Unhurried, Franco struck a match and lit his pipe. "Indeed she has. A surprisingly long time. So, what to do?"

She swallowed. "Disinfect the wounds?"

"And then what?"

"Ummm... stitch them up?"

Franco nodded. "A wise course of action. We must—"

"But what caused these marks?" Ursula interrupted. "It was no animal."

"An axe, most likely," said Henrik. He looked to Franco for approval.

"Appears that way. Too wide to be a knife, too blunt to be a sword." He turned to the nuns. "Where did you say you found her?"

"She came from the forest," said Isabelle. "She frightened us terribly."

"So she was on her feet?"

"Yes."

Franco nodded thoughtfully. "And did she say anything?"

"She tried to," said Ursula, "but her mouth was full of dirt."

"Dirt?" Henrik felt a chill wriggle through his bones. "It sounds like witchcraft."

"Witchcraft?" Franco scoffed. "This is the nineteenth century, Henrik, not the Middle Ages."

"True, but some of those mountain folk are—"

"A discussion for another time." Franco puffed on his pipe. "We need to take this girl somewhere warmer and more comfortable for surgery. My dear nuns, you know this building better than I. Any suggestions?"

"You can use my cell," Ursula volunteered. "It's above the kitchen, and the heat from the fire rises. It's one of the warmest rooms in the convent."

"That'll do splendidly," said Franco. "Sisters, run along and prepare the room. Henrik, fetch my bag from the coach." He glanced out the door at the worsening storm. "We have to be quick if we wish to leave this godforsaken mountain before springtime."

Ursula gasped at his language.

"I do apologise, ladies," he said, and smiled. "Sometimes I forget myself. I'm sure your God has not forsaken *you*."

Henrik buttoned his coat and braved the snow. Already it lay an inch deep, and he took each step carefully on his short journey to the coach.

He passed the stables and looked in on the horses, then retrieved Franco's bag and trudged back with the white powder crunching beneath his soles. Visibility was down to fifty yards, with worse yet to come. God, they should have left by now. Waiting until morning was not an option, for once the snow started to fall, it would not stop.

He entered the convent and kicked his snowy boots against the doorframe. The nuns' quarters were off-limits to the doctors. Usually, Henrik and Franco sat in the rarely used visitors' room behind steel bars, and spoke to the sisters only under the supervision of the abbess. But with a young girl's life hanging in the balance, there was no time for such trivialities.

He headed left in search of Sister Ursula's quarters. She had said her room was above the kitchen, which he knew to be in the east wing beside the refectory. The corridor was long, with a single window at the far end, and numerous smaller hallways branching off to the right. With little decoration other than scattered crosses and statuettes, the convent interior made Henrik think of the labyrinth from Greek mythology.

He located a staircase and jogged up the well-worn steps. Emerging on the upper level, he spotted Sister Isabelle pacing back and forth. She waved him onwards.

"This way!"

Henrik followed Isabelle into Ursula's cell, where the unconscious girl lay on the bed. As promised, the small room was marginally less chilly than the rest of the convent. It was certainly a more agreeable temperature than Gertrude's lodgings.

"Ah, perfect timing," said Franco. He took his bag from Henrik and rummaged inside. "She's got lesions on her stomach, back, and thigh. Which reminds me," he added, looking at Ursula and Isabelle, "I need water, as much extra bedding as you can find, and several clean rags."

Ursula nodded, her fingers fidgeting with her cross. "When we return, will she be... unclothed?"

"Of course she will," Franco replied curtly. He winced. "Of course, I forgot your religion forbids you from seeing human beings in their natural state. In which case, knock upon arrival, and furnish Henrik with what I require. Now go!"

The nuns left the room, and Franco shook his head. He produced a pair of scissors from his bag and used them to slice through the girl's tunic.

"Make sure those two stay outside whilst we're operating," he said to Henrik, as he laid out a reel of surgical thread and a needle. "This procedure is going to be most unpleasant."

5

———

Ursula and Isabelle split the doctor's tasks between them.

While Isabelle headed to the well to fill a bucket with water, Ursula fetched armfuls of bedding from the storeroom on the ground floor, fending off probing questions from her fellow sisters about what was happening and who the girl was and where had she been found and was she going to die and... and...

She couldn't blame them for their inquisitiveness, for it wasn't every day something interesting happened in Sant'Arcangel, and she promised to explain all once she had performed her important duties for Dr Franco.

Was it her imagination, or had he seemed impressed by her knowledge in the entrance hall? The idea thrilled her, and quite honestly, she could not recall the last time she had felt that particular emotion. Excitement, in the hallowed opinion of the Mother Superior, carried the risk of sin, which was why she expected the nuns to thrive on routine and mundanity.

And yet, as Ursula raced up the stairs with her footsteps

reverberating off the walls, she was struck by a revelation. Perhaps Sister Isabelle was right after all?

Sinning *was* fun.

She arrived at her quarters to find Isabelle peering through a crack in the door.

"Sister Isabelle, really!" Ursula hissed, and the woman turned to her, ushering her onwards.

"He's sewing her up!" she whispered incredulously. "Like she's a torn blanket!"

"I don't wish to know," Ursula replied, which was entirely untrue. If she hoped to work in the medical profession, she would need to become accustomed to such gruesome acts. She raised a fist to knock and announce her return... and then, with Isabelle's stare burning into the back of her head, she peeked through the thin gap.

The girl lay on Ursula's bed. She was naked, her ribcage visible through the bruised, discoloured skin. Crimson rivers flowed down her side as Dr Franco laboured over her, carefully piercing a curved needle through her flesh.

It was fascinating to see, and Ursula was surprised to discover the sight neither shocked nor repulsed her.

You could be in there. You could help.

But not in her current capacity. As a nun, she was forbidden from being in the same room as an unclothed person. She shouldn't even be looking!

Dr Franco lifted the needle, pulling the thread through and drawing the skin—

Isabelle thumped her fist against the door, and shouted, "Ursula's here!"

Ursula leapt back and fixed her sister with an angry stare. Isabelle, being Isabelle, only laughed.

She heard heavy boots stride across the floor, and then the door opened.

"Did you bring the bedding?" asked Henrik.

Ursula nodded and held the bundle out to him. Unable to help herself, she glanced over his shoulder at the girl. She had never seen a naked person before — the nuns wore clothes even when washing themselves — and nor had she ever seen so much blood.

"Will she survive?" she asked.

"She'll be fine," Dr Franco answered without looking up, his pipe fixed between his teeth. "Now hurry, Henrik. I need you to clean her up. And fetch a lamp; it's getting hard to see what I'm doing in this light."

"Coming," said Henrik. He took the bedding from Ursula and slammed the door in the nuns' faces.

Ursula turned to find a wide-eyed Isabelle grinning at her. "Did you see?"

"I did," replied Ursula. She shouldn't have looked. It was wrong of her. A terrible sin. Oh, but how she wished she could have been in there, rolling her sleeves up and helping!

"So horrid," Isabelle was saying.

"The doctor said she'll recover," said Ursula. "He's so skilful."

"Well, he'd better hurry, or he and Henrik shall be trapped here all winter. Not that Sister Gertrude would care, I imagine..."

Ursula sighed. "Trust *your* filthy mind to turn to matters of the flesh at a time like this."

"And what would you suggest I think of, dear sister?"

"That young girl's recovery." She turned and walked

down the corridor. The urge to run was frighteningly strong. "We should visit the chapel and pray for her."

Isabelle followed close behind. "Yes, I suppose we *could* do that."

"It's the correct thing to do."

"Absolutely. We should pray together, you and I. Sister Ursula, I completely agree."

"Then why don't I believe you?" asked Ursula.

"Because you lack faith in me, and I find that most hurtful."

Ursula felt cold, and hugged her arms around her chest. "Nonsense," she said, as they descended to the ground floor. "I have an abundance of faith."

"I know you do. More than enough to go around." Isabelle stopped at the foot of the stairs. She was trying to hide a smile. "In which case, might I offer a suggestion?"

"Do continue."

Isabelle placed her hand on Ursula's shoulder. "Why don't *you* go and pray for both of us?"

Ursula may have been a nun, but she was no fool. "Do you have somewhere more important to be?"

"Well, now that you ask... I fear that Sister Maria will be upset over today's events, and pining for counsel with a trusted sister."

"Sister Maria is truly a sensitive soul," Ursula said dryly.

"Indeed. Which is why, while you seek solace in prayer, I believe my time would be better spent seeking solace... elsewhere."

Warmth spread through Ursula's cheeks. "Oh, just go!"

"Thank you for your blessing," Isabelle said, and playfully slapped Ursula's bottom through her habit. "And don't worry." She could no longer suppress her grin. "I may not be praying, but I promise you... I *will* be on my knees."

6

———

The surgery was complete.

Henrik stood in the confines of what Sister Ursula referred to as her 'cell' — such queer language these nuns used, although the room's similarity to a prison could not be disputed — and inspected Franco's handiwork as the doctor crouched by the bucket and scrubbed the blood from his hands. During the procedure, the pipe had never once left his lips.

Using what little medicines and ointments remained in the medical bag, they had cleaned and disinfected the wounds, then sutured the skin together as best they could. The results were not pretty; due to the age of the injuries, they had to stretch her skin near breaking point in order to reattach it. But, with the right care and attention, she could go on to live a healthy life.

Franco dried his hands on some bedding and pulled a gold fob watch from his jacket. "Good god, man, is that the time? If we don't leave now, we'll never make it home. What's the weather like out there?"

Henrik strode to the window and undid the latch. He

may have been unafraid of heights, but as he gazed out over a straight drop of hundreds of feet, he could not help picturing some poor soul plummeting from the open window and being dashed to shreds on the rocky cliffs.

"The *weather,* dear boy," Franco entreated. "If it's not too much trouble."

Henrik shook the ghastly image from his mind. "The snow's lying, but the worst is still on the horizon." He shut the window and turned to the doctor. "I'd say there's still time for us to reach Cerbesca."

"Good." Franco snapped his bag shut. "We shall leave at once. Ready the horses and—"

"Going somewhere, Doctor?"

The voice may have come from behind Henrik, but he knew it all too well. His heart sank. He had hoped not to hear it again until their return.

"Ah, Mother Superior," Franco replied without missing a beat. "What excellent fortune! I was just about to seek you out."

The abbess stood in the doorway. With her hunched posture and fragile, bony limbs, the men had always agreed she was born to lurk in the shadows like a cadaverous ghoul. How such a chilling presence had ended up running a convent was beyond either of them.

"How is the girl?" the Mother Superior asked.

Franco smiled, and puffed on his pipe. "Recovering. I've done what I can with limited means. Rest and recuperation are what she now requires."

He spoke slowly, his posture relaxed. They may have been in a hurry to leave, but Henrik understood they could show the abbess no weakness.

She hesitated in the doorway. "Cover her up. I won't have her brazen nakedness corrupting my flock."

Franco turned to Henrik. "Put a sheet over her," he said, and Henrik did as asked, draping a blanket over the girl, whom they had wedged on her side with the bundled bedding. Once he had accomplished this simple task, the abbess deigned to enter the room, accompanied, inevitably, by Sister Claudia, a flesh-crawling limpet of a woman with obvious designs on the Mother Superior's position. The joke was on her, however, as Henrik sensed the aged matriarch would last another century and outlive them all.

"Corruption within my walls," she muttered as she crossed herself.

"Disgusting," Claudia added needlessly.

"Poppycock," said Franco. "I had to disrobe her to save her life, and in doing so, destroyed her meagre clothing. Perhaps you would be so kind as to furnish your patient with new attire? Judging from her weak bones and pale complexion, I'd say she's of peasant stock, so anything you can spare will suffice."

The abbess didn't respond. She stood before the girl, staring at her and clutching the cross she wore around her neck. Unlike the other nuns, hers had a golden Jesus affixed to the wood. "Remove this girl at once," she said. "She does not belong here."

"Impossible," said Franco dismissively, and Sister Claudia gasped.

"This is *my* convent," the Mother Superior said. "You will do as I command, and take this outsider with you."

Claudia stepped forwards. "It's *her* convent."

"Quiet, girl," hissed the Mother Superior.

Franco tapped his pipe against his boot and casually placed it in his pocket. "And I tell you, that's quite impossible. The child is just out of surgery, and would never survive the journey. Therefore, I must do what's right and entrust the pitiful creature into your care, where you shall bestow upon her all the love and mercy you have shown your flock."

She gazed at him through icy-blue eyes. "Do you expect my untrained sisters to nurse this wretch back to health?"

"I've left all the medicine I can spare, and I shall write instructions on how and when to take or apply it. Other than that, what she requires most is the one thing this convent has in abundance." He smiled at her, and placed his hat on his head. "Absolute silence."

"I cannot allow it." The woman's hands trembled. "I *forbid* it."

At first glance, Henrik had assumed she was furious. But the tremor in her voice, and the way she gripped her crucifix with a white-knuckled fist, suggested otherwise.

He thought she was afraid.

"My... my flock do not have time to attend to—"

"The needs of others?" Franco interrupted. "Dear Mother, if a nun cannot look after those in need, then what, may I ask, is her true purpose?"

"To serve God," said Claudia, and the abbess slapped her across the back of the head.

"Hold your tongue, foolish girl," she said, and glared at Franco.

Henrik would have withered under such a fearsome stare, but Joseph Franco was the most obstinate man he had ever met.

"My assistant and I," he said calmly, "will shortly be making the treacherous journey down the mountain. It will be just the two of us in the coach, as I'd prefer not to murder an innocent girl immediately after healing her. That will be the end of the discussion, and I sincerely trust that you and your sistren shall pray for our safe passage."

The abbess reached for the blanket and drew it up over

the sleeping girl's face with a withered hand. "You're not listening to me, Dr—"

"What if *I* stayed?" asked Henrik. The words were out before he could stop them. The Mother Superior regarded him with contempt, and Franco with confusion. Then, Henrik saw the realisation dawn on his old friend's face.

"A sterling suggestion," said Franco. "My young charge shall remain here over winter and tend to the girl until she is well. Then, when spring arrives, I shall return them both to Cerbesca."

"I can stay in the gardener's cottage," Henrik added before the abbess could raise her objections. "It'll be cold, but there's a fireplace, and I'm confident you can spare some blankets for my comfort."

And one of your nuns, he thought wickedly. Oh, to see Gertrude's face when she found out!

"A man in such close proximity to my flock," said the Mother Superior with a shake of her head. "It's not right."

"He'll be a temptation," added Claudia.

"I'm sure your nuns are strong-willed enough to resist Henrik's charms," said Franco with a twinkle in his eye. "Bountiful though they undoubtedly are."

Henrik stepped confidently forward. "I shall chop my own firewood, make my own meals and eat separately, and avoid all contact with the sisters unless absolutely necessary."

"If anything," Franco said, the two men working together to bludgeon the abbess into submission, "having a doctor around during these dark days would be a real boon. I'm rather surprised by your reluctance."

The woman faltered. "I fear," she managed to say, "the child shall succumb to the rigours of winter."

It was a weak argument, and Henrik pounced. "Then at

least she shall die in this most holy of places." He looked at Franco, and the man nodded at him, a thin smile crossing his lips as Henrik delivered the killing blow. "That alone should come as no small relief to a simple peasant girl."

The abbess backed away from the bed, her wide-eyed gaze fixed on the slumbering shape beneath the blanket. She had lost the battle, and everyone knew it.

"Very well," she mumbled at Henrik. "I will leave her in *your* care... and you, *alone,* shall be responsible for burying her when she passes."

With that, she exited the room.

Sister Claudia shook her head. "An outrage," she said, then turned on her heels and scurried after her superior.

Only once they had left did Henrik notice his heart was pounding with exhilaration. He broke into a wide grin, and Franco laughed.

"Congratulations, dear boy," he said. It always tickled Henrik when Franco referred to him as such. Certainly, the doctor was two decades his senior, but Henrik was still thirty-three years old. "You've claimed your first victory over Satan herself."

"You softened her up," said Henrik, though he welcomed the warm words. Praise from Franco was as rare as hens' teeth.

"There's no softening that crone. She's as old and hard as the walls that surround us, and twice as decrepit."

Henrik pulled the blanket down from the girl's face. She looked so peaceful. "Strange, isn't it? The abbess really didn't want this poor thing to stay."

"The only creatures more difficult to understand than women are nuns," said Franco. "I'm sure she has her reasons, however foolish they may seem to men of science such as ourselves." He opened a closet, the only piece of furniture in the room other than the bed and a single wooden chair, and pulled out a floor-length white tunic. He drew back the blanket, and the two men carefully dressed the girl so as not to disturb her wounds.

After, Franco lit his pipe once more. "Henrik, are you certain you've made the right decision?"

"Why do you ask?"

"Well, do you honestly wish to spend all winter with a bunch of nuns? And, more importantly, with no good brandy?"

"Ah, that's where you're wrong," said Henrik, reaching into his jacket and removing a metal hip flask. He held it aloft, the liquid sloshing inside, and said, "I always come prepared for our visits to Sant'Arcangel."

Franco nodded appreciatively and clapped his friend on the arm. "My boy," he said, and produced a hip flask of his own. "It appears I've taught you well."

7

———

Sister Maria was on her knees in prayer when the knock came at her cell door.

Though she hadn't witnessed any of the commotion that had shaken the convent — those supper dishes would not wash themselves, no matter how hard she prayed — she had heard the whispered rumours from that irrepressible gossip Sister Agatha.

A young girl, no older than eighteen, had been found in a near-death state and brought inside, where Dr Franco had performed emergency surgery to save her life.

Maria thanked God for ensuring the doctor was present to attend to the unwell stranger, yet she was finding it unusually difficult to concentrate on her prayers, for Sister Agatha had also informed her that Isabelle was one of the nuns who had found the girl.

Maria screwed her eyes shut and prayed with all her might.

She was aware that no single person should take priority in her thoughts, but she couldn't help focusing on Isabelle. They loved each other, and not just as sisters in Christ. They loved each other the same way as people outside of convents... in a profoundly *physical* manner.

Their union was against God's teachings. Wrong on every conceivable level. And yet... her heart yearned for Isabelle. Only when they were together did she feel complete; a whole person, rather than a servant of God.

It hadn't always been like this.

In the early days of their tentative relationship, she had feared the devil was at work within her, and prayed for the lustful desires to subside. In the monastic life, physical love between a man and a woman was forbidden. Between a woman and another woman? Why, that wasn't just forbidden. That was, according to the Mother Superior, the greatest sin of all.

Greater, even, than murder.

So why did it feel so good, and so right? Why was she never happier than when she spent time alone with Isabelle? And not just the kissing and the other, more intimate matters. Simply talking to her, or sitting together in quiet contemplation, filled Maria with incomparable joy.

So when she heard Isabelle using their secret knock — *tap... tap... tap-tap* — she happily paused her prayer and bid her enter. Unable to help herself, Maria embraced her lover before the door was even closed, tears of relief rolling down her cheeks.

"Fret not, Sister Maria," smiled Isabelle. She shut the door firmly, then took Maria's face in her hands and kissed her. "I am perfectly well. Sister Ursula and I came across an injured girl in a terrible state, but Dr Franco is tending to her now. There was a lot of blood, but I'm quite certain she will survive."

"Thank you for putting my mind at ease. I feared you'd been attacked by wolves, or... or worse."

"What could possibly be worse than a wolf?"

Maria tenderly stroked Isabelle's hair. "A man. Where I came from, if a woman was hurt or bleeding, it was usually at the hand of a man."

"I'm afraid you may be right. This girl had been repeatedly struck with an axe. Someone had tried to kill her."

Upon hearing that, Maria felt sick. She would never understand mankind's limitless capacity for violence.

"Were you frightened?" she asked.

"A little. The girl appeared like a spectre, gripping onto dear Sister Ursula as if the very devils of hell were on her tail. And... and I thought..."

Isabelle cast her eyes down. The light from the bedside candle rippled across her face.

"Go on," urged Maria. She gently squeezed Isabelle's palm. "You can tell me."

"I never spoke of this with Sister Ursula, because it all seemed so unreal, so fantastical. It may have been the snow, or the fright and the surprise of finding her... but as we were carrying the girl through the gardens, I had the notion that something else was out there."

"Whatever do you mean? A person?"

"No, not a person. A presence, as if a thousand eyes were watching from afar. Oh, I know it's all frightfully silly, isn't it?" She laughed, and the hollow sound bounced eerily off the bare walls.

Maria shivered. That alone was not unusual, for the cold seeped from the convent walls like a foul odour. But this was a different kind of cold. Isabelle's words chilled her, and she felt a gnawing dread deep within her bones. She held Isabelle tightly and kissed her cheek. She knew not how the other nuns made it through the desperate loneliness of winter without someone to hold.

Someone to love, and to make them forget about everything for a short while.

Isabelle angled her head to meet Maria's lips, returning the kiss. They sat on the bed, and Isabelle raised the hem of Maria's underskirt. Fingers traced along her thick socks, seeking flesh and finding it, fingertips brushing the sensitive skin of her thighs.

Maria shut her eyes and groaned as Isabelle lowered her onto her back. The bed creaked beneath the weight of their bodies, and she glanced to make sure the door was indeed fully closed. "I was so worried about you," she whispered, as Isabelle's curious fingers danced lightly up her thighs. Isabelle could be a brash woman, but as a lover, she was delicacy incarnate.

"I'm here now," said Isabelle, her amorous caresses causing Maria to fidget with pleasure. They shared a kiss, tongues brushing together, and Maria raised her tunic higher, her body tingling as Isabelle kissed her left breast.

"And you'll never leave me?" Maria whimpered, her passions inflamed.

Isabelle slipped two fingers inside her. "I promise, I'll never—"

She hissed, and roughly withdrew her hand.

Maria gasped in pain and surprise. "What is it? What's wrong?"

"I don't know." Isabelle stared curiously at her hand. "Something stung me."

"Here, let me see." Maria took her lover's hand and inspected the wet, glistening fingers. There, on her index, was a thin red slit between the lower knuckles. "You've cut yourself," she said. "No wonder it hurt."

Isabelle nodded dazedly. "Oh yes, I remember. I cut it right before we found the girl."

Maria looked closely at the mark. A barely perceptible black line surrounded the laceration, from which dark, vein-like threads originated. She pinched the cut. A drop of blood trickled down Isabelle's finger, dispersing into the lines of her palm.

"It looks infected. Does it hurt?"

"No. I hardly feel it at all." Isabelle smiled. "Anyway, why are we still talking about my finger?" She leaned in for a kiss, and Maria shuffled out of reach.

"You should show it to the doctor."

Isabelle laughed sweetly. "Don't be silly, Maria. I already told Ursula I shan't bother anyone over such a trivial matter. Not when we've got much more exciting things to do."

Maria glanced down at Isabelle's finger. She supposed the burning sensation she felt on her labia was unrelated, and doubtless caused by the rapid withdrawal of Isabelle's fingers, but the idea of touching that wound, and of those little black threads...

"No, I really would like you to see Dr Franco. I'm sure he'll have a remedy for it." She patted Isabelle's thigh. "You don't want an infection over winter."

Isabelle waved her concerns away. "I don't know why you're so concerned over nothing. And, might I add, if you'd rather not make love to me, you just need to say so. I'd prefer not to listen to your feeble excuses."

"Isabelle, that's not—"

"If you need me, I'll be in the chapel praying." And with that lie, she stormed out of the room, dotting the floor with tiny red bloodstains.

"Please, Isabelle, don't—"

The door slammed shut with enough force to extinguish the candle. The flame blinked, plunging the cell into darkness, then cautiously returned.

Shocked, Maria sat on the edge of her bed and wept. Oh, she hadn't intended to upset Isabelle! She was only looking out for her. An infection like that, however small, could easily...

Her thoughts trailed off. She sniffed the air. What *was* that rotten stench that caught in her nostrils? Wiping her eyes, she glanced at the bed and located the loathsome miasma; a bloody mark on the bedsheet, left by Isabelle's finger. Pinching her nose, she looked closer. Even against the white fabric, the blood appeared darker than normal. Muddy brown, verging on black.

She scratched irritably between her legs, and stripped the sheet from the bed. If only Isabelle could have seen the mess she had left! Then, mayhap, she would understand why Maria was so concerned for her welfare. An unchecked infection could spread quickly, and the fact Isabelle could not recall *how* she had injured herself was doubly concerning.

It's like Sister Ruth, she thought, and shuddered at the memory.

A few years prior, Sister Ruth had cut her foot on some rusted metal in the stable. That had been the first week of December. By the time spring arrived, the sisters had been forced to amputate her monstrously diseased leg in an attempt to save the woman's life.

Maria would never forget that day.

It had taken six nuns to restrain Ruth, and a seventh to hack her leg off with the woodchopping axe. Severing the limb proved more difficult than expected, and only after the fifth blow did the leg finally slide off the table and thud to the floor.

But that hadn't been the worst part.

Because no one had been prepared for the amount of

blood contained in the human body. So much blood, in fact, that when the desperate sisters had attempted to cauterise the wound by forcing the dying woman's stump into the fireplace, the blood had gushed in pulsing waves onto the angry flames, extinguishing the fire.

Maria gagged. Was that the grim fate awaiting Isabelle? She closed her eyes in prayer, asking... no, *begging* God to show her the folly of her ways. She prayed, and she prayed some more, pausing only once to reach up her underskirt and rub her vagina.

Good Lord, she itched *terribly* down there.

8

———

Only Henrik and Sister Gertrude braved the snowfall to see Dr Franco off.

In the hours since the first flake fell from the sky, the temperature had plunged dramatically, and now Stygian clouds threatened an approaching blizzard, casting darkness across the land.

"Are you sure it's safe to travel?" asked Henrik, as the three stood by the entrance hall doorway. He gazed out over the unblemished snow, where Franco's coach awaited, the lanterns illuminating his blanketed horses and little else.

The doctor hugged his coat around him. "If not now, when?" He puffed on his pipe, releasing a cloud of smoke. "If the snow keeps falling, and it will, then tomorrow morning the mountain road shall be intraversable, even in daylight."

Henrik smiled. Franco was right, of course. The pragmatic doctor usually was. "Then it seems I must bid you farewell, my friend."

"It appears that way." Franco turned to Gertrude and offered a shallow bow. "A pleasure as always, Sister

Gertrude. Pass on my regards to your Mother Superior for her," — he cleared his throat — "*hospitality.*"

"I shall," she said knowingly, her hand skimming against Henrik's. "And thank you for your help, Doctor. You are always welcome within our hallowed walls. Safe travels."

She smiled at him, shared a glance with Henrik, and took her leave.

Once she was out of sight, Franco chuckled. "You'd better be more subtle than that."

"Excuse me?"

The older man laughed. "Be wise, dear boy, and try not to get caught in the comely arms of Sister Gertrude. Or any of the nuns, for that matter. Our beloved Mother Superior does not take kindly to those who corrupt her flock."

"I wouldn't dream of it."

Franco raised his eyebrows. "Really?"

"Of getting *caught,* I mean. I fully intend to spend all winter in those comely arms, as you so eloquently put it."

"In that case," laughed Franco, "I suggest you confine your nocturnal activities to the cottage, for the sake of your own skin. I don't think any nun would dare enter and risk being alone with a handsome brute such as yourself." It was sound advice, and easily practicable, for Gertrude's cell was on the ground floor around the side of the building. With the storm restricting the nuns to the convent, he should have no trouble sneaking her out after hours.

"Oh, stop smiling at your impending foul deeds," said Franco, "and help me to the coach. I crave the comfort of my own bed."

They walked through the snow with their breath steaming before their faces. Henrik shielded his eyes and squinted at the coach.

"I can tell by your startled expression you've noticed I'm

missing a horse," said Franco. "Don't worry, I've left my sturdiest nag in the stables in the unlikely event the snow melts and you require a quick getaway."

Henrik glanced at the stables, then back to Franco. "Thank you, Joseph," he said. He rarely used his friend's first name, but it felt appropriate in the moment.

"Not at all. And don't ever say I'm not good to you."

Before they got too sentimental, Henrik placed Franco's medical bag onto the coach, then helped him up to the seat, aware that the old bullet lodged in his friend's leg played havoc with his joints during cold spells.

"Much obliged," said Franco. He took a drink from his hip flask and handed it to Henrik. "Keep this, my dear boy. I shall return in the spring, or earlier, should the snow clear."

"Then let us hope for unseasonable weather, for my supply of brandy is not inexhaustible." Henrik offered his hand. "Farewell, old friend. And godspeed."

Franco grunted, and reached beneath his seat. Snowflakes clung to his coat, turning it white. "Here, I have something else for you."

"More brandy, I hope?"

"Even better..." He leaned over, almost losing his balance, then righted himself. In his gloved hand, he held a Colt revolver. "Best to keep this between ourselves for now. I doubt the old hag in charge would approve."

Henrik took the weapon and turned it in his hands. The metal was freezing against his skin. "What the devil is this for?"

"Protection. It's about time the nuns had some."

Henrik admired the gun a moment longer, then pocketed it. "Very well, but I doubt I'll need it. You are far more likely to encounter wolves on your way down the mountain than I am."

"It's not wolves I'm worried about," said Franco. He took the reins, staring ahead. "Someone did that to the girl, Henrik. A madman, or a sexual deviant. He may be dead, or he may still be out there. Either way, I'll sleep easier knowing you can defend those poor women." He turned his head and they locked eyes. "And yourself."

Henrik nodded resolutely. "I'll look after them."

"I'm certain you will. You're a very hands-on doctor. Although hands on *what,* I don't care to know," he chuckled. "Now step down. And at least wait until tomorrow night to sneak Gertrude into your bed. Have *some* sense of decency."

"I make no promises," smiled Henrik, and Franco cracked the reins, the three remaining horses taking off at a canter. The coach trundled towards the tree line, before disappearing into the whirling storm. Henrik's pocket sagged from the weight of the revolver. His friend was being overprotective. There was no danger here besides the risk of being found in a compromising position with Gertrude.

Or was there?

For Franco was correct in one regard. Someone *had* attacked that girl, and the assault must have taken place nearby. In her condition, she could not have survived more than half a day on the mountain, which meant her assailant could still be close. They could be watching from the trees, or behind the blackberry bushes. Hell, they could be inside the convent right now, chopping up nuns with an axe while he stood pontificating in the snow.

He turned to look at the imposing building, and smiled to himself. He was acting foolishly. But then, that was what happened up here on the mountain. *Devil's brain* was what the old timers in Cerbesca called it; a combination of thin air and extreme isolation that played tricks on the mind. He wasn't sure how the nuns managed it all year round.

Perhaps they didn't? A touch of madness likely went some way to staving off complete insanity. It was an idea worth pursuing, and maybe he would? Goodness knows, he would have little else to occupy his days over the next four months, and if he could emerge from hibernation in the spring with at least the vague notion of a medical paper, then it would be time well spent.

With a final glance in the direction of the forest, he turned and trudged towards the gardener's cottage. Inside his lodgings, he lit and stoked the fire, running through tomorrow's errands in his head.

Firstly, he would need to check on the patient. Afterwards, he would discuss the washing and eating arrangements with the abbess, a task he did not relish. It would also be wise to visit the library and pick out some reading material to pass the time while Gertrude was engaged in her duties. He had brought no books with him, and all he had found in the cottage was a journal overflowing with blank pages.

"Perhaps I'll write some poetry," he said and half-smiled.

Had he made a terrible mistake in volunteering to stay? Gertrude hadn't thought so. When he told her of the arrangement, she had squealed with delight and whispered in his ear of the awful things she had planned for him.

She really was the worst nun in the world.

And as he lay back on the bed, with the fire crackling and the snowflakes drifting outside, he realised how powerful his love for Gertrude truly was, and how badly he wished to take her away from this place. With agreeable thoughts of her smile and kisses in his mind, he rolled onto his side, and winced as the gun pressed into his ribs. Uneasily, Henrik removed the Colt from his coat pocket and checked the chambers.

Fully loaded.

He recalled the foreboding words of his friend.

Someone did that to the girl, Henrik. He may still be out there.

It was unlike Franco to be so overly cautious.

"Don't worry about me," he said, and laid the revolver on the bedside table before tossing another log onto the fire, secure in the knowledge that if the maniac didn't show tonight, he never would. No man, no matter how warmly wrapped, could withstand the arctic temperatures of the mountain overnight.

9

THE GIRL WAS IN THE THROES OF A DREAM.

Ursula watched from the discomfort of her wooden chair as the prostrate figure anxiously jittered in her sleep, emitting soft, disgruntled moans. Was she dreaming of the attack? Or of wandering, lost and bleeding, across the mountain, seeking sanctuary? Ursula couldn't begin to comprehend the hardships the girl had endured. What would she have done under similar circumstances? Would she possess the stamina and the will to survive? Or would she lie down in the snow and accept the fate God had planned for her?

She rose from her chair — there was only so long she could sit in its wooden embrace without her limbs aching — and stood by the window, watching the storm. She would pray for Dr Franco's safe passage. Henrik, on the other hand... well, he was exactly where he wished to be.

She smiled. For once, it was going to be an interesting winter in the convent. How could it *not* be? For the foreseeable future, she would, for the first time, be sharing a room. It didn't bother her that the girl had taken her bed. She had borrowed a spare mattress from the storeroom and laid it on the floor, covering the old, dried stains with a clean sheet. Perhaps, when the girl's condition improved, they could become friends. Ursula liked having friends. It made her feel — and she did not mean this blasphemously — less like a nun and more like a woman.

With the wind whistling through a gap in the window frame, she walked to the bed and placed a hand on her patient's forehead, checking for a fever and finding none.

It was amazing how things worked out. Here she was, eager to help others in a more direct fashion, and out of nowhere an ailing girl was entrusted to her care. It was no coincidence.

This was God's will.

Clearly, he meant to test her. And if she passed, surely it pointed the way towards her future? Not even the Mother Superior would be able to deny that her prayers had, quite literally, been answered.

She dipped a cloth into the bucket and gently mopped the girl's face and dry, chapped lips. She was very pretty, with curly blonde hair and smooth skin. What on earth was she doing up here in the middle of nowhere? The convent rarely received visitors. Other than Dr Franco and Henrik, only the young novices made their way up the mountain track to join the flock. But even if that were the case, and the girl longed to devote herself to God, why had she foolishly undertaken the journey on the cusp of winter?

It was, to put it bluntly, a suicidal endeavour.

So no, Ursula did not believe the girl had come of her own volition. More likely, someone had brought her here for nefarious reasons. Though it pained her to consider it, the mountain was the perfect place to commit a murder, especially at this time of year. The snow would bury the body for months, and if hidden far enough from the track, chances were high the corpse would never be found.

Ursula returned the cloth to the bucket with a light splash. When she stood, the girl's lips were moving.

She was trying to speak.

Ursula panicked. What to do? Should she fetch Henrik? No, no, that would take too long! It was up to her now. "Umm, would you like a drink?" she asked.

The girl nodded weakly. Ursula dipped her cup in a second, smaller bowl full of clean water and held it to her mouth. The girl's eyes drifted lazily as if failing to focus, and when she tried to move, she cried out in pain.

"Stay still, please," said Ursula. "Dr Franco stitched your wounds only recently. Do you know of him?"

Her question was met with a blank stare.

"I ask," she continued, "because Dr Franco is Cerbesca's resident physician, and I wondered if you were from there? Oh, that reminds me, he left medicine for you." She crossed the room to the closet and took a small bottle from the shelf. "You should take some whilst you're awake."

She decanted the liquid into a spoon, and the girl swallowed it with difficulty, her eyes wet with tears.

"Thank you," she croaked.

"You're very welcome." Ursula placed the bottle back in the closet. "I imagine you're wondering where you are. Well, this is the Sant'Arcangel convent. Sister Isabelle and I were picking berries in the garden when we found you."

The girl seemed to look straight through her.

"So..." said Ursula, "...are you from Cerbesca?"

Nothing.

"Do you remember what happened to you?"

A shake of the head. Almost imperceptible.

Ursula looked upon her kindly. "No matter. I'm certain it shall all come back in time. What's your name?"

"My name?"

"Yes. Mine is Sister Ursula, and yours is...?"

A pathetic sound escaped the girl's lips. She lay for what felt like an eternity, then whispered, *"I don't know."*

Ursula's heart broke. She really should find Henrik. But what if the girl lapsed into unconsciousness while she was away? Better to keep her talking and try to jog her memory. She scooped more water from the bowl. "Don't worry about your recovery," she said as the girl sipped. "It's been arranged that you shall live with me until you're well. Then, after the winter, we can take you back down the mountain. Unless, of course, you wish to remain in the convent."

"A convent," the girl said, water dribbling down her chin. She blinked for such a length of time that Ursula thought she'd fallen asleep. "Are you a nun?"

"Can't you tell by my wimple?" Ursula smiled.

"I thought... I thought nuns were old?"

"Not at all. There are lots of us here, young and old alike. All are welcome. Well, all *women*, I should clarify. There are no men here, except for the doctor's assistant Henrik, and even that is *highly* irregular. He's staying in the gardener's cottage to help me look after you. Or, I suppose, I'm helping *him* look after you. He's a doctor too, but we all still think of him as Dr Franco's assistant. I imagine he finds it most vexing. But we have strict rules about men in the convent, so you'll be spending most of your time with me. We're going to be great friends, I'm certain of it."

A simple nod was all the girl managed. Ursula wondered if she was even listening.

"When you're feeling better, I'll fetch some books from the library, and you can read by the window. Won't that be nice? The view is lovely, especially once the snow lessens. In the meantime, perhaps I can read to you—"

A vicious gust rattled the window in its frame, and the girl's eyes opened wide.

"It's here," she said. The pockmarks of colour drained from her face, leaving her skin a pale, ghostly white.

"What is?" asked Ursula.

A hand clamped on her wrist.

"The *evil*," said the girl. "I can feel it. It's close." She stared at Ursula, and through gritted teeth, snarled, *"The evil is here!"*

"What evil? I don't understand. Do you need..."

But the girl's head sank back into the pillow, her tight grip on Ursula loosening like shrivelling vines. Seconds later, she was snoring softly, a healthy pink blossoming on her cheeks.

It's here.

The storm battered the window, and Ursula cast her mind back to the strange presence she had felt in the entrance hall.

The evil is here.

Had Isabelle felt it too? She needed to find out. Urgently. And if she interrupted Isabelle and Maria doing, well, whatever it was they did together, then so be it. This was too important to wait.

She backed away from the slumbering girl and turned to leave. As she reached the doorway, she froze.

For there, in the lonely darkness of the hallway, skulked a sinister, shapeless figure.

Ursula screamed.

It was staring right at her.

10

———

"Hush, child," the Mother Superior snapped irritably, as she stepped into the dim glow of the candlelight. "Or am I so frightening that my own flock shriek in horror upon sight of me?"

Ursula squirmed with embarrassment. What a fool she had made of herself!

"No, Mother Superior," she said, and took a breath to compose herself. "You startled me. My nerves have been rattled by—"

"I'm not interested in your nerves. Tell me, how does the girl fare?"

Ursula bowed her head. "She suffers greatly from her injuries."

"It's a woman's lot in life to suffer." The abbess walked closer, stopping at the doorway. "As a nun, you should know this. Do you think she suffers more than Christ did on the cross?"

"No, Mother Superior."

The woman nodded. She peered inside. "I heard talking. Has she awakened?"

"She stirred briefly. Would you like to come in and see her?"

The abbess remained rooted to the spot like an old tree. "If I wished to enter your cell, Sister Ursula, I would have done so without invitation. The Lord may work in mysterious ways, but *I* do not. Come hither and speak with me in the hallway."

Ursula stepped out of her room, leaving the door ajar in case the girl called out.

"Now," the abbess said, lowering her voice. "What, precisely, did she say to you?"

"Something about—"

"*Exact words,* child. I did say *precisely,* did I not?"

"Yes, Mother Superior." Ursula wondered how long the woman had been listening in the doorway. "She remembers nothing. Not her name, nor what happened to her, nor why she's here."

"Good. What else?"

Ursula wasn't sure what was 'good' about that, but she continued. "Well, I didn't understand it, but—"

"It's not your place to understand, child. Your only task is to tell *me* so that *I* may understand. Unless, somehow, *you* are now the Mother Superior of this convent? Is that the case, Sister Ursula? Should I refer to you as Mother Superior and bow my head in deference to your infinite wisdom?"

Ursula shook her head. Tears pricked her eyes as she fiddled with her corded-rope belt. "No, Mother Superior. I apologise for my insolence."

"You're lucky Sister Claudia isn't here. She's been looking for fresh meat for her cat o' nine tails. Unless that's what you want?"

Ursula said nothing. She trembled in shame, tears

rolling down her cheeks.

"Well, is it? Answer me!" Her raised voice reverberated throughout the corridors. "Do you long for Sister Claudia to punish you? Do you lie awake at night, praying for the crack of her leather whip against your plump, sinful flesh? Well? Do you?"

Humiliated, Ursula sobbed, her chin resting against her sternum. "No, Mother Superior. I wish only to please you and God."

"Then stop playing with your cincture and answer my question, and answer it *accurately*. What else did that *thing* in there say to you?"

Ursula dropped her hands to her sides and looked over her shoulder at the sleeping girl. "She said... the evil is here."

A long silence followed, punctuated only by Ursula's intermittent sniffling. She hated to cry in front of the abbess, and wanted to crawl into a deep hole and die to spare her blushes.

The Mother Superior's brow furrowed, deep lines creasing her forehead like knife wounds as she clutched her crucifix tightly to her bosom. She rubbed her thumb across the gold Christ's well-worn torso.

"Don't you have chores to perform?" she asked.

"I... I thought it best to stay with the patient until—"

"You thought you knew better than I, is that what you're saying?"

"No, Mother Superior. I would never be so bold."

"Then get out of my sight, you snivelling cur."

Ursula shuffled aside, and the older woman stopped her with a hand on her shoulder. For a fraction of a second, her face softened. "May God have mercy on your soul, Sister

Ursula," she said grimly, and then the hard lines returned to her skin.

"Thank you," Ursula said, before turning and heading down the corridor. She blinked, unleashing the full flood of salty tears, and stepped in a puddle. With a heavy sigh, she glanced up to where murky water dripped from the ceiling. On the long winter nights, if she listened closely, she could sometimes hear the melting snow trickling through cracks in the walls. The convent was in dire need of repair, but who would pay for such things? It had been five years since the storm had destroyed the old chapel in the west wing, and with each passing year the once-impressive building fell further into decrepitude.

A door groaned shut behind her.

Ursula wiped the last of the tears with her sleeve and looked back. The Mother Superior had entered her cell.

But why now? Why wait until she was alone? Something was amiss.

Ursula pivoted on her heels.

What are you doing? Disobeying a direct order from the Mother Superior is a sin!

True. But wasn't deliberately making someone cry *also* a sin? If the matriarch of the convent was unwilling to abide by her own rules, Ursula reasoned, then why should *she* be bound by them?

Stepping out of her sandals, she held her tunic at her knees to prevent her robes from swishing as she soundlessly tiptoed towards her door. It was partly closed, and for the second time that day, Ursula found herself peering through the gap.

She didn't feel bad about doing so. After all, it *was* her cell.

Closing one eye, she watched the abbess stand over the

sleeping girl, caressing her crucifix with both hands. The polished golden Christ sparkled in the candlelight.

"Immundus spiritus," she whispered. *"De profundis clamo ad te, domine."*

Unclean spirit?

Ursula leaned closer. Her head bumped against the door, and it creaked. She ducked out of sight as the Mother Superior turned.

"Is someone there?"

Every part of Ursula was still except for her heart, which hammered uncontrollably. She pressed up against the wall, her fingernails scraping the stone, sweat dripping down her forehead and soaking into her head covering. There came a cautious footstep from inside the cell... and then nothing more. She heard more whispered murmurings, and against her better judgement, she crept to the door and peered through again.

With one hand on her crucifix and the other on the girl's tunic, the Mother Superior raised the garment, revealing the young woman's nakedness.

Ursula could not believe her eyes. This was against all the holy order's teachings.

"Ecce crucem domini."

The abbess spat twice and removed the crucifix from around her neck, letting the beaded cord dangle from her fingers.

To Ursula's right, frantic footsteps hurried up the stairs.

Someone was coming.

Clutching her sandals, she scurried to the closest cell, slipping inside Sister Augusta's quarters and closing the door.

Ecce crucem domini.

Behold the cross of the Lord.

The footsteps pounded along the corridor. Ursula knew they belonged to Sister Claudia, for it was she who patrolled the corridors every night at bedtime, and among the nuns, only Claudia walked with the leaden steps of the haughty.

"Mother Superior?" she called out. *"Are you there?"*

Ursula snorted. She wouldn't be surprised if one day Dr Franco had to surgically remove Sister Claudia from the abbess. The nun followed her around like a living shadow. It was obvious she desired a position of power, yet most of the sisters agreed that should the Mother Superior ever be relieved of her duties, Sister Claudia would be an abominable replacement. Her proclivity for punishments was legendary, and while Ursula herself had never provoked such wrath, she knew of several nuns whom Claudia had lashed severely for minor infractions.

"Ah, there you are," she heard Claudia say, and pressed her ear closer to the door. *"I couldn't find you."*

"That was intentional," the Mother Superior replied. *"I'm quite capable of performing my duties without you hanging off my tunic."*

"I'm... I'm only trying to help."

"It's too late for that. We're beyond help."

Whatever did she mean? Ursula strained to hear through the heavy wooden door. Thankfully, Sister Claudia sounded equally baffled.

"Too late? Too late for what? Enlighten me, Venerable Mother."

"You'll understand soon enough." She muttered something else. To Ursula's ears, it sounded like, *"Omnis satanica potestas."*

Then more footsteps. The two sets grew louder as the women left Ursula's cell and carried on along the corridor. Ursula reached for the door handle, ready to—

"Stop following me!" the Mother Superior roared at Claudia, an outburst so unexpected that, behind the door, Ursula had to bite back a scream. *"I can walk unattended, you louse. Now leave me alone!"*

Stunned, Ursula waited until the Mother Superior's footsteps subsided before carefully opening the door. Sister Claudia stood motionless in the candlelit hallway, facing the opposite direction and visibly shaking.

"That old *witch,*" Claudia seethed, and surreptitiously followed the abbess's echoing footsteps down the corridor, stepping lightly until she came to the stairs.

Only once she had started down them did Ursula dare leave the safety of Sister Augusta's cell. She slipped her sandals on and snuck across to her cell, shutting the door behind her and drawing in a deep, and very welcome, breath.

Sleety rain hammered relentlessly against the window as Ursula dragged her chair to the bedside and took the sleeping girl's hand. She closed her eyes. It was only the first day of winter, and already things were unravelling. Usually, it wasn't until the new year when the cracks began to show in the sisters' polite facades. That seemed to be when the overwhelming sense of isolation set in; that indescribable feeling of being cut off from the rest of the world in a decaying building.

It affected all of them.

Even the Mother Superior.

"I'm glad you're here," said Ursula, and as she squeezed the girl's cold hand, she prayed to God to let this be her last winter within the hallowed walls of Sant'Arcangel.

11

———————

Sister Claudia was worried.

In all her years in Sant'Arcangel, only once had she heard the Mother Superior raise her voice in anger, and that had been the time Sister Fiorina had unexpectedly gone into labour during supper.

Though it had happened over a decade ago, Claudia still vividly recalled the day. She doubted she'd *ever* forget the sight of Sister Fiorina giving birth on the refectory floor while the abbess loomed over her, beating the screaming woman's arms and legs with the branch of a birch tree and yelling about succumbing to the devil's phallus, while the nuns looked on in uncomprehending horror.

But not even that happy memory was enough to banish the concern in Claudia's heart. The Mother Superior's ability to remain calm was what made her so intimidating to the other sisters. If she started to crack under the pressure, she risked losing the flock's respect.

More importantly, they would stop fearing her. And fear, in Claudia's mind, was the *only* way to maintain order.

As she walked the corridors of Sant'Arcangel, maintaining a discrete distance from her superior, she pondered what could have caused this change in behaviour. Had it been the confrontation with the doctor? That despicable man had humiliated her in their verbal sparring match, and refused to remove the interloper from the convent. Or had it begun with the arrival of the girl herself?

Claudia was determined to uncover the truth.

She rounded a corner and watched as the abbess strode through a doorway that led to the outdoor courtyard. The large square area was surrounded by covered walkways, the cross-vaulted roof of the ambulatories supported by wide columns. During more seasonable weather, it was mainly used as a recreation ground. The nuns enjoyed sitting on the circular steps around the ancient stone well in the centre of the courtyard, reading their books or simply enjoying the sunshine. In the winter months, however, the courtyard was nothing but a bother. As the snow deepened over time, they would have to dig a trench to the well to retrieve the water. And if the well froze over? Someone would have to be lowered down to chip away at the ice and send it up in a bucket to be melted.

It was a task Claudia gleefully reserved for her least favourite sisters.

She waited by the doorway, watching silently as the Mother Superior stalked through the courtyard. Sister Giovanna, Sant'Arcangel's resident cook, stood by the well, hauling a bucket of water up using the metal pulley that hung from the well's arch.

"Good evening, Reverend Mother," Giovanna said cheerfully, to which the Mother Superior lowered her head and kept walking as if she hadn't heard.

Claudia, who did not wish to be seen, waited as Giovanna painstakingly raised the bucket an inch at a time, while the Mother Superior crossed the courtyard, heading towards the old, disused chapel in the west wing.

"Strange," muttered Claudia, for no one visited the chapel anymore. Not since the great storm of 1891 had condemned it to oblivion.

That winter, fearsome winds had battered the chapel walls for seven days and seven nights. The stained glass windows had been the first to go, exploding from a particularly violent gust and showering ten pews of nuns with glass. When sections of roof rained down atop them, the nuns had fled mid-sermon, an act of defiance that had ultimately saved their lives. For on the seventh and final day, three of the walls had crumbled, bringing the entire building down. Only the bell tower had emerged miraculously unscathed, the sparing of which the sisters took as a testament to God's holy power.

But why would the Mother Superior be heading there? To pray?

Sister Giovanna lifted her bucket from the well. She hoisted it into her arms and trudged through the snow towards the kitchen.

Finally!

Claudia made her move, sneaking from pillar to pillar beneath the stone awnings. She reached the doorway at the far end of the courtyard and stepped into the last corridor.

Ahead, the abbess left the passageway and walked amongst the devastation of the old chapel. A thick carpet of snow covered the ruined masonry and stonework from the collapsed walls. After the disaster, the sisters had rescued as many pews as possible and installed them in the new, much smaller chapel in the east wing, but dozens were still buried beneath rubble and glass and snow. Only one wall remained upright, although Claudia's favourite stained glass window, the one displaying Christ on the cross with a spear pene-trating his side, had long since perished.

The abbess stopped before the bell tower and gazed upwards. Without the support of the chapel walls, the imposing structure stood crooked, the spire stretching awkwardly towards heaven.

Claudia ducked behind a snow-coated pew. Surely the abbess wasn't considering *climbing* the tower? The stairs must have rotted to nothing over the years. And yet, through the blinding storm, she saw the Mother Superior enter through the arched doorway. Claudia waited... but the woman never came out.

She rubbed her cold hands together and moved from her hiding place. The snow soaked into her robes and chilled her feet as she approached the askew building.

Now, there was nowhere to go but up.

The evil is here.

Ursula sat by her bed, unable to shake the dread that had settled in her gut. Beside her, the girl twitched in the midst of a disturbed sleep.

Unclean spirit.

What did it all mean? And what in God's name had the Mother Superior been searching for when she drew back the blanket and exposed the girl's naked lower half?

There's a simple way to find out.

She glanced at the bare feet protruding from under the covers.

No! It would be best if she forgot what she saw. What-ever transpired here was between God and the Mother Superior.

But the abbess was acting so frightfully *oddly* today. From her insistence on entering Ursula's cell alone to the way she had exposed the girl, her behaviour was not only *wrong*...

It was downright sinful.

The sleeping girl's legs shuffled, and she whimpered in what sounded like pain. A single tear rolled down her pale, pretty flesh.

Ursula stood, wincing at the sound of the chair scraping across the floor. She looked once at the door, listened for movement in the corridor, and reached for the blanket.

What are you doing?

She had to know. It was as simple as that. And if she didn't act now, while fired up with righteous indignation, she never would. Gripping the blanket with trembling fingers, she pulled it back. The fabric slid aside and crumpled onto the floor.

"Father forgive me," she whispered, and lifted the hem of the girl's tunic. The skin on her ankles and calves stretched tightly across bone, and showed little evidence of muscle. Ursula raised the garment higher, her blood rushing madly through her veins. A headache pounded in her temples. So far, she had found nothing to interest the Mother Superior.

No signs, no symbols.

Unclean spirit.

And certainly no satanic markings.

Ursula knew she should stop. To lift the clothing any further would be a dreadful sin.

"She's just a woman," said Ursula. "Exactly like me. We're all created in the image of God." She took a deep breath and pulled the tunic up. "Beneath our clothes we're all the—"

Then she saw it.

"Good Lord," she said, as the fabric slipped through her useless fingers and rested above the girl's navel. She stepped back, tripping over her own mattress and falling to the floor. There, she bit down on her knuckles, hard enough to pierce the flesh and draw blood.

It was all she could do not to scream in horror.

Claudia stepped into the bell tower.

Two long, weathered ropes dangled before her, and she craned her neck to look at the rusted bell hanging high above. The only way up was a staircase that clung to the walls and spiralled all the way to the top.

Shielding her eyes from stray flakes of snow that entered through the belfry, she spotted the Mother Superior's hand sliding along the rail.

"Mother Superior!" Claudia shouted. "Where are you going? It's not safe!"

The abbess neither slowed nor stopped, and Claudia reluctantly placed a foot on the lowest step. It creaked alarmingly beneath her.

"Come down! We can talk about this!"

She started up after the abbess, her fingers trailing along the mouldy rail, and came across a broken step after the first sharp corner. The splintered wood had left a gaping hole.

"Mother Superior, please!"

Sobbing, Claudia took each step quickly, avoiding the middle sections where the wood would be most fragile and never letting her feet linger. Above her, the shadow of the abbess fell across the bell.

"It's dangerous!" cried Claudia. "Come down!"

The abbess was shouting something, but her words were stolen by the roaring wind. Flurries of snow billowed inside, stinging Claudia's face and eyes. She placed her right foot carelessly and felt the step crack beneath her, yet on she continued. The survival of the Mother Superior was of paramount importance. Without her guidance, the sisters would be lost, especially over the unforgiving winter.

But Claudia was tiring. She slowed to a jog, catching fleeting snatches of the Mother Superior's voice between the groans and shrieks of the rotten wood.

"...forsaken me? Why have..."

"Get down from there!" cried Claudia. She was halfway up the stairs when she looked up and saw the abbess perched on the edge of the staircase. The rail was broken, and the woman wavered uncertainly before it.

"...done all I can..."

"Mother Superior, stop! *Stop what you're doing this instant!*"

At last the abbess acknowledged her. She peered down, and for a moment, their eyes met.

"Our souls are damned," she said. "Do not let the—"

Thunder crashed, obscuring the words. The Mother Superior toppled forward, her head striking the bell with a melancholy clang, and then...

Down she fell.

Ecce crucem domini.

That's what the abbess had said as she lifted the sleeping girl's tunic and removed the crucifix from around her neck.

Ursula had thought little of it, for at that moment Sister Claudia had appeared and forced her to hide.

But now it all made sense.

A sick, twisted, *monstrous* sense.

Ecce crucem domini.

She picked herself up from the mattress and took two faltering steps closer to the girl. She didn't want to look again, but she had no choice. For there, nestled betwixt the girl's thighs, was a wooden crucifix with a golden Christ affixed to it. Ursula knew it belonged to the abbess. She knew, because she had seen it before.

And only the abbess...

...could have put it...

...where it was now.

Behold the cross of the Lord.

Ursula felt sick.

The holy symbol had been crudely inserted into the girl's vagina. Blood trickled down the polished Jesus and pooled between her thighs.

"An abomination," Ursula whispered.

What could have driven the abbess to such obscenity? Not only was it a vile assault of a young girl, but it was an affront to God. Bile rose in her throat, and she swallowed it down. She had to be strong. There was no time to find Henrik. She couldn't leave the girl here with that... *thing* sticking out of her.

And so, sobbing at the thought that such cruelty could be perpetrated by one of the Lord's staunchest admirers, Ursula reached for the crucifix. She pinched the tip, but the wood was smeared with blood, and she couldn't get a solid grip. Instead, she hooked her fingers under Christ's arms and slowly pulled. She had never seen the genitals of another person before, and though she tried not to look, she needed to ensure she didn't hurt the girl further. The crucifix slid out between the fleshy folds with a soft sucking sound. Curly, light-coloured hairs stuck to the blood.

It was all too much.

Ursula raced to the window, yanked it open, and hurled the tainted crucifix out. She leaned over the sill, watching the cross fall. Smaller and smaller it became, tumbling down the vast, imposing cliff upon which the convent rested. Long before it reached the bottom, the bloody talisman vanished amongst the falling snow, followed closely by the contents of Ursula's stomach.

With tumultuous thoughts rattling in her head, she staggered backwards on weak legs. She had to tell someone. But who would believe her? It was her word against the Mother Superior's, and in her panic, she had tossed the only evidence out of the window.

Then confront her.

How? The abbess would deny everything, and any punishment meted out for her insolence would be grave. She might even be banished! With a single word, the abbess could cast Ursula out into the snow to die a solitary, excommunicated death.

Who, then, would look after the young girl?

Ursula wept. She had never felt so alone. Oh, God was by her side, naturally, but he wasn't going to mop up the blood from the girl's—

She shuddered. More tears fell.

Ecce crucem domini.

Henrik. She should speak to Henrik. He was a kind man, and a godless man, and, more importantly, he was no friend of the Mother Superior. If anyone would be willing to help, it was surely he.

Behold the cross of the Lord.

Wiping her tears away, Ursula fetched the bucket and a clean rag. She spread the girl's legs apart and started to wipe away the blood.

"I promise," she said, as she wrung the rag between her hands and watched the bloody water splatter into the bucket. "I'll never let anything bad happen to you again. Do you hear me?" A teardrop fell onto the sleeping girl's pale, sutured thigh. *"Never."*

12

———

The Mother Superior was dead.

Sister Claudia hurtled down the stairs, her shoulder brushing the wet stone wall. She no longer cared whether the walkway shattered beneath her, because the Mother Superior was *dead*.

Dead, dead, dead.

No one could have survived that fall.

After her head struck the bell, the woman's body had gone limp. She sailed through the air like a diving bird, and though Claudia had reached out to grab her, to *save* her, the heavy robes slipped through her grasping fingers. Halfway down, the abbess smacked violently against the staircase, smashing the rail and plummeting downwards until she hit the floor with a nauseating crunch.

Dead, dead, dead.

When Claudia reached the bottom of the stairs, she found the Mother Superior lying face-down in the snow. The old woman's leg bent the wrong direction at the knee, and a steaming pool of red liquid formed around her head like a mocking, bloody halo. Dazed and weeping, Claudia knelt by her side. She peeled the woman's face from the icy stone and rolled her onto her back. As she did so, she heard the jumbled crackle of broken bones, a sound akin to stepping through frozen leaves in the dying days of autumn.

For the first time in years, the bell chimed quietly above them.

Shortly after the great storm, the Mother Superior had deemed the ruins unsafe for worship, and forbidden her flock from visiting. From that day on, the bell had lain dormant.

Until now.

Claudia backed out of the tower and turned, gazing at the snowy, wind-blasted remnants of the chapel, which had, some time ago, been one of the finest in Europe. Where she stood had been an altar on a raised platform, alongside the lectern and the baptismal font, which, to the best of her knowledge, had only been used once in the thirty-five years Claudia had spent in Sant'Arcangel. She looked skyward, remembering the magnificent fresco that had adorned the ceiling, and which now lay beneath her feet, lost to the dual threat of time and the elements.

They claimed everything, eventually.

Even the Mother Superior.

But what to do? What to do?

The toll of the bell filled her with an aching sense of loss. What was God's purpose in robbing the convent of its beloved matriarch? Without her steadfast leadership, the flock would be set adrift on a thrashing sea of confusion and despair. Who among the sisters would be able — would be *willing* — to step up and take her place?

No names sprang to mind.

Unless...

No.

Of course not.

You're not ready.

But who was? Which sister was best qualified to lead the flock through the challenges of winter? That filthy slut Sister Isabelle? Claudia scoffed at the idea. Or how about Sister Gertrude, whom she suspected had not a worshipful bone in her wretched body? Or the obsequious Sister Ursula, bending over backwards to please others as the convent fell to ruin around her?

None of them had what it took. Not a single one. They lacked both conviction and direction, and required strict governance. Claudia had devoted her life to studying the way the Mother Superior ran the convent. Surely... if *someone* had to take over...

She faced the tower. Snow whirled across her vision, grazing her cheeks and melting on her lips.

Could it be true? Could it *really* be true?

Had her time come at last?

Her legs trembled. Was the Holy Spirit entering her? Or was she just cold? She looked at the crumpled body of the Mother Superior, and as she did so, the clouds parted.

Claudia gasped.

A blinding beam of light shone down upon her. Bathed in the celestial glow, she fell to her knees, clasping her hands as the light soothed her frozen flesh and spread warmth within her.

"Thank you, God! Oh thank you, thank you, *thank you* for showing me the way!"

This was no coincidence. God's intentions were as clear as a drop of dew on a blade of grass.

Sister Claudia smiled and wept and basked in the heavenly glow.

God had chosen a new leader for Sant'Arcangel's unruly flock... and he had chosen wisely.

~

By the time Ursula returned to her room with Henrik in tow, the girl was wide awake. She sat upright, leaning against the headboard and crying, her bloodstained tunic bunched up around her waist.

"Lie down," said Henrik. "It's much too early for you to be sitting."

She gazed down at the crimson sheets beneath her thighs. "Something's wrong with me," she sobbed. Her eyes were less glazed than before, and blood coated her face and hands.

Ursula shared a worried glance with Henrik. She had already explained the situation on their way from the gardener's cottage, where she had found the doctor sitting by a roaring fire and staring at the blank pages of a journal. As they passed through the convent, she had spoken in hushed tones of the girl's brief awakening, and of the Mother Superior's blasphemous act with the crucifix. Henrik had listened and, to his eternal credit, seemed to believe her without question.

After all, nuns were forbidden to tell lies.

"How are you feeling?" he asked the girl, as Ursula filled a cup with water from the bucket. It was less than a quarter full, and she would need to visit the well before bedtime.

"I don't know," she replied, gratefully taking the water from Ursula with her bloody hands. She sipped, wincing as Henrik inspected her nether regions. "I don't know much of anything. My mind is like a parchment awaiting the stroke of the quill."

The words surprised Ursula, for the girl's educated tongue defied Dr Franco's assertion that she was of peasant stock.

"Quite," said Henrik, seemingly less impressed. "Now, Sister Ursula tells me you don't recall what happened. Is that so?"

"Yes. I remember... at least, I *think* I remember waking up... beneath the earth. Waking up and... and clawing my way out." She looked down at her red hands. "Though it may have been a dream."

"I don't believe so," said Ursula. "There was dirt in your mouth when we found you."

The girl looked aghast.

"And under your finger and toenails," Henrik added. He concluded his examination and pulled the girl's tunic down. "No lasting damage, thankfully. But we'll need new bedclothes and sheets. I trust you can arrange that, Sister Ursula?"

"Of course." She began stripping the sheet from her mattress on the floor. "For now, she shall use mine."

As Henrik prepared a spoonful of laudanum, Ursula took her nightdress from the closet and perched on the edge of the bed. "May I ask a question, if you're feeling up to answering?"

The girl nodded, though her eyelids fluttered sleepily.

"Earlier, when you awoke, you said something curious. You said... *the evil is here.*"

"I did?"

"Yes. The evil is here. I was wondering, whatever did you mean by such a thing?"

"I... I'm sorry. I have no recollection of that."

"Not to worry," smiled Ursula, feeling both relieved and

disappointed, and also a mite foolish. "It frightened me a little, that's all."

The girl swallowed Henrik's medicine, grimacing at the bitter taste. "I apologise. I can only imagine I was dreaming. I've been having such awful dreams."

"That'll be enough talk of night terrors for one day," said Henrik. "Now, let's get you washed and changed. Can't have you lying in all that blood." He raised her arms, preparing to lift her garment, and said to Ursula, "You may wish to look away."

"No, I'll help you."

He hesitated. "Isn't that against your vows?"

"I said," she replied firmly, her mind set, "I can *help*."

"Very well," said Henrik, and, working together, they cleaned the patient and dressed her in fresh bedclothes. Henrik helped her stand while Ursula changed the sheets, then laid her back down in a supine position. Lastly, he checked her temperature by placing his hand on her forehead.

"No sign of a fever, I'm pleased to report. But for the next few days, I don't want you sitting up unless you're eating or drinking. If you need anything, I'm certain Sister Ursula shall be only too happy to assist you."

"Of course," said Ursula. "Get lots of rest, and we'll have you on your feet in no time."

"I don't want to dream anymore," the girl said drowsily. Her eyes closed, then flickered open again. "Please... make it so I cannot dream."

Henrik patted her hand. "I'm afraid that's beyond my capabilities as a doctor."

"What do you dream of?" asked Ursula, and Henrik shot her a disapproving stare.

The girl moaned, tears forming in the corners of her eyes. "Hellfire... and damnation. Blood raining... from the sky. And a woman..." — unconsciously, she pressed one hand between her legs — "...an old woman performing unspeakable acts upon me."

"They're just dreams," lied Henrik. "Don't forget that. Your dreams can't hurt you. They're illusions. Phantasms. Nothing more."

"I'm sorry, doctor," she said, her eyes closing once more, and this time staying shut. "But I don't believe... that's... *true.*"

"Then may your slumbers be dreamless, little one," Henrik whispered as she drifted off. He turned away and knelt by the buckets, rinsing his hands. "Thank you," he said to Ursula.

"For what?"

"For allowing the girl to live in your room, in your bed, and in your clothes. And for assisting me in undressing her." He wiped his wet hands on his trousers. "I know it can't be easy for a nun to break her vows like that."

Ursula blushed. "I bent them rather than broke them, I think."

"You have a good heart, Sister Ursula." He smiled broadly. "Under different circumstances, you would have made a fine nurse."

Her cheeks burned, and she longed to tell him how much his words meant to her. Perhaps over the winter she would summon the courage to discuss her desire to leave the convent with him. She wished so *badly* to discuss it... but for now, she would exercise patience. There was no rush; it was only the first day of the storm, and if Henrik shattered her dreams, the rest of the season would be unbearable.

He stood by her window, gazing out forlornly.

Ursula, feeling equally pensive, joined him. Mist had settled across the mountains, and conspired with the snow to mask the peaks.

"Dr Franco will be safe," she said. She considered placing a hand on his shoulder, and decided against it. "He's made the journey to and from Cerbesca many times. More than anyone else on Earth, I'd wager."

"Do nuns wager?" asked Henrik.

"Nuns are people too."

He chuckled. It sounded forced. "I know Franco will be all right. The man is like a cat, always landing on his feet. It's something else that torments me." He took a breath. "Sister Ursula—"

"Please, call me Ursula. There's no need for formalities when the Mother Superior isn't around."

"Very well." He smiled thinly. "Ursula, I noticed a keyhole on your door. Do you, perchance, know where the key is?"

"Indeed. There's only one, and the Mother Superior keeps it on her at all times, tied to her cincture belt. She insists that only sinners need to lock their doors."

"Of course she does," he muttered wryly.

"Why do you ask?"

Turning from the window, he looked at her with keen eyes. "I can trust you, Ursula, can't I? I feel that out of all the nuns in the convent, it's you I can trust the most."

"More so than Sister Gertrude?"

It was Henrik's turn to blush. "I'm not sure I understand what you—"

"Don't worry, I won't tell." She trailed her fingers down the wooden cross around her neck. "We all have our little secrets."

"We do indeed," he said. "But please... reassure me that my trust in you is not misplaced. I need allies and confidants if I'm to make it through the winter; sensible people, with sound judgement and rigorous minds."

"You can trust me," she said, though she doubted how sensible and rigorous-minded she was.

"I'm glad to hear it. Because if I may be frank... I'm concerned."

"About the girl?" She lowered her voice as tears pricked her eyes. "Do you not think she'll make it?"

"It's not that. She'll be absolutely fine with you watching over her."

"Then what vexes you, Doctor?"

When Henrik spoke, his dry lips smacked together. "You heard what she said about clawing her way out of the ground. We both know that was no dream." He turned his head, and Ursula followed his gaze to the blood-soaked tunic on the floor.

"You think," whispered Ursula, "she was buried alive?"

"I don't *think*. I'm convinced of it. That young girl dug herself out of a shallow grave this morning. And I, for one, would like to know *who* buried her... and where they are now."

A shiver started in her extremities and snaked its way through her limbs. She looked out the window, where the snow continued to fall, and imagined a man tramping through the forest gripping a bloody axe with frozen fingers.

"We needn't worry," she said. "It'll be night soon, and once the temperature drops, no one outside will be able to withstand the cold."

"An inarguable statement," said Henrik. "Though perhaps I'm not making myself clear. My concern is not that the brute who attacked our young friend is somewhere out there."

He stole a glance at her, then turned away.

"I'm worried that whatever danger stalks the mountain is already here, with us... *inside the convent.*"

13

Sister Claudia passed through Sant'Arcangel unnoticed. An empty wheelchair rattled across the uneven floor as she guided the contraption towards the courtyard, accompanied by the distant sound of worshipful voices united in harmony.

It was time for choir practice, and the nuns had amassed in the new chapel, leaving the corridors devoid of activity. This was excellent news for Sister Claudia, who did not wish to be disturbed while carrying out her holy mission. She was sad to miss choir, for singing made her feel closer to God than even prayer, but she had more important work to attend to.

The wood and wicker wheelchair had originally belonged to the long-departed Sister Bartolomea, and was later used by Sister Ruth after her disastrous leg amputation. Since Sister Ruth's passing, the wheelchair had sat abandoned in one of the convent's vast storage rooms, buried beneath old bed sheets and farming tools. And yet despite the dank environs of its resting place, the chair was, with the exception of one sticky front wheel, still in perfectly workable condition.

God's plan was in motion, Claudia realised, and had been for years without anyone knowing.

She wheeled the chair through the courtyard and down the corridor to the derelict chapel. There, the snowfall lay thicker than before, and she had to drag the wheelchair rather than push it, but she soon found the Reverend Mother where she had left her. Snow had piled up around her crooked limbs, and the shallow pool of blood had frozen to an icy sheen.

Claudia knelt by her side, peering intently at the woman's face, watching for—

There.

A vaporous puff of steam emerged from between the blue lips.

The abbess was still alive.

She couldn't move, of course. Every bone in her body had shattered, the injuries so grievous she would never physically recover. Claudia had even considered putting the old woman out of her misery. It would be the merciful thing to do, and how could showing mercy be sinful? But, like the Mother Superior always insisted, it was a nun's lot in life to suffer. And if God wanted the woman to live, then he must have a plan for her, however obscure it may appear to a mere mortal. One thing, however, was certain.

Her days of leading the convent were over.

Setting the wheelchair against the wall, Claudia lifted the woman by her arms, grappling the loose body into the wooden seat. The Mother Superior slumped into position, and Claudia used rope she had found in the storage room to bind her waist, wrists, and ankles to the chair, tying the knots tightly to prevent her from sliding out.

"There," she said, standing back to admire her handiwork. Her expression darkened in revulsion. *"Oh."*

The abbess looked dreadful. Her face was a mass of swollen purple bruising, and her jaw sagged, revealing the broken remains of her front teeth. Frozen tears cleaved to her cheeks, and when Claudia gouged them off with her thumbnail, she took several layers of skin with her. The blood would have to be dealt with later.

Once she had thawed.

A thin wheeze escaped the woman's tumescent lips.

"No, don't speak," said Claudia. "Your time has passed, and God has chosen *me* as your successor. Isn't that wonderful?"

The woman said nothing. Her index finger twitched like a worm.

Smiling beatifically, Claudia reached for the digit. She placed her thumb on the knuckle, pressed hard, and — *crack!* — snapped the finger backwards. The woman's pupils dilated.

It was all she could do.

"No, no, no, don't even *try* to move. You had your chance, and you performed God's work admirably. I'm sure he's pleased. But now, it's *my* time to lead. Don't you understand? God showed me a sign. A holy light from heaven, shining only on me." She knelt before the woman. "So why do you refuse to pass on? Are you unwelcome? Has God barred the holy gates to you?"

She sighed.

"Well, I shall not hasten your departure. As long as God keeps you alive, you may help me, the way I helped you for so many years." She manoeuvred the wheelchair into position. "The way I'm *still* doing, it seems, despite my newfound superiority."

Sister Claudia pushed the handles, and immediately, the front wheels jammed in the snow. Grunting in annoyance, she spun the chair and tipped it backwards, dragging the Mother Superior through the ruined chapel as the wind pummelled them. Once they reached the corridor, movement became easier, and she made good progress. The old woman's head drooped to the side, bouncing limply as the rickety wheels rattled over the stones.

What purpose, Claudia wondered, could the abbess serve in her current vegetative state? Perhaps God had kept her alive to ease the transition of power? Claudia was in no doubt as to her unpopularity among the sisters. They thought her harsh, and her punishments excessive. Yet if they feared a flogging so badly, why, then, did they continue to misbehave?

It mattered not. For the time being, she would tell her sisters that the Mother Superior was alive but indisposed, and that she, Sister Claudia — *Mother Claudia,* she thought wickedly — would temporarily assume leadership. Few would dare challenge her authority, and if they tried, her trusty cat o' nine tails hung in the closet, craving the wet violence of leather splitting flesh. These women had to be kept in line by any means possible. A nun's life was one of determination and quiet perseverance; if they couldn't endure a flagellation for their indiscretions, then the monastic life, Claudia believed, was not for them.

She heard footsteps, and came to a stop. Who dared walk the halls during hymn recital? She left the wheelchair in the shadows and peered around the corner. In the candlelight, she saw a figure clad not in a habit, but in trousers and a long coat.

Dr Henrik.

What business had he in the nuns' sleeping quarters?

She narrowed her eyes in disgust. The doctor stopped and pulled an object from his pocket. Flickering light glinted off the dark metal, and Claudia's hands balled into fists. Was that...

Her heart pounded.

It was.

The insufferable doctor carried a *pistol*.

Quietly seething, she skulked in the darkness as Henrik checked the weapon, nodded, and placed it back in his coat. He resumed walking, and she receded further into the shadows, listening as the sound of his footsteps changed from the clack of the stone floor to the muffled thump of the entrance hall rug.

Righteous wrath boiled her blood. How *dare* that odious varlet bring a gun into the convent? And not just any convent.

Her convent.

The very act was an abomination against God! Only a man would have the unbridled temerity to bring an instrument of death into a holy building. Would *he* dare to question her God-given authority? Possibly. Claudia's jaws ached, and she realised she was grinding her teeth.

The sooner that doctor was gone, the better.

The front door closed, booming through the hallways, and that was when, for the first time, the voice spoke.

"...he's only here because of the girl..."

Startled, Claudia spun. "Who said that?" she hissed. "Who's there?"

But there was nobody except the Mother Superior in her wheelchair. The wind wailed mournfully.

"...if the girl were to die, then..."

She clamped her eyes shut. Was the voice inside her head? No, it was close, and echoed off the walls.

Slowly, she turned to the Mother Superior. The abbess gazed at the floor through bruised eyes; head tilted, jaw sagging, a string of blood-flecked saliva dangling from her chin. Claudia stared at her in silence.

"Was that... you?"

No reply was forthcoming. She kneeled before the abbess and placed her hands on the woman's broken knees. "Please, I beg of you. Answer me! Was that you who—"

"*...that doctor will destroy everything...*"

Had Claudia not been kneeling, she would have collapsed to the floor. Instead, she buried her face in the woman's lap, rapturous tears flooding down her cheeks and soaking into the frosty fabric.

"*...you need to stop him before he undoes all your hard work...*"

Of course! It all made sense now. Why hadn't she seen it before? The voice was coming from the Mother Superior... but it did not belong to her.

"Yes, God!" sobbed Claudia. Mucus ran from her nostrils, her lips drawn back in reverence. "Thank you for showing me the way!"

He was talking to her *through* the Mother Superior. That was why the living corpse still breathed! She was nothing more than a conduit, an empty vessel through which he could communicate with his Chosen One.

She took the abbess's hands in hers. They were cold, so very cold.

"*...the fate of Sant'Arcangel rests with you now, Mother Claudia...*"

"I shall guide them, my Lord," she said through her tears. She gripped the Mother Superior's hands so tightly she felt the bones shift inside the sagging flesh. "Speak to me through this woman, and I shall guide those strong enough to salvation. If I must, I shall guide them through the fiery pits of hell!"

The responsibility threatened to overwhelm her. God had spoken to her before, but only through signs, never in direct communion. His plans for her must be wondrously divine. Profound love flooded her heart and tingled in her chest. She needed to rest. To think, and to pray.

To let the shock wear off.

"I won't let you down," she whispered, and rose to her feet. She had already decided to move into the Mother Superior's cell, with its fireplace and writing desk and large, comfortable bed, *before* discovering the woman had become God's messenger. Now her plan made even more sense.

"This is the greatest day of my life," she said, and crossed herself once, twice, then a third time, stopping only at the shuffling of nearby feet.

Who dared disturb her now?

She turned, and there, several doors down, stood one of her sisters. A single candle glimmered in the sconce behind the woman, outlining her silhouette in a pale orange radiance.

Claudia shielded the wheelchair with her body.

"Shouldn't you be at choir, Sister?" she asked with all the authority she could muster.

The nun did not move.

"Run along now. This matter does not concern you."

Wreathed in darkness, the nun took a step closer. "My hand," she said.

Claudia recognised the voice. "Is that you, Sister Isabelle?"

"Please... *look at my hand.*"

Of *course* it would be Sister Isabelle. Who else but one of Sant'Arcangel's most poorly behaved sisters would dare play truant? Claudia had heard the rumours of her and Sister Maria. Of how they sinned together at night, and made a lustful mockery of God's teachings.

"I've no time for games, Sister Isabelle," she said, and stole a glance at the abbess. Usually, she would have dragged the sister to the refectory and whipped her raw for such a transgression. But right now? She could spare neither the time nor the energy. "Can't you see I'm busy? The Mother Superior... she had a fall. Her ankle is twisted."

Sister Isabelle advanced. She held her hand out almost as an offering. Liquid dripped from the appendage. It smelt like pus.

"It's getting worse," the nun said. "Every minute it gets *worse.*"

Claudia gagged at the stench and retreated behind the wheelchair. "Go to the chapel at once," she said. "And pray to God for forgiveness."

Isabelle stepped into the light, revealing thick, yolk-like stains down the front of her habit.

"You smell foul," said Claudia. "Forget about praying. Clean yourself up, then pay a visit to the doctor. If I find you like this again, there will be serious repercussions."

Without another word, she pushed the chair, leaving Sister Isabelle and her quiet sobs to the solemn darkness of the hallway. Strangely afraid that the nun was following, Claudia sped up. Each bump on the floor jostled the abbess's head from side to side, until at last they arrived at the Mother Superior's quarters.

Claudia's new home.

She opened the door and shoved the wheelchair inside. It rolled across the stone and bumped into the bed frame.

"My apologies, dearest Mother," Claudia said, and moved to close the door.

She halted, and sniffed. The malodorous stench of Sister Isabelle seemed to linger in the air. Cautiously, she stepped out into the hallway and glanced one last time down the corridor.

It was as dark and empty as a deep, dreamless sleep.

Claudia shut the door and leaned against it, but the grim odour persisted. It clung to her robes, so she stripped them and her undergarments off and laid them in the fireplace. Nude, she sat on the bed, watching her clothing burn and shrivel amongst the flames. Once they had turned to ash, she used the Mother Superior's private washroom to cleanse herself. It was, she thought, a baptism of sorts. For although the other sisters did not know it yet, and wouldn't for some time, Sant'Arcangel and its flock belonged to her now.

And she would not let God down.

14

DR JOSEPH FRANCO TUGGED HIS SCARF OVER HIS FACE, protecting his mouth and nose from the chill wind.

His coach bumped and shuddered along the mountain track. Despite the heavy snowfall and inclement conditions, he was making good progress. A glance at his fob watch told him he was well over halfway to Cerbesca, where a fire and a brandy awaited him in the tavern. Hell, he may even invite his favourite barmaid Veronica to keep him company tonight. Something about spending time with a bunch of frigid nuns always made him crave the warmth of a real woman.

He scratched his arm, keen to see the lights of Cerbesca shimmering through the mist.

Was Henrik regretting his decision to stay yet? Franco chuckled at the idea. The man had a job to do, and a woman to occupy his time, so providing the silly bugger didn't get caught in the act, he should be able to make it through the long winter nights without going mad. It was the lack of cigars and a dwindling supply of brandy that may prove to be his downfall.

He pulled on the reins, reluctantly slowing the horses. The further he rode down the mountain, the more the storm lessened, so with the worst behind him, there was no sense risking his life on the home stretch. Once he was free from this blasted fog, he could speed up and be in bed with Veronica shortly after midnight.

A wolf howled in the distance.

Franco glanced at the cloth-wrapped rifle in the empty seat beside him. He felt foolish for leaving his revolver with Henrik. What use would the man have for it? The chances of the young girl's attacker not only surviving the night, but following her to the convent, were practically nonexistent.

Still, if the weapon offered an additional feeling of security, then it would have served its purpose. It mattered not to Franco either way. He had his rifle, and in the event of an attack from a pack of wolves, a single shot was usually sufficient to scatter the beasts.

His arm itched again, and he burrowed his fingers beneath his sleeve to give it a damn good scratch. As he did, his thoughts returned to Henrik. Perhaps their time apart would inspire his assistant to open a practice of his own? Cerbesca was stifling his growth, Franco believed. If he wished to, Henrik could move somewhere far more appealing to a younger man. Torino, or even Roma. He was an excellent doctor, and only his love for Sister Gertrude kept him shackled to the mountain village of Cerbesca.

Franco smiled sadly.

The day Henrik convinced the girl to leave the sisterhood would mean the dissolution of their longstanding partnership. He would miss his friend dearly, but they could always write to each other, and it would be highly agreeable to have somewhere to stay in one of the cities should he ever need a holiday. Some time away from the countryside, where payment was notoriously scarce, would undoubtedly be good for his soul *and* his wallet.

The coach emerged from the mist, and below, in the valley, the town's faint lights twinkled like distant stars.

"Ah, there you are," he said, cracking the reins to encourage the horses from a canter to a gallop. Should he go straight to the tavern? Yes, he thought so. His own home would be as chilly as the grave, and the idea of waiting for the room to heat was most unappealing. Whereas in the tavern, he could sit by an already roaring fire and ogle Veronica's voluptuous cleavage while she furnished him with cheap ale. Then, once he was suitably defrosted, they would keep each other warm until morning the old-fashioned way.

He scratched at his arm again. "This is ridiculous," he muttered, and rolled up his sleeve. The air nipped at his bare skin.

Franco frowned.

Unfamiliar black marks dotted his forearm. They looked fungal, and when he prodded at them, his finger sank into the soft mass.

"What the devil are *you*?" he smirked.

Bemused, he pulled his sleeve down and cracked the reins once more. The lantern rocked by his head, the movement creating the impression of dancing flames in an open hearth.

The thought pleased him.

Warmth, ale, and a fine, stocky woman were what he needed now, and nothing — not the storm, not the mountain track, and certainly not any curious black marks on his arm — was going to slow him down.

15

As the newest member of Sant'Arcangel, Sister Beatrice was still finding her bearings in the convent. She had begun her novitiate period four months prior, and had hoped some unfortunate soul would join before winter to relieve her of the menial tasks she had been entrusted with.

No one had, however, which left Beatrice in her current undesirable position at the very bottom of the convent's hierarchical pecking order. Whether it was peeling potatoes or scrubbing the washroom floors, no chore was too humble for her... at least, not in the eyes of Sister Claudia.

That very morning, her superior had instructed her to clean the statues in Sant'Arcangel's prodigious network of corridors. The request surprised her, because she could not recall ever *seeing* any statues other than the frightening wooden Christ in the entrance hall that looked like it was about to climb down from its cross at any moment. But Beatrice, being a timid creature who was prone to staring at her feet as she walked, hadn't noticed the statues because they were stored up high in a series of nooks and recesses that dotted the corridor walls.

She stood at the foot of her wooden ladder, gazing up at a statue of a kneeling Mary. The head was missing, and the once-lustrous paint was faded and dusty. Beatrice wondered when last it had been cleaned, then dipped her cloth in the water bucket and wrung it out. Elsewhere in the convent, her fellow sisters were singing *Anima Christi*. It was her favourite, and she hummed along under her breath as she climbed. One day, she would be allowed to join in, but for now, she was happy just to be here. There was no hurry. At sixteen years old, she had her whole life to celebrate Christ and sing his praises.

The ramshackle rungs groaned beneath her as she placed her weight on them. With one hand on the wall for balance, she leaned over and wiped the cloth down Mary's blue cloak in long, even strokes. The statue's head lay beside her in the alcove, the painted eyes closed in eternal prayer.

Over the choir came the hiss of scuffed footsteps, and from her perch atop the ladder, Beatrice spotted a nun weaving towards her. "Good evening," she called, and waved. The woman staggered awkwardly, almost drunkenly, taking three quick steps and slamming against the wall as if drawn by some invisible force.

It was odd behaviour, but perhaps her sister was unwell? Beatrice did not wish to pry, so she resumed her scrubbing.

The nun stumbled closer, raking along the stone wall. She held one arm close to her chest and panted heavily. The sound reminded Beatrice of the strange noises her mother used to make behind closed doors whenever she was entertaining a gentleman friend.

"Excuse me," she called down. "I don't mean to bother you, but do you perhaps need any help?"

The nun looked up at her. In the dim candlelight, her eyes appeared badly bruised.

"Umm, my name is Sister Beatrice. I don't believe we've been introduced?"

The nun bowed her head and shuffled closer, resting her hands on the ladder. This concerned Beatrice. Was her sister considering climbing up?

"Oh, I don't think that's wise," said Beatrice. She laughed uncomfortably. "This ladder is almost as old as the convent. I wouldn't wish to fall."

The silence that ensued went on far too long. Beatrice nibbled on her lip, trying to think of something to say.

"Well, I'd better get back to work. It was nice to meet you." She turned away and brushed a cobweb from the statue. The choir had moved on to *Benedictus*. She sighed at the beauty of their voices.

That'll be you one day, she thought. *Standing with the choir and—*

The ladder shifted beneath her.

"Oh!" she shouted. The wet cloth dropped from her hand and slapped onto the floor as she pressed her palms against the cold stone to steady herself. The nun, with lips contorted into a twisted grimace, shook the ladder.

"Stop!" cried Beatrice, spreading her arms wider. "Who is that? Why are you doing this?" With tears in her eyes, she gazed down at the nun.

Her hand... Lord in heaven, what was wrong with her *hand?*

Afraid to move, Beatrice carefully placed her foot on the rung below.

"Stop! Please, I'm begging you!"

The nun started to climb.

"No, it's not safe!" Beatrice sobbed. "Please, leave me be!"

The repulsive hand gripped onto the side rail, the nun's

crusted lips curling into a lecherous sneer. She took the next step.

"What do you want? Just let me down! This isn't funny!"

Beatrice scrambled up the ladder, crouching on the second highest rung as the nun stretched, reaching for her. Up close, she noticed the woman's pale white skin, and how the black rings around her eyes spread outwards the way a droplet of blood seeps into fresh linen. Her hand appeared to be rotting; the fingertips withered, the knuckles cracked and weeping yellow pus. She thrust her leprous claw towards Beatrice's ankle and clung on, her ragged nails digging into the flesh. Beatrice wrenched her foot free, tearing the skin further, and lashed out.

Her heel caught the nun on the nose.

The organ split under the impact. A juicy burst of blood erupted, and the deranged woman's head snapped backwards. She lost her grip and fell, smacking loudly against the hard stone.

Beatrice took her chance. She clambered halfway down the ladder then leapt the rest of the way. She landed, stumbled, and somehow kept her balance. Blood oozed from her torn ankle as she ran, and only when she reached the far end of the corridor did she dare look back.

The nun was on her feet, her shoulders hunched, silently watching.

"*Sister Beatrice,*" she said in a bone-chilling trill, and gave chase.

Beatrice ran. Her sandals pounded the floor, sending waves of agony pulsing through her damaged leg. She took corner after corner, each successive hallway identical to the last, with their candles and doors and heavy, oppressive atmosphere. She tried to follow the sound of the choir, but no matter where she ran, it seemed to get further away.

Round another corner she careened. Where were the stairs? Panicking, she started to pray.

For what? For God to save you from a nun?

Yes! Precisely that! She was lost and alone and horribly afraid. Where *was* everybody? Her ankle throbbed, and the blood in her veins burned like poison.

In the distance, a thin shaft of light crept from under a door. Her prayers had been answered! Someone had to be on the other side. They simply *had* to be.

"Help!" she yelled. She worked her legs harder, ignoring the pain, ignoring the fear. "Somebody help me, please!" She was almost at the door when she chanced a glance over her shoulder.

The sick nun was following at speed.

Beatrice screamed. She reached the door and hammered her fists against the dense wood. "Help me!"

Her pursuer drew closer.

"Let me in!" shrieked Beatrice. "She wants to kill me!"

The words sounded ridiculous to her ears. Killed? By a nun?

"Help me, *please!*"

She was screaming now. Screaming and begging and crying. Her fist ached from knocking, her knuckles bruising from the onslaught. A shadow moved through the light beneath the door. *"Help me!"*

She rattled the handle, and the door swung open with a click.

Of course it did! It wasn't *locked*. None of the doors in the convent were.

She looked back. The nun was almost upon her. "Leave me alone!" she roared, and threw herself inside, slamming the door and pressing up against it. She waited for the handle to move, or for the door to push against her and knock her to her knees.

Nothing happened.

Her stomach churned, salty tears forming in her eyes. Had the nun given up? Or had—

Wait.

What was that noise? It sounded like a moist slurp... and it was coming from inside the room.

Beatrice let the teardrops roll down her cheeks. Wherever she was, it was large, the corners shrouded in impenetrable pools of inky blackness. A stubby candle by the window reflected ethereally off the glass, offering a scant radius of light. Melted wax trailed down the holder in thick white globules, reminding her of the nun's hand.

From somewhere nearby, a woman wheezed.

Beatrice glanced at the unlit corners. "Who's there?" she asked. She wanted nothing more than to flee this place. But what if the nun was waiting for her? Could anything in here possibly be worse than that awful woman and her revolting hand?

In the darkness, a wet object splatted onto the ground.

Yes.

Apparently, something *could* be worse.

Beatrice sidled to the candle and snatched it up, holding it in front of her like a talisman to ward off evil spirits.

In the far corner, she saw movement.

Shadowy limbs uncrossed themselves. A figure began to rise.

"I... I asked who's there?" she whimpered, shuffling backwards until she hit the wall and could shuffle no further.

A pair of eyes glinted in the candlelight.

Then another.

"Please," said Beatrice. "Let me go."

Damp footsteps squelched towards her.

"Oh God," she said, as the first of the figures staggered into the light. Unable to fully comprehend the nightmare that confronted her, Beatrice sank to the floor. The candle trembled in her hands, and she held it to her mouth and blew the flame out.

It was all she could do to keep from going mad.

PART II

16

Excerpt from the diary of Henrik Persson
10th November 1896

*Three days have passed since the snow began to fall, and in the
absence of interesting reading material — the convent library
consists only of dusty tomes on saints and the scriptures — I, Dr
Henrik Persson, have decided to amuse myself in the keeping of a
diary to pass the time. This is intended solely for my eyes, so if
you are somehow perusing these pages and you are <u>not</u> me,
kindly refrain from continuing. And yes, Joseph, that applies to
you, my friend.*

*As I write, seated by a roaring fire in the confines of the
Sant'Arcangel convent's gardener's cottage, the storm continues
unabated. Not since my short time in the Himalayas have I experienced such unremittingly dreadful weather. The wind never lets
up, rattling the door and windows, while each morning I have to
dig my way to the convent through the snow for my daily
provisions.*

It has also made sneaking Sister Gertrude out of her room all the more challenging, but so far, we have managed every night. Even now, I can hear her gentle snores as she lies within reach, and I am reminded that I really ought to return the sleeping beauty to her cell before her absence is noted.

I don't wish to, though, for our time together has been everything I dreamed it would be.

Before I continue, may I reiterate that this is my <u>private</u> journal, and should be read by no one other than myself. Got it, old chum?

Splendid.

So as I was saying, simply gazing upon Gertrude is enough to set my heart aflutter. Her presence is a constant, and very welcome, distraction from the misery of the mountain. Just yesterday, as she stood naked and washed herself from the bucket, the way she posed as she wrung her hair reminded me of nothing less than Titian's masterpiece Venus Rising from the Sea.

Currently, she lies with her back to me, and my eyes cannot help but trace the rolling curves of her shoulder, her waist, her wide hips. Her back bears faint white scars from Sister Claudia's whip, and though I cannot see them from where I sit, her breasts are also scarred. When we make love, I can feel the raised welts with my fingers and tongue. She's sensitive about them, perhaps believing they mar her beauty, but her scars matter not to me. My darling Gertrude is grace and elegance in corporeal form. How I long to touch her, to taste her, to slide my hand beneath those sheets and find the fullness of her buttocks...

Ah, but she is asleep, and I do not wish to wake her. The monastic life is an exhausting one, and Gertrude deserves all the rest she can get. Anyhow, that's enough thoughts of the flesh for now. Onto other matters.

Indeed, one thing I had not anticipated was my concern for Joseph. I know not whether he has made it to Cerbesca safely, and will likely not find out for several months. Only now do I under-

stand how Gertrude must feel whenever the doctor and I undertake the hazardous journey down the mountain after our visits to Sant'Arcangel. It's not the danger that gets to you, that needles your skin and reminds you of the fragility of our lives, hanging by a gossamer thread. It's the uncertainty. The insufferable what-ifs? All it would take for disaster to strike would be the slip of a hoof on the icy road, or a loose bolt breaking and causing a wheel to fall off. I try not to think of it, for down that path lies madness, but it's difficult not to let the mind wander, especially as the convent is particularly grim right now.

A strange malady has cast a pall over the sisters. My services have been greatly in demand, with each day worse than the last. Yesterday, in particular, saw me tend to seven different women, all of whom had fallen ill and shared similar symptoms. Their skin has grown pale, their throats sore, and their limbs are weak, confining them to bed. This alone is not unexpected; Sant'Arcangel is a draughty, hellish place at this time of year, and the common cold is as inevitable as ~~death~~ the rising sun. But this is something else entirely. There has been a shocking increase of sexual desire in the nuns, though I shall refrain from writing about that until I know more. For now, all I shall say is that I find the matter highly disturbing.

And it's with that grim thought that I draw my first, surprisingly painless diary entry to a close. Gertrude stirs, and I intend to keep this journal private, a place for my deepest, innermost thoughts. And also, if time permits and the mood takes me, for me to try my hand at writing erotic literature about the naked goddess in my bed.

Until then, life, I suppose, marches on.

Henrik tucked his journal into the desk as Gertrude stretched. The book was safely hidden by the time she rolled over and looked at him through tired, bleary eyes.

"Why are you awake?" she asked. Without waiting for an answer, she added, "Come back to bed."

"Too much on my mind. I can't sleep."

"Who said anything about sleeping?"

"Don't tempt me, jezebel," he smiled. "Shortly, the sun will rise, and I really ought to send you off in time for your morning prayers."

"To hell with prayers," she said, and slid grudgingly out of bed. The light from the log fire shimmered playfully across her breasts. "Mine have already been answered." She came to him, wrapped her arms around his neck, and kissed his stubbled cheek as he stared out the window.

He returned her kiss. "Perhaps, then, you could pray for warmer clothes for me."

"You can wear my tunic, if you like. It may be chaste, but it keeps the cold out."

"Thank you, but I doubt your Mother Superior would be thrilled to see me capering in the holy robes of her order." He rested one hand on the sizeable curve of her buttocks. "Speaking of the old devil, has anyone seen the abbess lately? I was supposed to discuss my eating arrangements with her, yet she's proven astonishingly elusive."

Gertrude shook her head. "No one has seen her for days."

"And is that common?"

"Not at all. She usually performs the reading at suppertime."

"The reading?"

Gertrude covered her mouth as she yawned. "During meals, we eat in silence while the Mother Superior reads from one of the books in the library. The biography of a saint, or a Bible passage."

"And she does this every meal?"

"Every meal," she nodded. "I don't honestly believe I've ever gone a day *without* seeing her disagreeable countenance, until now." She leaned her head against his shoulder. "It's quite pleasant, actually."

Henrik wished he shared her outlook. He gazed through the frosted window. The wood-chopping axe was still embedded in its stump, but only the top of the handle was visible. The rest was buried beneath the snow.

"It never stops, does it?" he asked.

"The storm? No, not up here. After a while, you start to believe it's never going to end."

He turned to her. In the glow of the fire, Gertrude looked radiant. He ran his hand through her hair, and before he had a chance to stop himself, said, "Marry me. Leave this awful place forever and come away with me to Cerbesca. I don't have much, but I've been saving whatever I can, and I think I have enough to open a—"

"You don't need to convince me," she interrupted.

"Uh, what?" His mind raced, his hands shaking. What was he doing, what was he saying?

"Of course I'll marry you, you big oaf." She smiled warmly. "I was beginning to think you'd never ask."

"I... I worried you'd say no."

"Look at me, Henrik. I'm a nun, and I'm naked as sin and wrapped up in your arms. What part of that suggests I would refuse your proposal?"

"True, but—"

She held a finger to his lips. "Your visits are all I look forward to in my bleak existence. But five or six days a year are not enough. I want more. I *need* more. I need *you,*

Henrik. Take me away from here. I care not where we live, nor how much money we have, for as long as we're together, I shall know true contentment for the first time in my life. I love you, Henrik. I've loved you from the moment I first laid eyes upon you."

They kissed. Urgently, passionately. The sun was rising, threatening to penetrate the mass of clouds, and Henrik drew the curtain as Gertrude undid his belt and pulled his trousers down.

On the wolf-pelt rug, they made love by the fire, exploring each other as if it was their first time together. With Gertrude atop him, Henrik grabbed her exquisitely plump bottom and kissed her lips, her neck, her shoulders, her breasts, their lovemaking intensifying until neither could contain themselves and they came as one, their sweating, spent bodies falling limp in each other's arms.

By late morning, they were still together, although they had retired to the bed for the sake of warmth and comfort. Henrik lay on his back in contemplation, while Gertrude trailed her fingers through his chest hair.

"You seem distracted," she said. "Does the idea of wedded bliss send a chill through you?"

He sighed happily. "Not at all, my love. I was just thinking about horses."

"We make love, and your thoughts turn to livestock?" She pouted at him. "Should I be insulted... or concerned?"

"Neither," he grinned. "Franco left one of his horses in the stables, in case of emergency. So you see, we *do* have a way off this mountain, should the need arise."

She looked at him with wide eyes. "You wish to leave?"

"Fear not, my sweet. I'm not going anywhere without you. However, I do question our decision to stay here much longer."

She laughed, the sound as smooth as velvet. "As strong as my desire is to elope with you, we both know it's too dangerous to travel."

"I worry it's becoming equally dangerous here. There's a sickness in Sant'Arcangel, and I don't know the cause."

"It's the time of year, that's all."

He nodded. How much should he tell her? He did not wish to worry his beloved, yet what he had seen suggested something far more malicious than a case of the sniffles. He trod lightly. "Have you by any chance noticed anything suspicious over the past few days? Anything unusual or untoward?"

She thought for a moment. "I suppose there were a lot of sisters missing from last night's supper. But it's nothing to lose sleep over. Oh, Henrik, is that what's bothering you? A handful of poorly nuns?"

"It's more than that. Of the seven women I looked at yesterday, three of them—"

A knock at the door.

They glanced at each other, neither sure what to do. Who was foolish enough to venture out into the storm at this early hour? The Mother Superior? Heaven forbid!

More knocking. Faster, frenzied.

"Doctor? Doctor Henrik? Please, you must come with me to see Sister Maria. She... she..."

Henrik grabbed his shirt. "What about her?"

A moment's silence. *"She won't stop screaming, Doctor."*

"I'll be right there," he said, pulling on his trousers. "Go on and wait for me in the entrance hall, and tell one of the sisters to prepare some water."

"I will," the voice said. *"And please hurry."*

Gertrude was already stepping into her underskirt. "Go," she said. "I shall bring you soup and bread shortly."

"Thank you." He kissed her, then turned to leave. As he reached the door and picked up his medical bag, he hesitated. "Stay in your quarters as much as you can today. Or better yet, stay here. Try to avoid contact with the others."

"Oh Henrik, I'm not afraid of catching a cold."

He looked at her, his new fiancée, in her underskirt and nothing else. It was a wonderful sight, and he wanted to smile and tell her everything was going to be alright. But he would not begin their engagement with a lie.

"Just do as I say. Please."

She studied his face. "Very well, my love. Anything you ask."

"Don't worry." He slipped into his coat. "I'm sure it's nothing to concern yourself with."

But as he closed the door to the gardener's cottage, he couldn't help thinking of those rotten, black marks he had seen on several of the nuns, and the mad, frenzied look in their bloodshot eyes.

"Please," he muttered, as the snow stung his face and the convent loomed over him like a gothic monstrosity. "I beg of you... be not a plague."

17

———

A MIDDLE-AGED NUN PACED ANXIOUSLY BACK AND FORTH AS Henrik entered the convent and shook the snow from his boots.

"At last," she said, rubbing her cross with both hands. "Where were you? No, it matters not. Follow me, please."

Without waiting for a response, she led him through the corridors as fast as the rules of her order would allow. Henrik tried to recall if Sister Maria was one of the women he had seen yesterday. The trouble with nuns was that, with their head coverings and wimples, they all looked alike. Only those with interesting personalities stood out to him, such as the medically inclined Sister Ursula. He wondered if there had been any further improvement with her patient, and made a mental note to check on her after meeting with Maria.

Maria, Maria, Maria...

That's it! He remembered now. Maria was the nun Gertrude claimed was in a forbidden relationship with Sister Isabelle. *Good for her,* he thought. He heartily approved of a little love to pass the time in this joyless building.

The nun paused at a door. "In here," she said, struggling to be heard over the screams and sobs from inside Maria's room. "Please help her. She's in such pain."

"I'll do my best," said Henrik. "Kindly wait outside, Sister. I'll call to you if I need assistance."

He entered and ensured the door was closed behind him. The room was, as expected, identical to the others. Maria lay on the bed with her back to him. Judging from the fierce movements beneath the sheets, she was energetically scratching herself.

"Sister Maria," he said softly. "It's Henrik."

He walked closer, and moved to place his hand on her shoulder. At the last moment, he stopped himself.

What if she carries a disease?

He banished the thought... for now. "What seems to be the matter, Sister?"

"I can't tell you," she said through gritted teeth. Her body tightened into a clenched ball of muscle.

"Of course you can. I'm a doctor. There's nothing you can say that will shock me. I've seen and heard it all."

She rolled onto her back, her eyes wet with tears. "But it's..." — her voice dropped to a frail whisper — "*...it's some-where I can't let you see.*"

"Come now. I'm well aware your religion forbids it, but you're clearly in much discomfort, and I can't help unless I know what I'm dealing with. Think of me as a doctor rather than a man, if that helps. My sole purpose is to help those in need. To *heal* them."

He heard the rasp of fingernails against skin as her hands moved frenziedly between her legs.

"You can heal me?" she asked. "Like... like Jesus?"

"Well... yes." He cleared his throat. "Something like that."

Grimacing, she pulled her hands out from under the sheet. Blood, and an unidentifiable black substance, stained her fingers. They balled into fists and she pressed them against her eye sockets. "Just make the pain go away. *Please.*"

Before she could change her mind, Henrik tore back the sheets. Her knees were drawn tightly to her chest, and she wore not a stitch of clothing.

"Straighten up," he said, and swallowed. From the smell alone, he knew this was not going to be pretty. "I need to see the... affected area."

"If you insist, Doctor," Maria whispered. With her mouth open in a silent scream of agony, she unfurled her legs and stretched them out, before sagging backwards onto the mattress. "How... how does it look?"

A chill ran down Henrik's spine.

Good god.

Sister Maria's genitals were a nightmare.

Her vaginal area looked like charcoal. The tissue cracked as angry red sores bubbled before his eyes. Between the pulsating abscesses, thick hairs sprouted haphazardly from the throbbing mass. The horror continued up to her navel and down her upper thighs, hardening into a crust from which dark lines emanated like thousands of tapeworms burrowing beneath her skin.

"What's wrong with me?" asked Maria. She scratched herself, and he noticed her bloody fingers were rotting.

"I'm not sure," he said, failing to hide the tremor in his voice. He started to sweat. "Umm, when did you first notice any itching or pain?"

"A... a few days ago."

"Can you be more specific? Do you perhaps recall how it began?"

"I don't remember. I don't... *oooh!*"

Maria's jaw dropped. Her nails snagged one of the sores, bursting it open. Rank yellow discharge leaked onto the bed sheet, filling the air with a suffocating odour. She rolled away from him, displaying thin black lines that threaded from between her buttocks like subdermal cobwebs. Henrik stepped back. Not since his days working in the leper colonies had he seen such a devastating infection. He fumbled for his handkerchief and held it over his nose as the pus squirted and splashed onto the floor near his feet.

Maria violently arched her back and continued scratching, rubbing her crotch with increased vigour. She cooed orgasmically, thrashing her body on the bed in the throes of what appeared to be rampant erotomania.

"Stop that," Henrik said weakly. She was the most advanced case he had yet seen. Of the seven women he'd attended to yesterday, three had shown traces of decay on their bodies. The other four had refused to disrobe for him, but he had to assume they bore similar marks, for all shared one highly alarming trait; an intense form of sexual aggression.

"Help me, Doctor," Maria panted. She rolled her neck in ecstatic reverie, and spread her legs, displaying her throbbing cysts in all their appalling glory. "I can't quite get them. You... you must try." She reached for his hand and he backed away, the handkerchief still pressed to his nose.

"Where are you going?" she spat. "Scratch me!"

Henrik opened his medical bag and rummaged through the contents.

"Scratch my cunt you rotten bastard!"

He produced a glass bottle and laid it, with shaking

hands, on the chair. "Apply this three times a day to the, uhh, infected areas." The room stank like the hollowed cavity of a corpse's belly, and he felt woozy, as if the smell was somehow spirituous. Maria screeched and bawled, but her words were gibberish. She clawed between her legs, cleaving her nails through the dark rot. The pop and hiss of the bursting abscesses sounded like logs splitting in a raging fire.

"I shall return to check on you," Henrik said. He backed into the door with a bump and fumbled for the handle. "Remain in your room unless otherwise instructed."

The older nun was waiting for him in the corridor and chewing on a fingernail. "How is she? Shall Sister Maria recover swiftly?"

Henrik nodded, only half-listening. Recover? Recover from what? In all his years practising medicine, he had encountered nothing quite like this. He wiped the perspiration from his brow. "Stay out of Sister Maria's room. No matter how much she cries or begs for you to enter, do *not* go in. She may be... contagious."

"But what if my sister needs help? I can't—"

"Just do what I say, goddammit!"

Wide-eyed, the nun took a step back and crossed herself. "Blasphemy," she uttered.

Henrik leaned against the wall, his mind swirling with jumbled thoughts. He closed his eyes, but when he did, all he could picture were the thin lines originating from Maria's diseased groin. The infection was spreading rapidly throughout her body. Armed with nothing other than a medical bag full of bitter drops, belladonna tincture, and gentian extract, how could he possibly hope to stop it?

And more importantly... was he too late to prevent the disease from rampaging through the convent?

~

Considering the time of day, Sant'Arcangel was curiously empty as Henrik strode through the lengthy hallways on his way to find the Mother Superior. He passed a handful of nuns, who offered friendly, if somewhat surprised, greetings, but mostly he felt like a forlorn ghost haunting the ruins of a long-abandoned abbey.

Outside, the storm was worsening. He paused by the main entrance, unable to see the cottage through the snow flurries. It was, he had decided, best for Gertrude to stay with him from now on. The idea of her wandering these desolate corridors alone filled him with an unspeakable dread.

Following the directions given to him by the nun outside Maria's room, he continued down the corridor, taking the first turn after the refectory. The aroma of breakfast wafted from the kitchen. He glanced inside and spotted Sister Ursula. She waved to him, and he waved back, but he could not entertain the idea of eating so soon after his examination of Maria. The sight of her diseased—

No, best not to think of it.

Instead, he considered how best to explain to the Mother Superior that her convent was rife with the plague, and that he needed her key so he could lock everyone in their individual cells until the danger, hopefully, passed. He doubted she'd appreciate the suggestion, yet steadfast he would have to remain. And what of the woman herself? No one had seen her for days. Could she also be infected?

The thought spurred a vague suspicion in Henrik's mind. According to Maria, her illness had begun around the time the injured girl was brought to the convent. Could *she* have carried the disease? The more he considered it, the more doubtful it seemed. He had seen the girl in a complete state of undress on multiple occasions, and could not recall any strange markings on her body. Ursula, too, had shown no signs of infection, and she had spent more time than anyone with her. Who else had been in proximity to the patient? Ah, Sister Isabelle, of course. How interesting. He hadn't seen Isabelle for some time, and if the rumours were true of her and Maria…

He heard a voice and slowed, all thoughts of Isabelle slipping away.

Only one door remained in the corridor.

The Mother Superior's quarters. The voice came from within. He raised his fist to knock, and hesitated.

"…*need guidance,*" someone was saying. The words were muffled. "…*won't you answer me?*"

Sister Claudia. What a lovely surprise. Now he'd have to deal with both of the miserable snakes. Henrik took a breath and rapped his knuckles three times against the wood. Claudia immediately silenced.

"Mother Superior? This is Dr Persson. I'm here on urgent business, please let me in." He waited in silence with his arms folded, then knocked again. "I know you're in there. I heard you talking to Sister Claudia. Would you open the door? It's very important."

Nothing. Dammit, he knew they were in there!

"There's an infection spreading throughout your flock, Reverend Mother," he growled, no longer trying to mask his frustration. "I believe it's *deadly* serious, which is why I require the use of your master key. Until I think of a more humane solution, I see no alternative but to confine anyone showing signs of this grim malady to their cells. What say you to that?"

Still no reply. With all pretences at civility out the

window, he tried the handle. The door was locked. That selfish fool, ensuring her own safety at the expense of others!

"Very well," he shouted. "I shall try again later, when hopefully you shall be more amenable to discussion. After all, the fate of *your* flock is at stake, you damnable woman." In anger, he slammed his fist against the door and stormed off in search of Gertrude.

The sooner he took her away from this infernal place, the better.

The doctor's footsteps receded down the corridor.

Sister Claudia let out a rattling breath, although only once she was certain Henrik had left did she allow her shoulders to relax. The cat o' nine tails drooped in her hand, resting in a pool of blood.

So, the doctor wanted the key? Of course he did. He wished to seal them away so that he and his band of infidel unbelievers could wage war against God. Well, not on her watch. She gazed at the key affixed to the Mother Superior's cincture belt, and smiled. If the doctor was going to be a problem, then she would just have to remove him.

And she would... soon.

"As for now, Reverend Mother," she said, as she faced the abbess and raised the whip high, blood dripping steadily from the fearsome leather cords. "I believe you were about to give me some guidance."

18

In her role as Sant'Arcangel's head cook, Sister Giovanna had found a purpose that had been lacking in her life. Although, it was fair to say, she was unable to prepare any culinary masterpieces with the limited meat and vegetables available to her on the mountain, she tried her best to vary the sisters' meals, for it was her staunch belief that a full belly was conducive to a productive day's work and worship.

In her old life, she had prepared food for counts and nobility, but the vocation left her unsatisfied. The rich were not good people; their hunger for food was exceeded only by their appetite for decadence and wanton debauchery. The last family she had worked for — a duke of ill-repute and his brothers — had been the worst of all. They had seated a human skeleton at the head of the table as a reminder to live life to the fullest before death claimed them, an admirable ethos they had used as an excuse to hurt and abuse those they saw as lesser beings. After seeing the heartless way they treated their staff, and experiencing their callousness firsthand, Giovanna had given it all up and joined the convent, where every day she prayed that the wealthy might see the error of their ways. Was it not Christ himself who warned of becoming choked by life's riches? Those men, who pretended to be decent, God-fearing folk, could learn a lot from Christ's teachings, if only they cared to.

She chopped another onion into thin slices and set them aside. In the fireplace, an enormous black pot boiled, hungrily awaiting the ingredients. Unlike the rest of the convent, which revelled in faded grandeur, the kitchen had been well-maintained over the years, and Giovanna insisted on a high level of cleanliness. After every meal, she scrubbed the large table and fastidiously cleaned the countertops that ran around three quarters of the room. It meant more work for herself, but it benefited the other sisters, and her mother had taught her to live with J-O-Y in her heart.

Jesus first.

Others second.

Yourself last.

She scratched at her thigh, then carried the chopping board to the pot and shook the onion into the water in a series of small but satisfying splashes. Over the past few days, there had been fewer sisters than usual at collation, but she put in the standard amounts because, much as she had done the day before, Giovanna would personally deliver the broth to anyone unwell enough to make it the refectory.

She left the chopping board on the table next to the kitchen knife and walked to the storeroom. From the piles of hessian sacks in the corner, she selected half a dozen good-sized potatoes and carried them back to the kitchen.

After a quick check of the soup, which was bubbling nicely, she returned to the chopping board and scratched her thigh again. The irritation in her leg grew more bothersome, and she hoped she wasn't coming down with what ailed her sisters. She wished to seek Henrik's advice, but had been unable to secure permission from the Mother Superior to bare her skin to him.

Would the abbess be joining them tonight? No one had seen her recently, which meant Claudia had taken over the suppertime readings. Though she would never mention it, Giovanna thought Claudia's reading voice lacked expression, which, combined with the sombre mood in the convent, made for some distinctly dreary meals.

"Forgive my unkind thoughts, Lord," she said, and placed a potato in the middle of the chopping board. She reached for the knife.

It was not where she'd left it.

"That's odd." She glanced across the bare countertops, scratching her leg as she did so. The knife couldn't have gone far. She must have mislaid it, or perhaps accidentally knocked it to the floor. Sighing, Giovanna bent into a crouch and looked under the table.

"Oh!" she said. "What are you doing under there, Sister—"

The knife plunged into her cheek.

The razor-sharp blade cut easily through the flesh and scraped across her teeth. As quickly as it had entered, the blade was withdrawn, roughly slicing open her tongue, and only then did Giovanna realise what had happened.

She fell backwards, screaming, as Sister Isabelle came crawling towards her from under the table, the kitchen knife clutched in her twisted, blackened hand. The metal clanged off the floor as she advanced.

Giovanna scurried back against a cupboard. She clasped a hand over her ruined cheek and felt warm spurts of blood against her palm. "What are you doing?" she cried, her mouth filling with blood. "Why—"

The knife arced down, puncturing the soft flesh of her belly. Then, with both hands, Isabelle dragged the blade towards Giovanna's crotch, sawing her open. It snagged on her intestines, pulling them out of position as great gouts of blood squirted madly. In desperation, she kicked out, knocking Isabelle backwards. The nun's head struck the heavy wooden table, the knife clattering to the floor.

Giovanna turned onto her hands and knees, clutching her torn abdomen. Blood flooded from the wound, and something slick brushed her fingertips. She heard the knife rasp across stone, and looked back to see Isabelle rising.

Using the countertops for leverage, Giovanna got to her feet. The movement made her entrails shift. They slimed against her palm, and she pressed them back inside and grabbed the closest weapon to hand.

A saucepan.

Isabelle stood before her, a picture of grotesque evil. Her eyes were crusted black rings that leaked down her cheeks and connected to rank, ghoulish lips.

Giovanna's vision blurred. She was losing too much blood. She swung the saucepan feebly, and it clanged off Isabelle's shoulder. The woman didn't seem to feel the blow. She lunged, the fingers of one hand finding Giovanna's throat and closing around it, bending her backwards over the table.

Releasing the saucepan, Giovanna clawed at Isabelle's wrist. She couldn't breathe, and as she tried to wriggle free, she felt her guts slide out of her and dribble messily down her legs.

Isabelle raised the knife, the blade dripping with gore, and brought it down. She stabbed Giovanna's breasts and belly, once, twice, *threefourfive* times, unrelenting in her ferocity. Then she lifted Giovanna's legs onto the counter, laying the woman out like raw meat on the butcher's slab, and slammed the knife into her shoulder, hard enough that the blade not only penetrated the flesh, but burst out the other side and embedded itself in the wood, pinning her to the table.

"*Isabelle,*" she gasped, coppery blood spilling down her chin. "*Please...*"

But that was not Isabelle. Not as Giovanna remembered her, anyway. Sister Isabelle was a delightful companion, the sort of sister who made the winter fly by with her humour and good cheer.

The Isabelle she knew would certainly never attack someone.

She would never *kill*.

Impaled on her beloved table, where she had prepared meals for her sisters twice a day for over three decades, Giovanna listened to her old friend raking through drawers of cutlery and cooking utensils. The wet, black smears on her face reminded her of the peculiar markings on her own thigh, the ones that had kept her awake with their incessant, painful prickling. She could still feel them now, as she bled out like a stuck pig, the constant irritation strong enough to keep her alive long after she should have passed out from excessive blood loss.

Giovanna's hazy eyes focused on the meat cleaver in Isabelle's hand. It hovered above her, briefly catching the candlelight, then thudded into her ankle. The bone cracked, but did not break. Giovanna screamed. Could no one hear her? The cleaver descended two more times, and she watched as Isabelle removed the sandal from her severed foot and tossed it aside. Nothing seemed real anymore.

In the fireplace, the pot of soup bubbled.

"They shall not hunger," Isabelle slurred through bulging, tumid lips, as she forced her hand inside Giovanna's stomach cavity and wrenched out a handful of entrails. Some squelched to the floor, while others were deposited in the boiling vat. The woman loomed over her, pus oozing from her mutated face, the meat cleaver twitching in her fist.

"For you are the bread of life," she said, and brought the cutting blade screaming down on Giovanna's neck.

19

Sister Ursula was pleased, for the girl's condition was steadily improving.

She had spent much of the three days since her arrival in the throes of tortured sleep, but now she was awake, and had been for several hours. She lay on the bed as Ursula inspected her wounds. As expected, the skin was healing well thanks to Dr Franco's expertise.

Careful to avoid the stitches, she dabbed a cloth around the injuries, removing any discharge. It was funny how quickly she had gotten used to seeing a naked body. The girl was considerably skinnier than her, but otherwise looked much the same, to the point she had begun to wonder what all the fuss was about.

"Thank you for taking care of me," the girl said.

"It's my pleasure," replied Ursula without a word of a lie. "Do you feel your pain is lessening?"

"A little, perhaps."

"Well, a little is better than not at all." She soaked up the last of the leakage around the girl's thigh before moving on to her stomach. "And what about your memory?"

The girl looked pained. She turned her head and gazed out the window at the unceasing snowfall. "Still nothing. Sometimes I think I see fragments of memories, but I cannot tell whether they're real or illusory."

"There's no hurry. You've got all winter to remember." Ursula wiped the girl's flat belly. Her ribs were plainly visible through the skin, and she looked in dire need of a hearty meal. "But in the meantime, I'd very much like to call you by a name."

"I told you, I don't remember it."

"That doesn't matter." Ursula set aside the wet cloth and dipped her finger in the jar of ointment. "In Sant'Arcangel, none of us use our birth names. When women join the sisterhood, they choose their own saintly name."

"Really? So why did you choose Ursula?"

"Well, in my case, I was too young to decide. My father brought me here when I was seven years old. I was a rather sickly child, and wasn't able to work the fields or milk the cows like my brothers."

"So your parents sent you to the convent to find fulfilling work? That was kind of them."

Ursula gently rubbed the ointment onto the girl's skin. "Well, I'd hesitate to call it an act of charity. They paid the Mother Superior to take me, because the small amount I was worth was cheaper than clothing and feeding me. My parents wanted another strong son, not a daughter with a nervous disposition."

"Do they ever visit?"

"Never. I don't know what became of them." She brightened. "But I found a new family in the sisters of Sant'Arcangel, and the sickliness in my early years instilled in me a passion for helping others."

"Like the way you've helped me?"

Ursula smiled at her. "Exactly."

"Other than the doctor, you're the only person who's looked after me."

"Well, some of the other sisters are shocked that you're staying in my cell. It's not allowed. Nor is the way I clean and wash your injuries, but I don't think any of them know about that, and I'd rather keep it that way."

"I won't say a word," said the girl. "And if you like, I can move to another—"

"Don't be silly," she interrupted. "You're staying right here with me, although you *do* need a name. At least until you remember your real one. Would you like to choose?"

"You've been so good to me, Ursula. Please, do me the honour of selecting a humble name."

Ursula pretended to think, though she had already decided on a suitable name that very morning. "Lucia," she said. "Because, to me, you've been a guiding light that has shown me the path I need to take. All my life, I've wanted to help people who were sick. And since your arrival, I've realised that, as much as I love God, it's not my calling. You have inadvertently shown me the way, Lucia, and for that, I am forever in your debt."

"Lucia," said the girl. "It's a beautiful name." She blushed. "Too beautiful for me, I fear."

"Nonsense. It suits you perfectly." Ursula laid the ointment aside. "There, all done. Now for your medicine."

"I hate it," said Lucia. "It tastes horrible."

"I know. But it'll be supper soon, and I can bring you bread and a bowl of hot soup. Would you like that?"

Lucia's stomach grumbled.

"Well, that answers my question," said Ursula, and both girls laughed. It felt nice to laugh in the dreary confines of the convent, especially at a time of year when good humour was thin on the ground.

Downstairs, the gong sounded for supper.

She helped Lucia dress, then tucked her in. The girl's eyes closed as her head touched the pillow, and Ursula waited a few minutes to ensure she was sleeping soundly. She would be late for collation, she knew, but that didn't bother her.

Sister Giovanna *always* made enough soup to go around.

Ursula did indeed arrive late to the refectory.

The heavy oak tables were, as ever, organised in the shape of a cross, but the altar at the head of the room, where the Mother Superior would read to the sisters as they ate in silence, stood unattended. Neither the abbess nor Sister Claudia was present, she was happy to note, for it meant she wouldn't get in trouble for her tardiness. And if there was to be no reading from Sister Claudia this evening... then that truly was one of God's small miracles.

Ursula hid her mischievous grin with her hand.

Most of the flock were already seated and dining heartily, so she joined the short queue by the serving pot, an enormous black cauldron on wheels which had been a gift from a generous benefactor many decades prior. The wheels allowed Sister Giovanna to slide the cooking pot to and from the kitchen without having to lift it, which made every-one's lives easier.

Giovanna was nowhere to be seen — another victim of the illness, Ursula supposed — but the convent's newest novice, young Sister Beatrice, was on hand to help ladle the soup into ceramic bowls.

With no one to silence them, a light murmur of discussion buzzed around the room. Ursula picked up a bowl and glanced at all the empty chairs. The refectory was half-full at most, and she counted her blessings for avoiding the strange disease that had befallen her sisters.

The queue moved slowly, for the women ahead of her were too busy gossiping about the absences to pay attention, and she watched enviously as her sisters at the table tucked into the delicious-smelling soup. She planned to eat fast, refill her bowl, and bring the serving to Lucia. The girl needed sustenance more than anyone, for a good layer of meat on her bones would be essential to surviving the harsh mountain winter.

At last, the sisters in front of her received their portions, and then it was Ursula's turn. She smiled at Sister Beatrice, who didn't smile back. Instead, the girl clumsily ladled some soup into the bowl, spilling half of it onto the floor. Ursula noticed the black mark around one of Beatrice's eyes. A bruise?

"What happened to your eye?" she whispered.

The girl said nothing and turned away as if ashamed. Ursula wondered if Sister Claudia was responsible. The cruel nun liked to exert her authority over the newcomers.

"If you ever need someone to talk to, my name is Sister Ursula, and I'm a good listener," she said, not wanting to linger and embarrass the girl further. She carried her steaming hot bowl to the table, where she took a seat next to Sister Virginia.

"Good afternoon, Sister Ursula," the woman said quietly, as if afraid Claudia would appear from nowhere brandishing her whip as punishment for speaking.

"Good afternoon," said Ursula. She leaned towards her bowl and inhaled its aroma, letting the rising steam warm her face. Was Sister Giovanna trying a new recipe? It *looked* like tomato soup, yet smelt strongly of an ingredient she couldn't place. She dipped her spoon and stirred, then raised it to her lips.

"Ah," she sighed, and placed her spoon back in the bowl.

She had forgotten her bread.

Ursula excused herself from the table. The bread tray was next to the soup pot, and she picked two thick slices of Giovanna's loaf — one for her and one for Lucia — before heading back to her seat.

"Forgot my bread," she said to Sister Virginia as she sat down.

"Ugh," Virginia said in response. Her shoulders jerked, and she burped loudly.

"Sister Virginia!" laughed Ursula. "What would the Mother Superior say?"

Virginia turned to her. Soup dribbled down her chin. She gagged, her eyes watering, and placed both hands on the table. "Ack!" Her face was turning purple. *"Ack!"*

Ursula stood, sending her chair skittering across the floor.

Sister Virginia was choking.

She clapped the woman on the back as the rest of the nuns stopped eating to watch. "Go to the cottage and fetch Henrik!" she shouted, and hit the woman harder between the shoulder blades in an effort to dislodge whatever was caught in her throat.

No one moved.

"Somebody fetch Henrik, please!" she called again, and this time a woman at the table got up and ran from the room. "Tell him Virginia's choking!"

Virginia's hands clenched into fists, bunching up the white tablecloth. She pulled on the fabric, wrenching the cloth towards her and causing soup bowls and cups to fall to the floor and smash. The assembled nuns gasped.

Few had ever heard quite so much noise in the refectory.

"Really, all this fuss over nothing," tutted Sister Carmela, the only nun in the convent rumoured to be older than the Mother Superior. Ursula ignored her, and struck Virginia across her back again.

This time, it worked.

The woman spluttered and spat out a reddish lump. She leaned forward, panting and crying.

"How do you feel?" Ursula asked. "Is it all gone?"

The nun beside Virginia screamed.

"Quiet, please," said Ursula. All the excitement was giving her a headache.

But the woman would not stop screaming. "What is that?" She pointed at the scrunched tablecloth and slowly backed away. *"What in God's name* is *that?"*

Someone else screamed.

"Sisters, this is most unhelpful," said Ursula... and then she saw what the woman was pointing at.

"No," she whispered, for there was no mistaking the flap of meat on the table. The soft bud, the circle of pinkish skin surrounded by pale white flesh...

Sister Virginia had choked on a nipple.

The woman vomited. Lumpy soup and undigested morsels of bread splattered across the table, and several other nuns started to gag.

Ursula gazed down at the liquid that flooded the floor, at its dark red colouring and surprising thickness, and staggered towards the soup pot. With Sister Beatrice curiously absent, she reached for the wooden handle on the side of the pot.

Another nun emptied her belly across the supper table.

The sound and smell were revolting. Ursula tried to ignore them. She raised the handle and tipped the pot, slices of onion and potato detritus flooding out in a chunky torrent.

Then came the parts.

Toes.

A hand.

Part of a breast.

The screams followed, a wailing cacophony of horrified nuns shrieking as a human being poured out of the pot in hundreds of pieces. And when the beloved Sister Giovanna's severed head tumbled across the floor, her mouth locked in an eternal grimace, Ursula could no longer help herself.

She turned away, dropped to her knees, and vomited with the rest of her sisters.

20

WHERE THE DEVIL *WAS* EVERYBODY?

Henrik strode the empty hallways of Sant'Arcangel, his hands in his pockets to stave off the biting chill. The situation grew increasingly dire. Unable to find Gertrude, he had instead called in on the various women he had examined yesterday. In less than twenty-four hours, the black marks on their bodies had spread further. *Much* further. In the most extreme cases, the disease appeared to be rotting not only their skin, but their hearts and minds.

One woman, upon whom the mouldy fungus covered her torso and neck, had caught a bird on her windowsill, and plucked the feathers from its body before hurling it at the wall, where it dripped down the stonework. Another of the sisters exposed herself to him, fingering her sex and begging him to enter her. The third lay prone, gazing lifelessly at the ceiling and crying blood-flecked tears. Only when Henrik peeled back the bloody sheet did he find she had carved a cross from her navel to her sternum and across both breasts. She possessed no tools, using her fingernails to scratch and tear the uneven lines into her flesh.

The contagion brought madness to all it touched.

More disconcerting was the realisation that he knew not how many were infected. Short of stripping every nun in the convent stark naked, there would be no way for him to know who was safe to be around until their minds began to deteriorate.

And that included Gertrude.

The idea horrified him. They would need to inspect each other's bodies thoroughly to ensure they carried no trace of the rot, and once that was established, they would sequester themselves in the gardener's cottage until the first chance of escape.

Before that, however, he wished to look in on Ursula's patient. Sant'Arcangel's reckoning had begun around the time of her arrival, and although he doubted she was the cause, Henrik was a man of science, and he required proof.

There was no answer from Ursula when he knocked on her cell door. He waited a moment, then admitted himself into the room.

The girl was asleep in Ursula's bed. He shook her awake.

"Whaaah?" she mumbled.

"It's Henrik. I've come to check your progress, if I may."

"Mmm-hmm." Her eyes refused to stay open, and she fell back into the dreamy embrace of sleep.

It was for the best.

Henrik drew back the covers and rolled her tunic up, casting his gaze over her body. He opened her legs and checked her thighs, then around her breasts and under her armpits. Rolling her onto her front, he looked at the soles of her feet, the backs of her knees, and between her buttocks. But for all his searching, he could find no markings.

She was clean.

In addition, he noted her wounds were healing well,

which was testament to the care and attention lavished upon her by Sister Ursula. When he had told Ursula she would make a fine nurse, he had been telling the truth. She was a highly competent assistant, and he would need her by his side if this malaise was to sink its fangs further into the convent. She alone among the sisters had proven her worth in medical matters.

He only hoped she had not yet fallen prey to the disease.

At the sound of distant voices, he raised his head. Someone was screaming. More than one person, actually. What the blazes was going on now?

He tugged the girl's tunic down and walked to the door. Downstairs, more women joined in the cacophony. Henrik had grown sadly accustomed to the ghoulish lamentations of the infected, but these cries were worse. It was the dread wail of the damned, dozens of nuns shrieking in horror... as if the entire convent had suddenly awoken from a ghastly shared nightmare.

21

———

Far from the carnage of the dining hall, Sister Maria's body was in revolt.

"Isabelle!" she cried. *"Isabelle!"*

Her discarded bedsheets and nightgown lay crumpled and reeking on the floor, soaked in her own juices.

What in the name of the Holy Father was becoming of her?

Gazing across the appalling spectacle of her mutinous form, she prayed for death. A swift one would be welcome, but it mattered not, as long as her torment ended.

The rot had set in, spreading downwards from the source in squirming black striations, and writhing snake-like over her belly and breasts, mutilating and deforming them. She prodded at the black substance and yelped in pain as her fingers broke the spongy, wet tissue. Hair grew from between porous cracks, and pustulent boils sprouted like obscene, bloated mushrooms. Scratching — her only relief — was no longer an option. Moments earlier, the last of her fingernails had snapped off in the decomposing flesh of her breast. It was still there, jutting out and mocking her.

"Isabelle, please!"

She recalled the tapestry that hung in the old chapel, the one that read, THE ROAD TO HEAVEN IS PAVED WITH SUFFERING, and wept.

The itch was driving her mad. She rubbed her stubby digits against the trembling cysts. Was God punishing her? Even her tongue felt swollen and fuzzy, as if coated in a thick pelt of fur. She glanced out the window at the falling snow and fantasised about freezing to death, a fate infinitely preferable to this itching nightmare that could not be quelled. It felt like thousands of tiny insects were crawling through her body and stinging her beneath layers of skin.

With her wretched fingers, she pinched one of the boils and squeezed, desirous of the vulgar sensation when it burst. But she was weak, and lacked the strength.

"I hate you," she said to God. Was he listening? Did he care? "Do you hear me? *I hate you!*"

She despised herself for saying so, but if this was how God chose to treat his stalwart disciple for the sin of loving a being other than him, then God could go to hell. Yes, she had broken her vows by sleeping with Isabelle. But how did that affect God? She could understand the Mother Superior being angry, for the woman was beholden to archaic ideals. But didn't Christ preach of love?

Or was it all a lie?

With a mighty effort, she rolled over and tumbled out of bed, landing on her bottom with a painful jolt. She gasped in agony as the crust that coated her buttocks splintered, the pain turning to pleasure as warm, steaming pus seeped from the cracks.

"Ohhhh... ohhhh," she sobbed in ecstasy, as the stinking ooze leaked from her most private crevices. Yet as soothing as the release of her bodily excretions was, she could not remain here. She needed help.

She needed Isabelle.

And so, naked and expelling pungent discharge, she clambered onto her front and dragged her rotten body towards the door, groping for the handle.

"Isabelle!" Maria shouted, spilling out into the corridor like a monstrous creature washed up on the seashore. *"Isabelle!"*

But much like her God, it seemed even her lover had forsaken Sister Maria in her hour of need.

As a doctor, Henrik was no stranger to death.

The first time he had borne witness to the cessation of a life was the day his younger brother Bernhard had dashed in front of a coach. Before Henrik even realised what had transpired, the thunderous hooves of four horses had trampled his brother's frail body.

All six-year-old Henrik could do was watch.

He was supposed to have been looking after Bernhard, and had promised their mother he would not let go of his brother's hand for even a second.

One momentary lapse in concentration had been enough.

The memory tormented him for years, and still did on occasion, for despite the passing of decades, the brutal, calamitous death remained the most gruelling atrocity he had ever seen.

Until now.

For the sights and smells that greeted Henrik in the refectory, as he fought through a stampede of howling nuns, were enough to turn even the hardiest of stomachs. Covering his nose to mask the smell of recently regurgitated food, he made his way towards Ursula, stepping over large puddles of soupy vomit, in which languished what appeared to be human remains. Bile rose in his throat.

"What... what happened here?" he asked hollowly, gazing at the mess. The parts flooded across the slick floor, and his first thought was that a pack of wolves had torn a nun to shreds. Yet even at a glance, the finely chopped flesh and gristle suggested the devastation had been caused not by teeth, but by repeated blows from a sharp object.

"The soup," whispered Ursula. Her skin was so pale it blended perfectly with the white head covering that framed her face. "Sister Giovanna was in the soup."

Henrik nudged one of the chunks with the toe of his boot. It slid across the mosaic-tiled floor.

"She was in the soup," Ursula repeated disbelievingly.

He placed a hand on her shoulder. She did not flinch, did not even notice the contact, for her eyes were fixed on the grisly splatter that had once been Sant'Arcangel's cook.

Someone had slaughtered her. But why? And why place her remains in the...

Good god.

A chill prickled the hair on Henrik's nape.

Good... god.

"Ursula," he said softly, his mind racing with dreadful possibilities.

She turned to him with eyes that betrayed a cosmic sadness. "Who would do such a thing to Giovanna?"

Henrik tried to compose himself. "Ursula, there's something I need to look for, and if you feel up to the task, I would be most grateful for your assistance."

She didn't respond. She was in shock.

"Ursula... can you hear me?"

"Yes," she breathed, her lip trembling. "I... I can help. What do you need me to do?"

He glanced around the room. The nuns had cleared out, leaving just the two of them. "Go to the kitchen," he said, "and bring me a sack. The ones you keep the potatoes in will do." His gaze darted across the lumps of meat. "Oh, and two of the longest, sharpest blades you can find."

With a nod, Ursula disappeared through to the kitchen. As Henrik crouched to take a closer look, he heard the acute grind of metal against metal as she raked through the drawers, followed by the thumping of potatoes being emptied from a sack.

But it was all for naught. Already, with only a cursory glance, Henrik had located that which he hoped not to find.

A shadow fell across him.

"I did as you asked," said Ursula, two knives clutched in one hand, a dusty hessian sack in the other.

"Thank you," he said, and clenched his jaw. "Ursula... did you eat any of the soup?"

"Pardon?"

"The *soup*." His heart pounded, but he had to ask. He had to know. "Did you partake of it?"

"No, I don't believe so."

In the dim candlelight, her face was difficult to read. He stood and looked her in the eye. "Think hard. Did you or did you *not* eat the soup? Even a sip? It's very important."

"No," she said confidently. "I didn't. I was late to collation. Most were already seated, and I joined the queue and received my portion. But when I sat down, I realised I'd forgotten my bread. Then Virginia started choking, and..." She shuddered. "No, I didn't eat anything. I'm not sure I ever will again."

"Good."

He took a knife from Ursula and stabbed it into a slab of meat. He wasn't certain where it was from — most likely a thigh or a buttock — but he lifted the weighty piece from the floor and angled the knife so that the flesh slid from the tip. It plopped onto the table and wobbled like raw chicken, displaying the leathery decay and deflated pink boils of the disease.

"Look closely," he said. "Have you ever seen anything like this before?"

Ursula shook her head.

"Neither had I," said Henrik, "until a few days ago. But several of your sisters have been falling ill, and each one carries a similar mark. Over a remarkably short time, I've watched it grow on their bodies."

"Is it contagious?"

"I believe so, yes. Highly contagious, which is why I'm not touching it with my hands." He stabbed one knife into the chunk and sawed it open with the other. Inside, the rot had permeated the tissue. Mossy fungus spread through the muscle above a layer of fetid yellow pus that leaked onto the table like egg yolk. "See how deep it's burrowed under the skin? If that reached the brain, it would explain the severe personality changes I've witnessed."

"Is it fatal?"

"No one has died from it yet."

"That's not an answer."

He looked at her, studied her face. "Allow me to speak plainly, Ursula. This new development alarms me. I know not what it is capable of, nor how to treat it, let alone *cure* the damned thing." He paused. "I need your help."

"Then you shall have it. Anything you require."

"I was right to place my trust in you, Ursula. But now I

must ask that you return the favour by putting your faith in *me,* for what I am about to ask of you may be... unpleasant."

"Go on."

There was no easy way to say it. "I need to check your body for any traces of this rot."

"Oh, I'm unaffected. I would have noticed—"

"I need to examine *everywhere,* Ursula." He let the words sink in. "Everywhere. And if I can't find Gertrude soon... *you* will have to examine *me.* I know that flies in the face of your vows, but it's imperative we confirm neither of us carries this disease."

Her cheeks reddened. He was glad to see colour returning, even if it was under appalling circumstances. "Must it be done?" she asked.

"It must. I'm deeply sorry."

She thought for a moment, then nodded. "So be it." She reached for her wimple.

"Oh, I don't mean here! In private, naturally. And before that, I suggest we tidy up dear Sister Giovanna."

They both turned and looked at the mess on the floor.

"We should burn her," said Ursula. "Cremation may be forbidden, but in this instance, I doubt God will mind."

"On that, we are in mutual agreement. Fire seems the surest way of dealing with a contagious disease. Here, hold the sack for me, and I'll..." He gestured vaguely at the floor. Picking up Giovanna piece-by-butchered-piece was too grim an act for words.

Despite years of medical practice and a hardy constitution, Henrik's stomach churned as he stabbed the knives into the various hunks of meat. For the head — the largest, heaviest part — he had to insert one blade into the eye socket, and the other into the neck stump to lift it securely.

Blood soaked through the sack, forming a puddle on the tiled floor.

"We should take her to the courtyard," said Ursula. "At least then she may rest on consecrated ground."

"Then let us not tarry," said Henrik, eager to leave the stifling confines of the rancid-smelling refectory. He grabbed the top of the sack and dragged it towards the door, leaving a trail of dark blood across the elegant mosaic. They would need to clean that up. The blood could carry the infection, and...

He stopped, the sack slipping from his hands.

"What's the matter?" asked Ursula.

Henrik's throat was dry. His tongue cleaved to the roof of his mouth, and a tremor that began in his heart passed throughout his limbs. "Ursula, when I asked if you'd eaten any of the soup, you said you hadn't, am I correct?"

"Absolutely. I never touched a drop."

He turned back to look at the table. "And what about everyone else? Who among those present supped from their bowl?"

Ursula stared at him. She seemed to understand the dreadful implication.

"Everyone," she said, and visibly shivered. "As far as I know... they *all* did."

22

IN A GLOOMY CORNER OF SANT'ARCANGEL, SISTER BEATRICE stood, dazed and alone and staring at a ladder that lay across the floor beside a bucket of filthy water. She had been gazing at the scene for several minutes, and while, to the casual observer, it may have appeared she was deep in contemplation, in fact the opposite was true.

Barely a thought flitted through her numb, empty skull.

Since serving the last of the soup, Beatrice had wandered the maze-like corridors in a trance, oblivious to all around her. The sight of the ladder had jogged a memory. But a memory of what?

Oh, she was so very, very tired.

Her neck itched. As a novice, she wore no wimple, which allowed her to shove two fingers between her chin and her head covering to scratch at her prickly skin. Sweat soaked into her tunic as she scraped her fingernails against the strange lumps on her flesh. She longed to lie down, but for the life of her, she could not remember where she slept. She dimly recalled dishing out supper, but anything before that was tantalisingly out of reach.

Thank heavens Sister Isabelle had been there to help. She had looked rather frightening, with her face wrapped in bandages so that only her eyes were visible, but not only had she already prepared the soup for Beatrice's arrival, she had even wheeled it into the refectory. All Beatrice had needed to do was ladle the nourishment into the bowls.

Shortly after serving the last sister, she had left, wandering the convent in search of her cell. She wanted to rest... so why could she not stop staring at the ladder? And why did it make her tremble so?

Fleeting images shimmered through her mind; visions of a closed door, and of something dreadful behind it. But the full memory, if it even existed, evaded her. She knelt by the bucket and gazed at her reflection in the murky water. A tear fell, rippling the surface and breaking the image into gentle waves.

That door... what was behind that door?

She couldn't remember. For some obscure reason, she wasn't sure she *wanted* to remember.

And so Sister Beatrice righted herself, dusted off her knees, and drifted through the corridors like a leaf caught on the breeze, scratching and crying and trying to remember. She might have walked forever had she not come across the naked woman crumpled on the floor by an open door.

Beatrice hurried to her side, focusing on the woman's face rather than her shocking state of undress. "What ails you, my sister?"

The woman looked at her through half-lidded eyes ringed by darkness, and a shudder of recognition passed through Beatrice. In the back of her mind, a voice suggested she leave the woman lying here, but Beatrice was a young woman in need of a purpose, and now one had presented itself.

"My bed," the woman said. Beatrice could have sworn she was smiling. "Help me... to my bed."

She gazed through the open doorway, where a single candle illuminated an empty, unmade bed.

Don't go in. Don't go through that door.

"You're Sister Maria, aren't you?" she asked, looking anywhere but at the nun's naked body. "You showed me to my cell on my first day here."

"Yes," the woman croaked. "Now show me... to mine. *Please.*"

What could she do? Leave Sister Maria for someone else to find? This woman may have been unclothed, but it was Beatrice's duty to help her sister. And so, with guilty thoughts of penance occupying her mind, she hooked her arms under Maria's shoulders and half-lifted, half-dragged the woman through the door and onto her bed. The wooden frame groaned, and in the faint candlelight, Beatrice, who was a curious young thing, and innocent in the ways of the world, could resist the temptation no longer.

She stole a quick glance at the woman's nakedness.

"Oh God," she gasped, drawing in a breath so sharp it stung her tender heart.

Black marks covered Sister Maria's body from her knees to her breasts, and her womanly parts were a festering mass of cysts and sores. Beatrice felt sick, for beneath her novitiate clothing she bore similar marks, which itched terribly and grew larger and more vile by the day. Without thinking, she scratched at her neck. Was this the terrible fate that awaited her?

"I... I must fetch the doctor," she said, taking a small step back. The words caught in her throat. "We must both seek his counsel."

"No," Maria hissed. She reached out and took Beatrice's

hand, placing it on the splintered, perished flesh of her stomach. "I can't find Isabelle… but *you* can help."

"Don't," said Beatrice, tears forming in her eyes. She prayed for forgiveness and understanding from the Lord for this malfeasance. "Please, unhand me, I beg of you."

But Maria did not. She slid Beatrice's hand lower, over the swell of her belly and down, much further down, until it scraped against rubbery boils that quivered at the unwanted touch.

"Sister Maria, stop! This is wrong!"

The spongy rot throbbed against her hand, hot and wet and pustulent. She managed to pull away, but Maria rose up, oily liquid spilling from beneath her eyelids, and seized Beatrice's head covering with both hands, ripping the fabric and yanking the young nun down towards the grotesquely infected area between her legs.

"You must!" screamed Maria. "It makes the pain go away!"

Tight fingers clutched Beatrice's exposed hair, tearing at her scalp. "The doctor! The doctor will know what to do!"

"No," Maria sobbed. "He refused me!"

Beatrice was inches from the woman's mouldering crotch. Long, wiry hairs tickled her nose, and a cyst bubbled tremulously as if in anticipation. The smell was worse than rotten fruit, worse even than a country privy. It stank of death and decay and foul, malodorous secretions. The black, spoiled flesh pressed soggily against her face, and when she tried to scream, the layer of bulging tumours absorbed her cries. Her tongue brushed something abhorrent, and she gagged.

Maria clamped her thighs around Beatrice's ears, locking her in position.

"Burst them!"

Beatrice shifted her head, but there was no escape. The cysts pulsated against her cheeks, and although the soggy rot muffled her hearing, she could still make out the awful, horrible words.

"Use your teeth!"

Lights danced across her vision as fists pounded the dome of her skull, each vicious blow jarring her already foggy brain.

"Bite them!"

Desperate for a way out of this terror, Beatrice opened her mouth and wrapped her lips around the mound of swollen abscesses. Pressing her face hard into the woman's crotch, she placed the fluid-filled vesicle between her teeth and bit down. It burst, expelling rancid, bloody pus. The taste on her tongue brought up bile, yet when she pulled away, believing her awful work to be complete, Maria's thighs tightened around her.

"More!" she moaned. *"More!"*

Beatrice angled her neck, fastening her teeth over another throbbing blister. This one was not as ripe as the first. She bit down on the rubbery growth, grinding her teeth until the membranous tissue tore, and rank liquid leaked onto her tongue.

Maria pulled hard on her hair and screamed. "Suck it out! Suck it out!"

Could no one hear her? Did anyone care?

Beatrice closed her mouth over the abscess and slurped on the flaccid cyst, drawing the liquid out.

"It's working," Maria sobbed. Her fists loosened, the punches turning to open-handed slaps. *"Keep going!"*

Weeping, Beatrice nibbled at the next pustule, tearing it free. She found another nestled in the folds of Maria's labia and took it in her teeth, chomping down hard with her molars and grinding them together until the blister ruptured. Flesh tore and blood pooled, for she had bitten off more than just the cyst.

Sister Maria did not seem to mind. She bucked in the throes of lustful ecstasy and lifted Beatrice by her hair. "Come to me," she said, yanking the young novice onto the bed and clambering atop her like a feral ghoul.

Beatrice lay utterly still, barely flinching as the mad nun tore her tunic open with gnarled, bark-like fingers, and saying not a word when Maria's furry tongue lapped up her own noxious emissions from Beatrice's lips.

"Look at me," Maria growled.

Beatrice opened her eyes, watching helplessly as Maria dug her twisted hand into the sodden, crumbling flesh of her chest. She forced the broken digits deeper, blood and venomous discharge frothing to the surface and gushing down her belly.

"Join me," said Maria. She scooped out a handful of her rotten breast and forced it into Beatrice's mouth. "Taste my flesh."

All at once, the memory of that day up the ladder, and of what lay behind that door, came back to her with nauseating clarity.

She recalled Sister Isabelle with her rotting hand chasing her through the corridors, and hurtling through a door to find three nuns engaged in a ghastly erotic tryst, the women naked and dragging their nails through each other's decaying skin, unleashing torrents of blood and diseased slime from their gaping wounds.

And she recalled the way all three women had slowly turned to her, cruel smiles breaking out across their ravenous faces. At first, the horrors they subjected her to had seemed unimaginable. They had disrobed her, and debased her, and forced her to drink from their festering lesions. The taste had been at once putrid and divine, and the more she had sipped, the more her worries and fears had dissipated, replaced by an intense, base desire for physical stimulation.

The women had infected her with their disease, and she had let them.

For as she gorged on Maria's mutilated flesh, and tore out a chunk of her own breast and offered it to the woman in return, she remembered not the fear nor the agony nor the horror she had experienced that day.

All she recalled... was how much she had liked it.

23

EXCERPT FROM THE DIARY OF HENRIK PERSSON
19th November 1896

First, the good news. This shall not take long, for there is little of cheer to report, other than that Ursula's patient, the young girl we found barely twelve days ago, is coming along nicely. She remembers little, nay, <u>nothing</u> of her ordeal, but slowly her strength is returning. Ursula has even bestowed the name Lucia upon her, and long may her recovery continue. And there, as my good friend Joseph would say, endeth the good news.

Sleep continues to elude me. How can one rest in such proximity to the dying and the damned, when their discordant screams echo across the mountain all night long? Not to mention the fearful thoughts that trouble my every waking moment. One in particular has caused me no end of sleepless nights. What if the women are <u>not</u> dying, but growing stronger and more deranged? In my naivety, I had assumed the dreadful virus would claim the first victim. But Sister Giovanna, the only confirmed casualty of this long winter of misery, was brutally slain by human hands, *and her murderer lurks within the lonely, winding corridors of Sant'Arcangel. Is it the same person who attacked young Lucia? I don't believe so.*

For I have witnessed with my own eyes the level of degeneracy the disease has reduced the sisters of the convent to. It has addled their minds and crippled their morals, and the way that Sister Giovanna was placed in the soup suggests a deliberate attempt to poison the rest of us, an attempt that, I add with a shudder, was almost entirely successful. To the best of my knowledge, only myself, Gertrude, Sister Ursula, and young Lucia remain untainted. We gather in Ursula's chamber each morning to look for the disease on our bodies, leaving no patch of skin uninvestigated. Any shred of dignity we possessed was cast aside the first time we bent forwards and spread our buttocks as our partner probed for signs of what we have taken to describing as 'the rot.' Gertrude believes there are more of the uninfected somewhere in the convent. She clings to this hope like a talisman, while I fear that the inmates are now well and truly running the asylum. I insisted that Ursula and Lucia move into the cottage with us. There is a good-sized bed, a fire, and I have even constructed a crude lock to keep any unwanted visitors at bay. But Ursula, for whatever reason, refused. I can only hope she reconsiders.

My dear Joseph, if you're reading this in Sant'Arcangel and I stand not by your side, then I urge you — nay, I <u>beg</u> you — to get the hell out. Run from this place and never look back. Or better yet, burn it. Raze these hallowed walls to the ground and let the mountain wind scatter the ashes, for whatever macabre terror stalked these halls when first we arrived... is no longer alone.

～

The door to the cottage opened, and a gust of wind flipped the pages of Henrik's journal. Gertrude entered, wrapped in a woollen blanket, and struggled to close the doors against the pounding gale. Hurriedly, Henrik stuffed the journal back into his desk.

"What are you writing?" she asked, as she slotted a heavy wooden plank into Henrik's makeshift lock.

"Oh, just some theories based on medical textbooks I found in the library. Nothing exciting, my darling."

"A shame," she said, brushing snow and hay from her blanket before draping it over a chair by the fire. "I was hoping for some poetry to pass the long nights." Snowflakes clung to her hair and lashes. Gertrude no longer wore her wimple, though she continued to dress in her tunic, for she owned no other clothes.

"How's the horse?" asked Henrik.

"He's managing. But the snow weighs heavily on the stable, and I worry the roof may collapse."

"I'll clear it this evening," he said, and smiled for her benefit. "I'd prefer the horse did not have to move into the cottage with us."

Gertrude shivered by the crackling fire, saying nothing. Surrounded by a stone hearth, the flames spat embers into the air as Henrik approached from behind and wrapped his arms around his lover's waist.

"All will be well," he whispered. "I promise."

"I wish I could believe that."

He held her tighter. "We're safe in here."

"And what about out there? Every time I leave the cottage, I feel eyes upon me."

"Then from now on, perhaps it's wise not to stray from each other's side, even for a short while. And," he added quietly, "I would like to show you how to operate the gun."

She turned to him, shadows dancing across her pale, haunted face. He thought she was about to refuse. Instead, she closed her eyes and leaned against him. "I pray I never have to use it."

The door rattled, and they both fell silent. "Is someone there?" called Henrik. The wind answered with a keening lament. He eyed the door, waiting for the handle to turn.

It never did.

"I'm so frightened," said Gertrude. She trembled in his arms.

"As am I, my love." He kissed her head. "But we must stay strong. Once the snow melts, we can ride down the mountain, and I shall return with Franco and his coach to retrieve Ursula and Lucia."

Gertrude turned her face towards the fire. "When the snow melts? That may not be for months."

"We shall wait as long as it takes, Gertrude." He gripped her shoulders. "Days, weeks, even months. We have no other choice."

She smiled joylessly. "And what state will the sisters of Sant'Arcangel be in by then?"

"If their rapid rate of decay is any indication, I believe they shall all be dead."

"And if they're not?"

He glanced out the window. The axe handle was no longer visible, buried deep beneath the snowdrifts.

Then perhaps it is time for us to start praying, he thought, but did not say so. Instead, he ran his hand through Gertrude's hair, and whispered, "Then we wrap ourselves in a dozen blankets and take the horse down the mountain, weather be damned. I'll protect you, my darling. On that, you have my—"

Gertrude stiffened. They locked eyes.

"Do you hear it?" she asked. "Or have I gone mad?"

"No. I hear it too." The fire roared beside him, but Henrik had never felt so utterly cold as, outside, a church-bell tolled, the pealing chimes ringing out across the mountain. "Where's that coming from?"

"The old bell tower," said Gertrude. "It still stands."

"Impossible," said Henrik, yet unless his ears deceived him, Gertrude was correct. He had seen the ruined chapel only once, during a midnight tryst with Gertrude one hot summer evening, the pair of them sneaking off to make love amongst the ruins. That had been two years ago, and even then the bell tower had looked within days of collapse.

Gertrude stroked his face. "Please don't say it, my love."

"Say what?"

"That we must investigate. I can see it in your eyes. A desire for answers. A hunger."

"Are you not in the least bit curious?"

"Of course I am." She cast her eyes down. "But Henrik, to reach the chapel, we must traverse the length of the convent. There could be *anything* in there, awaiting us." She held him tightly. "I don't think my heart can bear it."

She was afraid, and understandably so. Yet while Henrik did not wish to quarrel with his beloved, he could not let the call of the bell go unheeded. To do so would be to admit that their situation was indeed hopeless, and he would not accept that. And anyhow, in the worst case-scenario...

He strode to the desk and retrieved Franco's pistol, checking the chambers the way he did every evening before bed. All six were loaded. "Enough talk," he said. "We have no choice but to investigate. But be not afraid." He tucked the pistol into his waistband and patted the handle reassuringly. "You're safe with me, my darling. I promise you that."

24

———

Sister Ursula was in the pantry, stuffing loaves of bread and handfuls of berries into a sack, when the toll of the bell broke the heavy silence.

The convent corridors had been mercifully deserted as she wandered in search of supplies. She had already filled several large jugs with fresh water from the well and carried them, one-by-one, to her cell. Now, all that remained of her plan — if she could be so bold as to call her half-formed notion a 'plan' — was to bring at least one month's reserve of food to her room, before sealing her and Lucia inside until rescue arrived or the snow thawed... whichever came first.

Of course, without the Mother Superior's master key, the door would not lock, but if she were to position the closet and the bed in front of it, then that, she hoped, would act as a sufficient barricade. The door was the only way into the room, unless some unhinged person clambered along the narrow ledge around the building and climbed in through her window. But not even a diseased, mind-rotted murderer would be foolhardy enough to attempt *that* risky endeavour.

As the bell pealed, the hair on her arms stood on end. Never before had the call to worship sounded so chilling. That bell had not rung for five long years. So why now? And who was ringing it?

She clutched the kitchen knife in her trembling hand. After glancing around to ensure she was alone, she tied the sack with rope and hoisted it over her shoulder. More than anything, she wanted to be back with Lucia in the relative safety of their shared cell.

Furtively, she slipped out of the pantry and into the kitchen, where the fire crackled softly. She had lit it a while ago, hoping the heat would rise and warm her cell, but with no one to tend to the logs, the flames would soon die out. Ursula, however, had prepared for the cold. In addition to food and water, she had already fetched extra sheets and blankets from the storeroom. At worst, she and Lucia could cocoon themselves and hibernate until spring.

The idea amused her, but she did not laugh. Mirth was impossible in the room of Giovanna's slaughter. Her dried blood had soaked into the tabletop and left a permanent stain, while a meat cleaver, blunted from sustained blows against flesh and bone, lay discarded on the floor, surrounded by its own muddy brown smear.

Gripping the knife in her white-knuckled fist, Ursula hefted the sack from the kitchen and into the corridor, praying each door she passed remained closed. The sun had almost set, and the candles had burnt themselves out days ago, plunging the corridors into perpetual gloom. Yet on she walked, her eyes focused on the stained glass window at the end of the hallway, through which the last vestiges of dying light bled. Her heart thumped in time with the bell as she neared the stairs. One of the doors was partly open, a splinter of candlelight cutting across the corridor like a wound. From inside came wet sucking sounds and low, pleasurable groans.

Steeling herself, she pressed against the wall. She would have to sneak past. God, what was happening to her beloved sisters? She swallowed her fear. This was not the time for hysteria. Lucia needed her, and—

The sliver of light widened.

The door was opening.

Ursula backed away.

A bare arm, marred by bloody abrasions, groped across the floor. The fingertips hooked into the stone, dragging the unseen body forwards, and Ursula fled in the opposite direction. She kept her steps light, for if her sisters knew she and Lucia were living, safe and uninfected, in her cell... well, she wasn't sure what they would do, but she was not keen to find out.

The sack of supplies bounced against her spine as she ran. The tolling bell had seemingly brought the convent to twitching, ghoulish life. She heard shuffling feet, sibilant whispers, moans and grunts and screams. But worst of all was the laughter, for it was fiendish and wicked.

Above her, in the main sleeping quarters, doors opened and closed. The sisters were leaving their rooms. Where were they going? Ursula's mind raced. Should she hide somewhere and wait it out? What if they discovered Lucia in her room and—

She tripped.

The knife clattered onto the hard stone as Ursula went sprawling. Her sack opened, spilling bread and berries, and sending lumps of cheese rolling across the corridor. She lay a moment, listening, tracing her hands over the floor in search of her supplies. She located the knife first, and clutched it to her bosom. Then, she found the obstacle she had stumbled over. It was heavy, and wet, and clad in fabric.

A corpse.

Shoving what food she could recover into the sack, Ursula got to her feet and carried on towards the far set of stairs. They were located outside the Mother Superior's quarters, and for that reason were rarely used. They would make the perfect hiding place until the sisters were gone.

A single melancholy candle burned outside the abbess's room. Judging by the lack of melted wax, it had been lit only recently. As she trod carefully by, Ursula noticed the door. For the first time in days, it was unlocked and slightly ajar.

She paused. No one had seen the Mother Superior or Claudia for some time. Were they in there right now?

Were they infected?

Cautiously, she placed her sack of supplies by the stairs and returned to the door. With a gentle push, it swung wide open. Inside, the crackling fire illuminated a centuries-old walnut desk, the blaze giving life to the intricate religious carvings on the panels. It was the only room in the convent with wooden floorboards, and a large cross hung on the wall betwixt oil paintings of Christ and St Peter. And there, with her back to Ursula, sat the Mother Superior in a wheelchair.

Go in.

Absolutely not. She was wasting time. Lucia needed her. *But the key…*

Of course! The key the abbess carried could lock and unlock every door in the convent. With it, Ursula could secure Lucia and herself in their cell. It was their best chance of survival. Surely even the Mother Superior would understand that?

"Excuse me," she said, taking a tentative step across the threshold. Her heart pounded. "It's Sister Ursula."

The woman did not stir. What if she refused to help?

"Reverend Mother?"

Dried blood stained the floor. Her legs felt weak, and she gripped the door handle for balance.

"May I... may I enter?"

It mattered not whether the abbess agreed to help. Ursula had promised Lucia no harm would come to her, and it was a promise she intended to keep. If the Mother Superior refused to part with her precious key, then...

Then what, exactly? The woman *terrified* her.

"Please, are you listening? Can you hear me?"

Fearful of alerting the other sisters, she kept her voice low and walked fully into the room.

The abbess was motionless. An open Bible lay on the bed, the pages torn and scattered across the bloody floor.

She stepped closer.

"Reverend Mother?"

A pungent stench filled the air.

Ursula reached the abbess, peeling her sandals from the sticky floorboards. She placed her hand on the woman's shoulder. It felt thin.

Skeletal.

And when the head drooped lethargically onto her hand, Ursula bit back a scream. She took a long, wheezing breath, and rotated the wheelchair, slowly turning it until the orange glow from the fire lit the Mother Superior's lifeless face.

Was she dead?

At first, it appeared so. Beneath the thick coating of dried, cracked blood was a smashed face and a nose so severely broken it was practically pulped. The jaw sagged, revealing toothless gums, while loose flesh subsided over gaunt purple cheeks.

Ursula placed two shaking fingers on the woman's neck. Was that a faint pulse she detected? With all the blood rushing through her own head, it was difficult to ascertain.

The key! Take the key!

She looked down, and there it was. A rusted black mortice key, attached to the cincture cord around the Mother Superior's waist. Ursula reached for it, and a low, gaseous rumble escaped the abbess's lips, followed by a stream of runny black bile. The liquid splatted onto her lap, and one swollen eye flickered open.

Ursula's head swooned. She felt sick, but she could waste no more time.

"I'm sorry," she said, laying the knife on the desk. "But I need that key."

She leaned over the woman and fumbled for her cincture. Each nun wore one, a simple cord tied around the waist with three separate knots to represent the vows of poverty, chastity, and obedience. The Mother Superior's belt looped through the key, securing it between the second and third knots.

Digging her nails into the closest knot, Ursula attempted to lever open the bond.

"Please," she muttered, scratching at the cord. It wouldn't budge. She doubted it had been unfastened even once in the last fifty years. No matter. She reached for her knife, lifted it, *gripped* it.

Over the relentless toll of the bell, she thought she heard a faint sound.

"It's nothing," she told herself, and held the blade to the cord. Before she started cutting, she heard it again.

Footsteps.

They echoed insistently throughout the corridor, getting louder... and getting closer.

The knife trembled in Ursula's hand. She looked over her shoulder at the infinite darkness beyond the open door, and shuddered in fear.

Someone was coming.

25

Henrik and Gertrude left the cottage and laboured through the waist-deep snow, shielding their eyes from the frequent flurries. The moonlit convent loomed forebodingly, the front door swinging open on rusted hinges as if beckoning them into its dismal bosom.

Once inside, Henrik shut the door with a satisfying *clunk,* offering a welcome respite from the weather. His hands throbbed from the cold, and he flexed his raw, pink fingers before drawing his weapon. Though it had been some years since he had fired a pistol, he felt safer with the gun in his hand. No nun would dare attack an armed man. The deadliest weapons available to the sisters were farming tools, and while pitchforks and scythes could be deadly at close range, the gun offered the advantage of distance.

Presuming he could *see* any potential assailants.

"We need light," he said.

"There are candelabras in each corner. Wait there." Gertrude shuffled through the darkness, her sandals scuffing the floor, and returned to him with a single candle.

Henrik fumbled in his pocket for his matchbook, and lit

one on the second try, holding the flame to the wick. The weak light felt inadequate, but any illumination was preferable to none at all. Through the murk, a doorway shimmered into view. Henrik and Gertrude approached side-by-side, entering the ominous twisting labyrinth.

Lit only by the modest glow of the candle, they wove through the corridors in a somnambulant fugue, passing no one in the deserted hallways, and hearing not a single voice nor pained cry. It was as if they were all alone, the last survivors of the unknown disease that had ravaged Sant'Arcangel and brought God himself to his knees. Had death finally claimed the nuns? Their feverish, agonised wails had turned the convent into a purgatory over the past few weeks, and if this brooding silence portended the end of their time on Earth, then it was an act of mercy.

No one should have to suffer the way those poor women had.

Henrik's breath steamed through the candlelight. Every door they passed was open. He stepped towards the nearest, and Gertrude gripped his sleeve.

"What are you doing?" she asked.

"Checking the rooms."

"And what of the bell?"

"It's not going anywhere. I simply wish to ensure the sisters are where they're supposed to be."

Inside, the cell was as dusky as a moonless night. The light from the candle failed to reach the walls, illuminating only a vacant bed. The once-white sheets had been drawn back, a pool of shimmering gore nestled in the body-shaped impression left in the mattress.

"There's no one here," said Gertrude.

Henrik glanced at the dark corners of the room, and

slowly backed away, ushering Gertrude out first. "Indeed. Let's try another."

The next room was also empty, and judging by the freshness of the blood, only recently abandoned. A long, thin blade nestled amongst the creased sheets. Gertrude reached for it, and Henrik stopped her.

"Touch nothing in these rooms." He looked at the pus-stained bed, wrinkling his nose in distaste. "Nothing at all."

They tried two more cells. Both were unoccupied, and bore traces of blood and rot and faeces. Where had everyone gone? A few days prior, the diseased nuns had been bed-bound and incapable of supporting their own weight. And now they had simultaneously found the strength to leave their rooms? It couldn't be.

The bell tolled.

"Let's go back to the cottage," said Gertrude. "We're safer in there."

"We shall," he said, and squeezed her hand. "But not yet. *Someone* is ringing that bell, my love. And I, for one, cannot rest until I find out who is responsible."

26

———

Ursula *needed* that key.

She placed the knife against the rope and started to saw, fighting against a rising tide of panic. Her senses heightened, each nerve standing to attention as the footsteps echoed through the corridor.

They could only belong to Sister Claudia.

"Almost there," she whispered, stretching the rope taut. She glanced at the door, expecting to see someone coming for her, someone diseased and rotten and hideously misshapen. Distracted, her hand slipped, and the blade sliced her finger open. Blood trickled onto the abbess's lap as Ursula scraped the knife back and forth over the fraying cord. She was nearly done, the bloody strands unravelling. But the footsteps... oh, the footsteps grew harsher by the second.

She continued cutting. She couldn't stop, not even for a moment. The rope split into thin sections, and then — *snap!* — it broke. She laid the knife aside and yanked the key free, then tucked the belt around the Mother Superior's waist to disguise the breakage.

The footsteps were almost upon her.

Her mind raced. What to do? She had the key, yet if she stepped out into the corridor, she would surely be seen. Could she run? Could she defend herself?

Hide.

Her stomach turned somersaults, her bladder full and painful. She ran to the closet and reached for the handle.

Wait!

She looked back.

The wheelchair was facing the wrong way.

In an anxious frenzy, she raced over and spun the chair into position. With only seconds to spare, Ursula threw open the closet door and shoved the hanging clothes and vestments to one side, forcing herself into the cramped space.

The first thing that hit her was the smell; a terrible, rank funk of decay. Pinching her nose, she gagged and pulled the door shut.

"The bell!" Claudia cried as she stormed into the room. *"Who dares ring that bell?"*

The stench in the closet leached insidiously into Ursula's nostrils. Blood pumped through her veins.

"I ask for guidance," Claudia was saying, unaware of her presence. *"And I receive none. Is this ringing some sort of sign? Why won't you talk to me? I await your answer, you wretched God!"*

Ursula's hand dangled by her side, clutching the key tightly. Her knuckles brushed something wet and rotten, and she recoiled, bumping the door with her shoulder. Too late, she realised it was simply a stained, putrid tunic. The door whined open, and her stomach dropped. The gap was less than half an inch, and through it she watched Claudia stomp across the room. She gripped the Mother Superior's shoulders, shaking her.

"*Tell me what to do! Speak to me! Am I not good enough?*" She struck the abbess's cheek. "*Have I not proven my piety? What more can I do to earn your trust?*" She walked around the desk and opened a drawer.

Ursula's eyes widened in horror.

The knife.

She had left the knife lying on the desk.

Claudia rummaged in the drawer. "*Where is it?*" she snarled. "*Where have you hidden it?*"

Ursula had never experienced such dread. The sensation draped across her like a blanket of ice, and she bit down on her finger to prevent her from passing out in a dead faint. As she did so, she prayed Claudia would perceive neither the knife nor the missing key, and that, should the unthinkable happen, God would protect her dear friend Lucia from further harm.

"*Not here,*" said Claudia. She slammed the drawer shut, causing the knife to wobble. She didn't seem to notice, for her attention had turned to the closet.

Ursula shuffled sideways into the stinking, pus-stained clothes. There was nowhere to go, nothing to do but stand here and wait for—

Claudia walked past the closet and out of sight. Closing her eyes in relief, Ursula forced out silent tears that had waited patiently for their moment of release. She unclenched her fists, her fingers aching from the pressure.

Seconds later, Claudia reappeared, striding towards the abbess. A vicious-looking whip dangled from her hand, the tarnished leather handle splitting into nine knotted, blood-stained cords that rasped across the floor.

A cat o' nine tails.

"I'll prove myself to you," said Claudia. *"Then you'll believe me."*

Slowly, almost ceremonially, she removed the cross from around her neck and wrapped the cord around the handle of the cat o' nine tails. Then she raised it to her lips, kissed the cross, and laid the vicious lash down. With her gaze fixed firmly on the Mother Superior, she removed her wimple, then lifted her robes over her head and tossed them on the desk.

The garments landed on top of Ursula's knife.

Clad in nothing but a yellowing underskirt and head covering, Claudia stood before the Mother Superior. Lattice-like scars covered her back and breasts, from older, faded white lines to fresh pink welts encircled by maroon bruising. And there, on her side, was a patch of black rot.

She knelt before the abbess and lifted the cat o' nine tails. *"Is this what you want?"* she cried, and cracked the whip fiercely over her own shoulder. The nine cords split her skin with resounding smacks. Claudia grimaced, but did not cry out. She whipped herself again, the self-flagellation opening old wounds and creating new ones. Blood gushed down her back and drenched the seat of her underskirt. *"Are you happy?"*

Again and again she lashed herself, swapping hands and strapping the bloody cords against her stomach and her chest and her shoulders, until the whip splatted to the blood-slicked floorboards and she hung her head, panting and weeping, her upper half a mass of ravaged tissue and exposed, glistening muscle.

In the closet, Ursula could not tear her eyes from the repulsive spectacle. She realised she was holding her breath, and let out a slow, deep exhalation as Claudia reached for the whip once more.

The bleeding woman staggered to her feet. *"You,"* she said, and pointed the cat o' nine tails at the Mother Superior. *"You* will *give me guidance."*

The nine wicked cords screamed across the old woman's face, rending her skin and slicing her open. Blood sprayed from the whip and spattered the walls, some landing in the fire and sizzling like fat in a saucepan.

"Talk to me!"

Another blow sheared the skin from the Mother Superior's face. It hung in curled ribbons from the exposed bone. *"Talk to—"*

She froze. The whip swung at her side.

Ursula's eyes widened. Had she somehow been noticed?

"Yes?" said Claudia. She fell to her knees before the abbess, clutching the woman's bound hands and staring at her as if listening intently. *"Her? She's responsible? Yes, yes. I understand."* She punctuated her words with knowing nods, tears flowing down her cheeks. *"I hear you, heavenly Father."* Weeping, she buried her head in the Mother Superior's lap. *"I will do it. You can trust me, Lord. You can trust me!"*

She unwrapped the cross from the whip and placed the wooden idol around her neck, where it soaked up the blood between her mangled breasts. And only when Claudia stood and reached for her robes did Ursula remember...

Her knife was lying beneath them.

She gasped, almost cried out.

This was it. The moment of discovery. When Claudia saw the knife, she would know someone had been here.

And still *was* here.

With her heart in her throat, she watched through the gap as Claudia grabbed the crumpled robes and slid them towards her, unaware of the knife moving with them.

Please God don't let her find me.

Claudia snatched her clothing from the desk, turning away to face the door.

The knife teetered on the edge.

Petrified, Ursula leaned forward. Her nails scratched at the closet walls as the knife tipped.

Down it fell, tumbling to the floor.

And at the precise moment Claudia hurriedly threw her robes on, the sharp point of the blade embedded itself between the wooden floorboards... and there it remained, the handle vibrating soundlessly.

Ursula's body trembled uncontrollably. She wanted to weep, to scream, but her relief was short-lived.

For as Claudia tied her cincture and gripped the wheel-chair handles, she muttered words that froze her to the marrow.

"I'll kill her for you, my Lord," she sobbed through a deranged devotional smile. She pushed the abbess towards the door. *"I promise you... the devil child shall not live."*

27

———

THE SNOWFALL HAD TURNED INTO A BLIZZARD BY THE TIME
Henrik and Gertrude reached the courtyard. The old well
lay hidden beneath the drifts; only the stone arch with the
pulley system protruded from the snow, standing tall above
the deep, dark pit.

They stuck to the east wall, moving from pillar to pillar
towards the corridor that led to the ruined chapel. The bell
tolled mightily, and Henrik wondered whether the wind
would carry the sound all the way to Cerbesca. It was a pipe
dream, he knew, but with hope swiftly evaporating, dreams
were all that remained.

Gertrude shivered next to him, her cheeks red with frost-
nip. "Please let us turn back," she said upon reaching the
final stretch. "No one is ringing that bell with virtuous
intentions."

"Turn back? And do what?" He kicked his boots against
the wall to dislodge the snow. "Return to the cottage to
warm ourselves by the fire while someone in need dies a
pauper's death in the cold?"

"Yes," she said emphatically. "Yes a thousand times over. No good can come of this."

He sighed and walked on. Poor Gertrude. She was not cut out for adventure. If he could have left her in the cottage, he would have done so, but he placed little faith in the flimsy lock he had constructed.

"We'll just take a quick look," he said. "If it appears dangerous, we shall retreat to safety."

With no light to guide them — the candle would never have survived the gale — they took the final corridor slowly. Hand-in-hand, the young couple shuffled across the cold stone until they rounded the last curve and arrived at the ruined chapel. Rays of moonlight struggled through gaps in the clouds, isolating pockets of snow in pale blue streaks through which the flakes whirled and spun.

Henrik marvelled at its crumbling beauty. Unlike Sant'Arcangel itself, which was typical of sixteenth-century Roman architecture, the chapel had been built years earlier in the Gothic style so popular in Europe during the Middle Ages. A grandiose place of worship, it had been an extraordinary sight atop the mountain, especially as Gothic architecture had never been common in Italy.

Now, only one wall remained. Icicles plunged from the window frames like underground stalactites, while broken pews lay overturned by the wind and coated in layers of snow. And behind it all, somehow still standing, was the bell tower.

"There's nobody here," said Gertrude. She sounded relieved.

They stared through the snowstorm at the tower. Shadows cloaked the entrance.

"We've come this far," said Henrik. The pistol felt like ice in his hand. "No sense in backing out now." He started towards the tower, yet for all his bravado, he was no longer sure who he was trying to convince.

Gertrude... or himself.

~

Ursula staggered from the closet and plucked the knife from the floor.

She wept, unwilling to accept that God would allow unfettered malignancy to thrive within his holy temple. Did he not care that such distemper profaned his daughters? The sight of the naked and rotting Claudia whipping the skin from the Mother Superior should have broken her mind, and yet the nightmare she had borne witness to in the refectory had seemingly inured her to such atrocities. But reflections on her mental condition could wait for another time. She must be prudent, and hasten back to her cell.

Fearful of leaving footprints, she avoided the freshly spilled blood as she walked unsteadily to the door. Thank heavens Claudia was in such a hurry, for she had not the foresight to try to lock it. Ursula looked at the key, which she clutched in her left hand. In her right, she held the knife. With God unwilling to intervene, she would put her faith in these two modest objects and pray they would be sufficient to hold the deranged sisters of Sant'Arcangel at bay. But she would have to make haste, for it did not take a scholar to surmise where Claudia and the Mother Superior were going.

I'll kill her for you, my Lord.

Ursula's heart pounded an irregular rhythm as Claudia's parting words rang in her ears like the mad toll of the bell.

The devil child shall not live.

~

Henrik gazed up at the bell tower in awe. How the blasted thing remained erect while the walls around it had fallen to ruin mystified him. From his low angle, the imposing structure tapered towards the belfry like an obelisk, and horizontal snowfall obscured the surrounding mountains as if the tower was located amidst a sinister white hell.

"Stay behind me," he said to Gertrude, flexing his trigger finger as they trudged through the snow. His limbs felt leaden from the cold, and he longed for a stiff drink. On their way to the tower they passed not a soul, and inside, snowflakes drifted through the open belfry and eddied through the moonlight. A wooden staircase, rotted from years of neglect and exposure to the elements, clung to all four walls and spiralled upwards. Was it safe to climb? He pinched the bannister and the damp wood crumbled between his fingers.

"Henrik..."

"One moment." He tested the first step and felt it bend. If he were to go higher, conditions would only worsen. Would his resolve be strong enough, or—

"Henrik, *please.*"

He turned to Gertrude. She was staring at her hand, at the smear of blood she had wiped from her cheek like a bloody tear. Another drop fell, dotting her shoulder. Beneath her feet, scarlet stained the snow like crushed berries.

"Step back," he said. "And for pity's sake, don't look—"

Too late.

Gertrude screamed.

"—up."

A dead nun hung from the bell ropes twenty feet above

them. She was naked, her belly cut wide open, intestines drooping from the wound. With each chime, the rope raised the dead woman higher before dropping her lifeless body back down, the additional weight offering enough momentum to keep the bell ringing long after it should have ceased. She started to rise again, and Henrik leapt and caught the woman's trailing ankles. He hung on, pulling hard to slow her ascent. The action caused the nun's guts to loosen, and the mass of internal organs slopped free, smacking onto the frozen ground in moist, steaming coils.

In silence, they watched the nun slowly spin on the rope. Her face was bloated, her tongue lolling out the side of her mouth.

"Who did this?" asked Gertrude.

Words failed him. Only the reassuring coldness of the pistol anchored his mind. "We should cut her down," he managed to say.

Gertrude shook her head. She couldn't seem to stop. "No. I want off this mountain. *Now.*"

"We can't—"

"Oh Henrik, *we must leave!*" She wrapped her arms around him, burying her face in his coat. "I'd rather take my chances in the storm than spend one more night in this awful place."

He held her close. "I agree. And we *will* leave. On that, you have my word. But night has fallen, Gertrude. Any attempt now would be tantamount to suicide."

"I don't care," she said, sobbing against him. She looked up into his eyes. "I don't... *Henrik, look out!*"

He spun, shoving Gertrude aside and raising his pistol in time to see a naked woman standing in the doorway.

In her withered hands, she swung an axe.

Henrik threw himself backwards to dodge the blow. He

landed on his posterior, the axe whooshing through the air where seconds before he had stood. The jolt knocked the gun from his hand. A shadow fell over him, and he looked up into the mad eyes of Sister Isabelle.

She was the worst case he had yet seen.

Coated in the fungal rot, she resembled a gnarled, mossy old tree, with rigid limbs like diseased branches and a face bulging with pus-spurting mould. With the axe high above her head, she shrieked in a mixture of agony and glee.

Henrik looked for the gun, but it was lost in the snow. All he could do as the axe came arcing down towards him was shield his face with his hand and prepare for death.

Thud!

He flinched.

"Henrik!" yelled Gertrude. *"Get the gun!"*

He looked up to see his fiancée had thrown herself at the rotting nun, slamming her against the wall. The axe lay at their feet, and as the two women grappled, he scrambled onto his knees, searching for the pistol. There wasn't a second to waste. Behind him, fabric tore. Or was it skin? Frantically brushing the snow aside, he located the weapon and snatched it up.

"Found it!" he roared, and turned to find Gertrude pinning Isabelle to the wall, the diseased woman thrashing in her grip and snapping her yellow teeth at Gertrude's face and neck.

"Shoot her!" cried Gertrude. She jumped backwards. *"Now!"*

Henrik aimed down the barrel. Time seemed to slow.

Do it.

The gun trembled.

Pull the trigger.

He used his other hand to steady himself.

Shoot her.

She was fully exposed. One shot was all it would take. So why couldn't he bring himself to do it?

"What are you waiting for?" screamed Gertrude.

He looked beyond the barrel and locked eyes with Isabelle. As if in understanding of his hesitation — of his *weakness* — her threadbare lips curled into a leering grin, and she darted from the tower.

"Shoot her, Henrik! She's getting away!"

He aimed the pistol at the woman's lesion-covered back as she loped through the snow towards the convent. The blizzard swirled around her.

"For god's sake, give me the gun and I'll shoot her!"

His finger hovered over the trigger. He closed one eye and squeezed.

The shot was deafening. Cacophonous.

It was also far, far too late.

Isabelle kept running until the whirling mist of snow enveloped her completely. Her crumbling body vanished into the whiteness... and then she was gone.

Henrik stared at the gun. His arm fell limp, the vibrations from the shot working their way up to his shoulder. He staggered backwards, and then Gertrude was upon him, pounding her fists against his chest.

"Why did you wait so long?" she cried. Weeping, she struck him again. "You could have stopped her!"

"I... I..."

"She's still out there!" Then, with a desperately sad shake of the head that broke Henrik's heart, she said, "You let her go. She tried to kill us, and you *let her go.*"

His heart beat fast. Too fast. What a fool he had been for believing that, should the time ever come, he could kill. As a doctor, he had devoted his life to *healing* people. It was what he did, and he did it well. But to take a life... to snuff a living creature out of existence... that was anathema to his belief system. It mattered not that Isabelle was insane, for the brain rot was not her fault. The disease had taken her forcibly, and it was the disease, not its victims, that needed to be stopped.

To be studied. To be understood.

To be cured.

He wanted to explain this to Gertrude, to help her understand his inaction. But as she leaned against the wall with her head tilted back, tears flooding her eyes, Henrik noticed the thin red scar on her neck, and the image swept all other thoughts aside.

It's nothing, he told himself. A small scratch, not too deep. Only a light breakage of skin. In all the excitement, Gertrude probably wasn't even aware. She came to him then, collapsing into his arms, and he held her, brushing her hair aside for a closer look. At first glance, he saw nothing but mild surface damage. The shallow wound wasn't even bleeding, for Christ's sake. And yet, when he spotted the minuscule black threads worming beneath his lover's flesh, Henrik started to cry, for he knew that his beloved was infected.

Gertrude dabbed at his tears with her sleeve. "I'm sorry," she said, and sniffed. "I shouldn't have hit you."

He nodded, barely listening. How long did they have left together before the rot took hold? How long until the filthy tendrils seized her brain and she degenerated into a sexually depraved, bloodthirsty maniac?

He broke down. Not realising why, Gertrude lovingly embraced him. "Don't cry, my love," she whispered. "Everything will be alright. I think I understand. We needn't kill unless forced to."

Should he tell her she carried the disease? Oh, to what purpose? With nothing but his useless bag of salves and ointments, he had neither the facilities nor the tools to seek a cure. He gazed out at the whirling snow and the cruel night sky, and a plan formed in his mind. Certainly, there was nothing he could do for Gertrude here in Sant'Arcangel. But back in Cerbesca, with Franco's limitless knowledge, and access to both his laboratory and his library...

Could they do it? Was it possible that he and Franco, working together, could find a cure and save Gertrude before she turned?

He kissed her forehead and said, "We shall leave tomorrow morning."

She looked up at him, her hopeful expression in stark contrast to the widening darkness of her neck injury. "Do you really mean that?"

"I do." He glanced one final time at the disembowelled horror hanging from the bell. The rope creaked as the dead nun rotated. "At first light, we shall abandon this dreadful place... and never return."

Ursula followed Claudia at a safe distance.

She stuck to the shadows, clutching the knife to her chest and remaining two corners behind. The noisy rattle of the wheelchair guided her to the opposite end of the convent, and she waited while Claudia struggled up the stairs with the Mother Superior. Was she planning on killing Lucia?

Ursula believed so. The woman had gone quite mad.

Her misguided belief that Lucia was the cause of the plague was understandable, for the malady had taken hold only a day or so after the girl's arrival. But Lucia was nothing more than an innocent bystander. Certainly, a presence had followed her to the convent; of that, Ursula was convinced. She had felt it on the day, and still did. But Lucia was not to blame. If anything, her innocence had protected them.

Ursula stared at the knife, then closed her eyes.

Lucia was her guiding light... and woe betide *anyone* who tried to harm her.

PART III

28

Excerpt from the diary of Henrik Persson
19th November 1896

It is shortly after ten, and in approximately nine hours, at the rising of the sun, Gertrude and I shall attempt the journey down the mountain. I doubt sleep will be forthcoming tonight, so ghastly were the transgressions we witnessed this grim, unforgiving evening, but I shall endeavour to rest my body in preparation for our gruelling descent.

As I write, my beloved perches on our bed, sewing blankets together with the aim of wrapping ourselves and the horse in as many layers as possible. The plan is to undertake the reckless expedition at a sluggish pace to minimise the risk of our steed taking a wrong step. The thought of our frozen corpses entombed in snow until next year's thaw sends — if you will pardon the gallows humour, dear Joseph — a shiver down my spine. We are acting in a foolhardy manner, but I am no longer convinced that staying in the convent is the safer option.

Death has laid claim to Sant'Arcangel.

We found another mutilated body, the details of which I shall not go into on the page, so heinous were the injuries. The killer in question, one Sister Isabelle, a most agreeable and quick-witted personality, was in an advanced state of decomposition. And yet, as the infection spreads, I fear <u>more</u> nuns will indulge their barbarous whims. Perhaps some already have? It is possible that in a matter of days, or even sooner, God forbid, the entire convent could be overrun by homicidal deviants. How many women call Sant'Arcangel home? Fifty? Sixty? More?

I should have listened to Gertrude. Had we left this morn, we would be home, and she would not have been scarred by Isabelle's claws. Does she realise she carries the disease? From her posture and attitude, I suspect not. She labours feverishly — a poor choice of words, I'm afraid — over her blankets, ensuring we will make the journey with the highest odds of survival. Were it not dark, we would leave now. The temptation is strong. But with no light to guide us, I can only pray that we endure whatever terrors the night brings, and that we reach Cerbesca and find a cure for Gertrude before she, too, succumbs to madness.

"Someone's coming," said Gertrude.

Henrik closed his journal and slid it across the desk. "From where?"

The double-thick blanket fell from Gertrude's lap and draped over her feet. Wordlessly, she pointed to the window. Through the frosted glass, a dark shape stumbled through the blurred white landscape, advancing on the cottage.

Henrik drew his gun. A visitor at this late hour portended nothing but misery. Had one of the nuns followed them?

The figure shielded their face from the snow as they

swept past the window. The door was locked, but Henrik could take no chances. Gripping the pistol, he stepped closer, feeling Gertrude's nervous gaze on him.

"Don't let them in," she whispered.

The handle rattled and turned, but the wooden bar sealed the door shut.

"Henrik! Are you there? It's Ursula!"

He turned to Gertrude. Frightened, she shook her head. "She could be infected."

Ursula hammered her fists against the door. *"Henrik, please! Claudia's trying to take Lucia!"*

He took a step closer.

"Don't do it," urged Gertrude.

"I have to," he said quietly. He understood her caution. They had settled on a course of action, and jeopardising it was foolish. But he also saw the conflict in her eyes, and knew that in her heart, Gertrude felt the same.

"Ursula? How do I know you're not—"

"Henrik, you bastard, Lucia is going to die! Do you understand me? I'll face death without you if I must, but I will not stand idly by and watch as a young girl is—"

"You've made your point!" he shouted. He removed the block of wood and threw the door open. Ursula stood shivering in the snow with Henrik's gun pointed at her face.

"I'm not infected," she said, and pushed the barrel aside. "I swear on the Bible itself."

Henrik knew he should check her body for infection. It could be another trick, like the tolling of the bell. But if Lucia was in danger, then time was of the essence. He had a decision to make, but what forced his hand was the fear that Ursula would perceive the black marks that tainted Gertrude's neck.

His beloved could not know about them, not until they

were safely off the mountain. There were no mirrors in the cottage, and he had made a grand show of cleaning her wounds to ease any lingering concerns.

No, of all the risks currently presenting themselves, that one he was least willing to take.

He backed away from Ursula. "Stay there," he said, leaving her standing in the doorway. He strode back to Gertrude and held the pistol out to her. "Take this. If anyone other than myself tries to enter, point the gun and pull the trigger."

"What? Henrik, no! You swore we would not part."

"I shan't be long. Please, take the gun."

She folded her arms and turned away. "I don't want it."

"Henrik, hurry!" said Ursula.

He placed the pistol on the bed beside Gertrude. "Lock the door behind me. And remember... let no one in but me."

Her lip trembled as she looked up at him. "Please come back. I can't face this without you."

His heart ached. She was on the brink of total mental collapse, and he wanted so badly to kiss her, to tell her she was safe, and that she need not worry. But when she moved to embrace him, the tears that fell from her eyes were black and clouded.

"I *will* return," he said, fighting back tears of his own. "And we *will* leave." He started towards the door, then turned back. "On that, my love, you have my solemn oath."

29

———

Henrik raced through the convent with Ursula trailing behind him.

Sant'Arcangel's sleeping quarters were the last place he wished to be right now, and without the pistol, he felt naked. Despite his reluctance to use it, the weapon had become a source of comfort over the previous week, and running headfirst into the lion's den unarmed was highly imprudent. But what was he supposed to do? Let young Lucia die?

He reached the top of the stairs and emerged into the upper-level corridor. Moonlight streamed through the stained glass window at the far end, revealing a bizarre tableau of figures: Sister Claudia, hunched over and dragging Lucia towards a wheelchair, in which sat what appeared to be a bloody-faced cadaver.

"Stop!" he shouted. "Leave that girl alone!"

At the sound of his command, Claudia turned to him. "This does not concern you, heathen."

A hand slapped down on his shoulder, and he spun. Ursula leaned against him, catching her breath. "She wants to kill Lucia."

"Insolent cur," said Claudia dismissively. She hoisted Lucia's prone body in her arms and dumped it onto the wheelchair atop the lifeless figure. "You dare question God's will? She *must* die. Don't you see? This foul wretch is a harbinger of evil. The devil's spawn, come to wreak havoc on us all!"

"Listen to yourself," said Henrik. He subconsciously patted his pocket, searching for the gun he had left with Gertrude. "You think your god speaks to a lowly servant like *you?*" He tutted, remembering the authoritative way Franco had spoken to the Mother Superior. "You have delusions of grandeur, Sister Claudia."

As he spoke, he sized her up. Physically, she posed little threat to him. But if an altercation ensued, he would have to end it decisively and with haste. If she was infected — and she surely was — then it would only take one scratch or bite to dash all hopes of survival.

Claudia smiled. Drool slobbered down her chin. "He does not speak directly to me, fool. He uses the Mother Superior as a vessel through which to commune."

She gripped the wheelchair handles and started towards him. Lucia lay prone across the Mother Superior, her toes scraping the floor.

Henrik maintained his ground. "I won't let you take her, Sister. I'll use force if necessary."

Claudia stared at him. "Then you shall make a fine offering." She turned her gaze on Ursula. *"Both* of you." She shoved the chair, forcing it against Henrik's ankles. He winced as the metal grazed his shin, and took a good look at the Mother Superior. Half of the woman's face was missing, the skin roughly flayed from her skull. One torn eyeball oozed down her tattered cheek. She had to be dead. But if so, why was Claudia pushing her around in a wheelchair?

Because she's mad.

She's utterly, stark raving mad.

"We must gather the sisters," Claudia entreated, "and burn the fiend alive. It's our last chance before she regains her powers and destroys us all."

Henrik pointed at Lucia. "This is what you fear? This poor child?"

"She's the devil." Claudia's eyes narrowed. "Now let... me... pass."

Lucia groaned, and he reached for her. With a shriek, Claudia lunged. He had expected as much, and punched the insane nun in the face. His fist connected with her jaw with a sharp *crack,* and she crumpled to the floor.

"You'll doom us all," she moaned, black blood trickling from her mouth. "All shall perish, and it will be your fault, infidel. Heretic!"

Henrik's knuckles stung from the impact of the punch, and he could only imagine how her jaw must feel. "Get out of my sight," he said, scooping Lucia from the chair, "and take your abbess with you. Give her a proper burial. Or better yet... burn her."

Claudia laughed at him. "Oh, she's not dead. You'll see. We shall return in greater numbers to claim what is ours. With each passing moment, more of my flock—"

"Hold your tongue," said Henrik, and he kicked the wheelchair down the corridor.

"No!" spat Claudia. She staggered to her feet and stumbled woozily after the Reverend Mother, while Henrik carried Lucia inside and laid her on the bed. He rescued the sheets from the floor and placed them across her.

Ursula closed the door and stood with her back to him, resting her forehead against the wood. "Thank you," she said.

Henrik watched her shoulders rise and fall. "She'll be back. Of that, I have no doubt."

"It matters not." She turned to face him, holding up a key. "I stole this from the abbess. Now I can lock us inside."

"Excellent. But will that be enough to keep them out?" He went to her and gently took her arm. "Listen to me, Ursula. Gertrude and I are leaving in the morning. Do you wish to accompany us?"

"Leaving?" She sounded incredulous. "You'll never make it. The storm..."

"To hell with the storm. Come with us, I entreat you. The horse cannot support three bodies, but if I walk alongside, we can—"

"And what about Lucia? I made her a promise."

"We will send help once we—"

"I won't leave her. You must understand, Henrik. I swore I'd protect her from harm."

"I *do* understand, Ursula. As a doctor, I understand better than most that I can't save everyone, no matter how much I'd like to."

She shook her head and walked to Lucia's side. "That doesn't mean I can't try, though, does it?"

"No," said Henrik. He sighed, and looked upon the nun with intense admiration. "Very well, then. Your commitment and bravery put my own to shame. At least let me leave my gun with you. Will you allow that?"

She smiled sadly at him. "I would like that very much."

"Good. I shall bring it in the morning. Shortly before we set off, I will knock three times to announce my arrival. Is there anything else you require?"

"I collected a bag of provisions earlier, but had to abandon it in the hallway outside the Mother Superior's quarters."

"Then I shall bring that too."

Ursula started to cry. "You're a kind man, Henrik. I know you don't believe in God, but I do, and I'm certain you'll be rewarded in heaven."

He smiled at her, pleased to note that her tears were untainted by the infection. "I shall send a rescue party the moment we arrive, although I'm sorry to say the men of Cerbesca lack strength of character, and may require some persuasion. In the meantime," he said, reaching into his pocket and removing his hip-flask, "there's a lot to be said for the healing power of good brandy." From the way the liquid sloshed inside, he guessed it was more than half-full. "Keep this. You may need it."

She took the flask, then threw her arms around him in a charmingly awkward embrace.

"Come now," he said. "We shan't be apart for long. In a matter of days, Gertrude and I shall host a delicious banquet for you and Lucia to enjoy."

"Will Dr Franco be there too?"

"Of course! He'll be seated at the head of the table, complaining the portions are too small."

"That sounds wonderful." She wept against him. "God-speed, my friend," she whispered, and as she did, he couldn't help wondering if, after tomorrow morning, he'd ever see Sister Ursula again.

30

Once Henrik let himself out, Ursula closed the door and inserted the key. The sound of the hefty bolt clunking rustily into place filled her with immense satisfaction.

She was safe now. And tomorrow morning, Henrik would bring the food and his gun, and she would thank him again and lock herself and Lucia securely away until rescue came. She did not know when that would be, but she would portion out the supplies sensibly, and if they were to run out of water, then in the worst-case scenario, they could drink melted snow, of which there would be no shortage.

The situation was far from ideal, but she would do what was required to survive. Lucia's life depended on her.

The girl stirred with a soft groan. Her eyelids fluttered open. "What happened?"

"Nothing," said Ursula. "But I have super news. In a few days, we'll be heading to Cerbesca." Her voice quivered, and she held the girl's hand. "Won't that be lovely?"

Snow battered the window. She would pray for Henrik and Gertrude tonight. Tonight, and tomorrow, and every day henceforth.

"It's getting worse, isn't it?" asked Lucia.

"The storm?"

"No. The other thing."

She nodded. "Yes, it is."

"Are we safe in here?"

Ursula climbed onto the bed and lay beside her. "We are. I have the only key now, and the door is firmly secured. Tomorrow we'll have food and water and... and a gun. We'll be very safe indeed."

"I'm glad," said Lucia. She put her arm around Ursula, who revelled in the warmth emanating from the girl's body. "I don't think I like it here."

"Me neither. But it shan't be for long, you'll see." She snuggled in closer. "Soon, we'll be far, far away from Sant'Arcangel."

She fought back tears.

"Forever."

Henrik stalked through the hallway, enshrouded in guilt.

Back in Ursula's cell, he had told a lie. For if he and Gertrude were to make it to Cerbesca alive, he would not, as promised, immediately return with aid. That would have to wait. His first order of business would be to work with Franco to seek an urgent cure for the disease.

A cure for Gertrude.

He was sorry for his falsehood, and he would, in time, return to the convent with coaches and a party of armed men to rescue Ursula and Lucia... but only once he had done everything in his power to help his love. After all, it was his fault she was infected. If he hadn't insisted on investigating that infernal bell, she would never have been attacked by Isabelle.

The shame gnawed at him, and he pondered other, more prosaic matters to wrest his mind away; visions of helping Gertrude with the blankets, of checking on and feeding the horse, and of getting as much rest as possible. Then, in the morning, he would bring the gun to Ursula's room, confident she would be safe overnight, and every night thereafter, behind her locked door.

He was keen to return to Gertrude, but Ursula had mentioned a bag of supplies, and he decided to pick it up while the hallways echoed in uneasy silence. It was only a matter of time before the nuns began to roam freely. And when they did...

He grimaced at the prospect, then snapped a candle from a wall sconce and lit the wick. Shielding the small flame with one hand, he descended the stairs, listening for movement and hearing nothing but the howl of the wind. The steps slurped beneath his feet, and when he reached the bottom, he lowered the candle and saw red, bloody footprints heading in the direction he was travelling in.

"This is most unpromising," he muttered. Keeping the candle low, he took furtive steps along the hallway, occasionally pausing to glance into the Stygian obscurity ahead of him. How many sets of prints were there? It was hard to say, for they intersected one another as if the nuns had stumbled to their destination in a befuddled, decaying revelry. His thoughts turned to the animal kingdom, and of how some creatures, aware of their impending death, leave their pack and go somewhere quiet to die. Even his old cat, Mittens, had hidden herself in the attic shortly before passing away, as if seeking peace towards the end of her short life. Perhaps the nuns, reduced as they were to a primal state, were following their own animalistic instincts?

The footprints, a mixture of dark blood and black, crumbled rot, led to a doorway, outside which Henrik paused. Lifting the candle aloft, he gazed inside. The light caught the brass handle of a pew.

The new chapel.

What had drawn them to this room? Did they seek salvation, or were they guided by some memory of their old lives? Judging by the silence, they had since moved on, but the question needled at him.

Why the chapel?

Leave it. Fetch Ursula's supplies. Gertrude awaits.

Yes, yes, of course. All in due time. But Henrik, like all good doctors, possessed an uncommonly curious mind. He wanted to understand the disease, and in particular its effects on the human brain. What remained of the victim once it had taken root? Could they be returned to their natural state? And was the process reversible? He had spent his life regarding every patient as a new mystery to solve, and now the stakes had never been higher. His own beloved was at risk, and the more he knew about the rot, the greater his chance of finding a cure.

And it was with this in mind that Henrik, against his better judgement, entered the chapel in search of answers. His first act was to use his candle to light the sconces. It felt reassuring to be out of the darkness, even for a minute, and once the room was suitably illuminated, he took a wary look at his surroundings.

The new chapel lacked the majesty of the storm-ravaged original. The hall, notable mainly for its vast floor-to-ceiling tapestry of the Last Supper, had been transformed into a place of worship by the addition of a lectern, a golden bas-relief cross that hung on the wall, and a confessional booth and pews salvaged from the desecrated ruins.

He walked carefully down the centre aisle. A Bible lay open on the floor, the pages dotted with blood, and in its place on the lectern was a heavy, leather-bound tome.

The Register of the Deceased.

The book was open at October 1858, though the scrawled lettering and stained, aged pages made the writing impossible to decipher. He closed the volume, his gaze falling instead upon the confessional. From inside came a damp, repetitive squelch.

Gooseflesh broke out on his nape.

Someone was in here with him. Someone he did not wish to meet. Backing away, he nudged a pew. The wood scraped loudly across the floor, and other than a persistent dripping, the moist sounds stopped. Henrik stood still, his gaze fixed on the confessional booth as two rotten feet lowered beneath the velvet curtain and settled on the floor.

He should not have come here.

A severed hand thudded between the feet. The index and middle fingers pointed forwards, the digits stained with green, soupy discharge, while the rest were broken and jutted out at unnatural angles.

Henrik retreated slowly. Perhaps if he kept quiet, he might—

The curtain drew open, revealing Sister Isabelle in all her foul, tainted glory. Murky green seepage dribbled down her naked thighs, and from the way the slime matched the fingers on the severed hand, he understood what blasphemy she had been performing in the confessional.

"Please excuse me," he said, and took a clumsy step in retreat. "I did not mean to disturb you, Sister Isabelle."

She rose from her seat, a foul parody of the bright young

woman she had been only a fortnight ago, and lifted a meat cleaver.

"Join us," she said, as she staggered from the confessional, holding her fingers up to him, offering a handful of her secretion. The colourful juices smelt rank.

Obscene.

For the second time that evening, Henrik reached for his gun and found nothing.

"Taste me," said Isabelle.

He bumped into the lectern. It toppled, the Register of the Deceased slamming heavily to the floor and sending up a plume of ancient dust.

"God, woman. What has *become* of you?"

"Be one with us."

"I'd sooner perish in the fires of hell."

"Yes, that too." She stumbled closer. *"All in good time."*

He couldn't let her touch him. Dammit, he had been armed all week, and now, when he needed the pistol most, he was entirely defenceless.

"Stay back, foul thing," he said, aware of the tremor in his voice.

Isabelle paid no heed. She held the cleaver in her rot-eaten hand and lurched towards him. Henrik raised his arm in defence, the cleaver arcing through the air and slicing his sleeve open. He hopped over a pew, and the blade thudded into the wooden backrest. Isabelle wrenched it free and followed, blocking his escape route. In the corner of his eye, he spotted the gold cross on the wall. The damn thing must have been three feet tall, but it was the only possible weapon he could see.

He sprinted for it. Isabelle swung, and he ducked.

He was too slow.

A sharp pain stabbed through his shoulder as Isabelle

buried the meat cleaver in his flesh. He spun away, dodging out of her grasp, hot blood spurting from the wound.

Keep away from her!

His shoulder throbbed mercilessly, and Isabelle's claws raked against his jacket. He kicked out, striking her hard, and when she staggered backwards, he grabbed the gold cross and tried to wrench the holy symbol from the wall.

It would not budge.

"Damnation!" he roared.

She came shrieking towards him. He reached over his shoulder, seeking the meat cleaver, his fingertips grazing the wooden handle. Isabelle was almost upon him when he yanked the weapon free and slammed the blade into the spongy tissue of her face. She stumbled, the momentum carrying her forwards until her head smacked into an iron wall sconce with a stomach-churning clang. Her lank hair whipped over and into the burning candle, the dry strands catching fire. She started to scream.

The flames spread over her rotten flesh, engulfing her in a monstrous pyrotechny. She whirled on the spot, searching for Henrik through the blaze of her own burning decay. With the meat cleaver embedded in her face, Isabelle fell against the Last Supper tapestry, igniting it in a violent frenzy. As the wall blazed, Jesus and his disciples withered and burned until the sizzling cords that held the tapestry aloft snapped. The intricately woven fabric detached from the wall, draping itself over Isabelle. She thrashed beneath her fiery prison, clawing and scratching and shrieking profanities until, at long last... she fell utterly still.

Henrik sat on a pew and placed his head in his hands. Even sitting by the smouldering embers of the tapestry, he felt impossibly cold. His shoulder ached. How deep had the blade cut? He would need to attend to it urgently. Oh, what a perfect fool he was for coming here in the first place!

Then he saw it.

"Good god," he whispered, and forced himself to stand. In disbelief, Henrik stared straight ahead through the dying flames and acrid smoke. For as the tapestry wilted to a mass of crispy threads, it revealed not only the burnt remains of Sister Isabelle... but a slender passageway cut into the wall.

Nudging Isabelle's corpse aside, he took a candle and peered through the gap. A flight of carved stone stairs led into the bowels of Sant'Arcangel.

Was this where the nuns had scattered? Underground, like rats?

He stepped fully into the passageway, and thought of his lover, and of their imminent escape, and of how worried Gertrude must be due to his absence. Had he learned *nothing* from his needless near-death encounter only moments before?

No, he hadn't.

For how could any man of inquisitive mind not have their interest piqued by the unexpected sound coming from the very depths of the mountain itself?

The nuns... they were *singing*.

Was it possible they had regained their faculties? Trepidatiously, Henrik started down the stairs. The passage reeked of death, and water dripped from the damp stone. One drop hit his candle and snuffed it out with a quiet hiss. The darkness engulfed him like a funeral shroud.

It was a sign.

He glanced back up the stairs, then followed his instinct and took another step. His foot plunged into water. The stinking liquid rose to his ankles, and he swept blindly through a flooded cavern, following a flickering light far in the distance.

The nuns continued their song. As a keen scholar of Latin, Henrik had always enjoyed the choral music of convents and monasteries, despite his lack of spiritual attachment to the subject. But down here, in this dank crypt, the music no longer sounded lovely to his ears.

It sounded evil.

Degenerate.

Focusing his gaze on the faraway torch, he plodded onwards, keeping his feet below the surface to minimise noise. The light grew brighter, the singing louder. Beneath it, he detected screams and moans and frenzied, orgiastic panting. What anarchic horrors were they partaking of below their cloister? What sacrilegious—

The ground shifted beneath him. He pitched forward, splashing into the water. "What the devil?" he spluttered, as he pushed himself up, his clothes drenched and dripping. He groped in the darkness for whatever had tripped him.

A pile of skulls.

Angrily, he kicked them loose, and then a dreadful realisation dawned on him.

The singing — that awful, ghastly caterwauling — had silenced. In its stead were hushed, angry whispers and barked orders that reverberated off the walls.

Turn around.

Good idea. He abandoned his mission, wading cumbersomely through the watery tunnel towards the stairs. A glance over his shoulder told him the nuns were following, their candles glowing orange down the endless stone passageway.

"*Kill them!*" someone cried. "*Kill them all and bring me the girl!*"

Claudia. Her booming voice rumbled off the walls like a feral roar, and Henrik knew beyond all doubt that everything was coming to an end.

It no longer mattered that it was night, nor that the storm raged on. He and Gertrude would leave this instant. They had the horse, and the blankets, and the gun, and anything that got in their way would be harshly dealt with.

This time, he promised himself, he would not hesitate to kill.

31

HENRIK EMERGED FROM THE PASSAGEWAY INTO THE SOFT
candlelight of the chapel. His wet clothes clung to him like a
second skin. Had he signed his own death warrant by
venturing into the catacombs? Undertaking the journey in
his current state was beyond dangerous.

It was suicidal.

And yet, had he *not* investigated, he would never have
known the crazed nuns were coming for them, and he and
Gertrude would have been slaughtered in their beds as they
slept. Hope may have been fading, but at least a glimmer, no
matter how microscopic, remained.

He left the chapel and ran towards the entrance hall, his
sodden boots leaving damp footprints in his wake. As he
passed the stairs, he skidded to a stop.

Ursula.

The poor woman would be utterly oblivious to the fast-
approaching horror. Would her door hold? He knew not the
strength of the diseased sisters, but he also did not believe it
mattered, for with no food, Ursula and Lucia would not last

the week, let alone the winter. He had to warn her somehow.

"Lock your door!" he bellowed up the stairs. *"And open it for no-one!"*

Would she hear? He could only hope. Had he been a religious man, he would have prayed, but god had long since left his heart, much as the supposed creator had abandoned his flock at Sant'Arcangel, allowing his devoted followers to become the devil's twisted playthings in their waterlogged subterranean hell.

With that small gesture to his ally, he raced for the entrance hall and exited the building. The snow and hail pounded his face, his soaked clothes seeming to freeze around him, chilling him deep in his wretched bones and distracting him from the ache in his shoulder. At least he could still curl his fingers, which meant the damage was only superficial.

Through the cottage window, he saw the roaring golden fire. He would have wept, had his frozen body been capable of producing moisture.

"Gertrude!" he called in advance. *"Open the door!"*

He crunched through the snow and reached the door. It was stuck. He tried to barge in, and his injured shoulder jarred against the wood. "Dammit, woman, let me in this instant!"

From inside came a faint voice. *"Go away."*

"Tis I, Henrik! We must leave, now!" He glanced at the convent entrance. No sign of the nuns yet. "They're coming for us!"

"Go away!" she screamed.

There was no time for this nonsense. He aimed a series of kicks at the door. It shuddered on its hinges, and on the fifth attempt, the handmade lock shattered.

"For god's sake," he roared as he entered, heading straight for his bag, in which he kept his spare shirt and trousers. Shivering, he stripped his outer clothes off and stepped out of his long johns. Naked, he carried his bag to the fire and hurriedly unpacked, glancing nervously at the doorway. "Are you ready?" he asked. "Are the blankets on the horse?" She sniffled quietly, and he angrily turned to her. "Gertrude, are you listening to—"

His clean shirt dropped to the floor.

"Gertrude, no." He stared at her in shock and confusion. "What are you doing?"

She sat on the bed, holding the gun in both hands.

The barrel pressed against her chin.

"Why didn't you say?" she asked.

His diary lay beside her, open at the latest page, the handwriting dotted with teardrops.

The gun trembled in her hands.

"Why didn't you tell me I'm infected?"

"Did you hear that?" asked Lucia. She was awake and lying on her side as Ursula, afraid to dip into their scant supply of water, mopped the blood from her wounds with a dry cloth. "It sounded like Dr Henrik."

"Indeed," she replied. As the only man in the convent, Henrik's voice was unmistakable, even if his shouted cry had been hard to decipher. He had sounded unusually agitated. Fearful, even. "Did he say to lock our door?"

As if in answer, his voice echoed through the corridors once more. *And open it for no-one!*

The two women exchanged glances. Lucia gripped Ursula's arm. "Is it locked? Is our door—"

"Of course it is." Ursula laid the bloody cloth down and strode to the door. The key, when she tried to turn it, would not budge. "See? Sealed tight." Her blood ran cold. "We're perfectly safe in here."

"Are you certain?" Lucia's complexion was bone-white. "Why would he say that?"

"Perhaps he wasn't talking to us?"

They both knew that was not the case.

"What do we do?" asked Lucia.

Ursula's head pounded. She walked unsteadily to the closet and removed Henrik's flask of brandy. "Lucia, I need you to be brave." She unscrewed the cap and drank. The liquid burned her throat. "I think we're in a lot of trouble."

"They're coming for us, aren't they?"

"I don't know." She took another swig and offered the flask to Lucia. The girl shook her head. "I believe so."

A troubled silence passed between them. Lucia looked imploringly at her. "Go," she said. "You can still get out. There's time."

"I swore I'd never leave you. That I'd let no harm come to you."

"Please," said Lucia. Her face creased. "Don't die on my behalf. I don't even know who I am."

"You will remember. I'll make sure of it." She laid the flask on the bed and took Lucia's soft hand. "Even if it takes ten years of trying, I promise I'll help you remember."

Lucia lay back. She was crying. "Don't make promises you can't keep," she whispered.

What to do? Ursula glanced around her cell for inspiration. If her sisters came for them, would the door hold?

Go to a different room.

For what purpose? They would find them wherever they went. And how long would it take her to move not only the buckets of water and the bedsheets to a new room, but the fragile creature that lay weeping on the bed? Lucia could barely stand, never mind walk. No, they would stay here and pray that God fortified the door. If it held, then that left only one way into her cell.

The window.

No longer trying to mask her fear, she ran to it, forcing the stiff frame open and leaning out. Through the intense gale and furious snowstorm, she peered down the cliff face, hundreds of feet of cragged rock leading into a chasm far below. Her stomach lurched, and she turned her head to view the ledge that snaked around the perimeter of the convent. There were no handholds, and the cracked, slippery ledge was littered with birds' nests.

She closed the window, secure in the knowledge that, as long as the door held firm, they would be safe from intruders. Her eye twitched.

And the door *would* hold... wouldn't it?

Henrik raised his hands.

"Gertrude, *please.*" He took a halting step closer. "Put the gun down."

She looked at him with bloodshot, tired eyes. "I don't want to be one of them, Henrik. I don't want to turn into one of those... *creatures.*"

"You won't," he said. "Not if we leave now."

Her finger coiled around the trigger. "No, it's too late."

"Please, Dr Franco and I can cure you!" He shifted, and she turned the gun on him.

"Stay back!" she cried. "Just keep away from me! I can't infect you too!"

A thunderclap boomed across the sky.

"There's still time," he pleaded. "It takes several days for the disease to take hold. I've witnessed as much with my own eyes."

She shook her head sadly. "No. You're wrong about that, my love." Her pretty countenance altered to one of pain and anger. "I can already feel it inside me."

"I tell you, there's still—"

"There's no time left!" she screamed. "Leave me to do what I must... whilst I still have the fortitude."

She leaned back, turning the gun on herself once more. Her hands shook as the barrel stabbed into her flesh, the tightening skin exposing burrowing black veins that wrapped around her throat in a septic chokehold.

"I can find a cure," he said hopelessly.

"In a matter of days? You know that's not possible." She glanced at his diary. "You said so yourself."

He was such a fool. A damnable fool. Ursula had come to him in such a panic that he had rushed off without tucking his accursed journal back into the desk. He hadn't been thinking straight, and now his beloved was... was...

"I won't let you," he said. Tears streamed down his face. "I won't let you kill—"

"It's in my head, Henrik. It's changing me." The gun wobbled, and she pressed it harder against her throat. Her voice dropped to a whisper. "It's making me think *terrible things.*"

"A psychological malady. It's this place, this—"

"It's making me hate you," she said. "Looking at you now, naked and frightened..." She bit her lip. "I want to *kill* you. Do you hear me, Henrik? Do you understand? I dream of cutting you open and bathing in your blood. I want to peel back your scalp and run my tongue across your skull." She panted as she spoke. "And more than that... more than anything... I want to bite off your cock and keep your ruined manhood inside my cunt forever." In the grip of hysteria, she laughed and wept simultaneously. "I won't do it, not yet. I'm still strong enough to resist. But it's wearing me down, Henrik. Even now I feel it rotting my brain. And the worst part?" She briefly composed herself, smiling through the tears. "The worst part is... it feels *so good*. Can you possibly understand that? I feel wonderful in a way that you could *never* make me feel."

"You don't mean that," he said. "I know you don't."

"I wish that were true, my love," she said, and closed her eyes.

Henrik took his chance. He reached for her, stretching his arm, fingers grasping for—

She pulled the trigger.

The blast was deafening in the small cottage. Gertrude's cranium cracked open in a smoky crimson spray. Somehow, she remained upright for several seconds, her eyes rolling into their sockets, blood fountaining from her shattered skull and flooding down her torso from her ruptured throat. A reedy croak escaped her, and then she slumped backwards onto the bed like a child's rag doll. Her body jerked, stiffened... and then breathed its last.

Henrik stared at her unmoving limbs.

"No," he sobbed, and dropped to his knees. *"There was still a chance!"*

The cottage door swung in the wind, thumping monotonously against the wall. Snow billowed inside, the flakes melting on his rigid, naked body.

"I could have saved you," he mumbled. "I could have—"

A long, twisted shadow fell across the bed.

Henrik glanced over his shoulder at the gnarled figure.

"I could have *saved* her," he said, and shook his head. The nun leered at him. A scythe twitched in her hands as she smeared her befouled tongue across sullied lips. Her torn tunic flapped open, while a second nun lurked behind her, kneading the woman's bare breasts, hooking her claw-like fingernails into the corpulent flesh.

"Look," the scythe-wielding nun said. The blade was sheathed in dried gore. "The godless doctor is on his knees praying."

"It's too late for prayers," rasped the dead-eyed woman behind her. She ogled Henrik lustily. "Succumb to us."

"Succumb to *all* of us."

Henrik pictured Gertrude's cold expression of acceptance as she shot herself. In the face of overwhelming odds, she had given up and sealed her own morbid fate.

And she was right to do so.

For as the scythe thrust into Henrik's lower back and lodged beside his spine, cutting through his internal organs, he realised, all too late, that they would never have made it down the mountain. All this time he had been fooling himself. Sant'Arcangel was doomed.

They all were.

The scythe-wielding woman — it was profane to call these devils 'nuns' — stood atop him, his bones grinding and cracking as she twisted the blade free. Several hands rolled him onto his back. There were more of them now, and he gazed up into their hungry faces.

"Make it quick," he croaked. "I beg of you... make it quick."

They laughed at him, and knelt by his side. At first, the assault was perversely pleasurable. Decomposing hands caressed his body, his chest, his legs. One woman kissed his face, while another took his cock in her mouth, her abrasive lips scratching his flaccid shaft. A repellent tongue probed his ear, and Henrik closed his eyes and tried to imagine Gertrude.

The fantasy could not last.

The woman sank her teeth into his earlobe. He heard it crunch. Another of the degenerates lifted his legs and spread them apart. Her stubby, flaking digits penetrated his anus, scraping in and out before they snapped off inside him. Others held his arms, gnawing chunks of flesh and muscle from his bones and chewing noisily on the gristly meat. They tugged on his cock, yanking it in circles, fighting over his limp member while yet another bit hard into his lower lip, tearing it free. Blood flooded his mouth, and as his penis tore off, he let himself drift towards the dreamless netherworld of death.

It couldn't come soon enough.

He lay dying, watching a woman bite his severed penis in half, holding the soggy remains above her bare chest and letting the blood trickle in rivulets between her mouldy breasts. She squeezed the cock, wringing it out like a damp cloth, and his thoughts turned to Ursula and Lucia. What nightmarish providence awaited those two sweet innocents? He should have killed them both. Smothered them in their sleep, then put Gertrude out of her misery, saving a bullet for himself.

Anything was better than this exhibition of atrocity.

The women stripped fully, moaning in ecstasy and plea-suring themselves and each other while rivers of blood, *his* blood, flooded across the floor. Using the scythe, they cleaved his stomach open, tugging handfuls of intestines free and wrapping themselves in his stinking guts.

Henrik accepted his fate, his life-force waning like the November moon. The only consolation was the fact that he and Gertrude were free from the infection. They would not have to live out the rest of their days as cannibalistic nymphomaniacs. No, they would die with their souls unblemished. It wasn't much... but it was something.

I'll be with you soon, my love, he thought, and smiled for the last time.

With Gertrude gone, and all hope lost... what was left to live for?

32

———

AT FIRST, THE KNOCK AT THE DOOR WAS PECULIARLY GENTLE.

Polite, even.

Knuckles rapped lightly on the wood, and Ursula sat up in her chair. She glanced at Lucia, who was awake in bed, and put her finger to her lips. They waited. Never before had silence felt so intolerable.

Another knock followed, more insistent this time. Together, the two women watched as the handle turned, rotating all the way until it met resistance.

The bolt was firmly in place.

"Urrsulaaa," trilled a voice on the other side of the door. *"Sister Urrrrsulaaaaa. It's Sister Claudia. Let me in."* A pause. *"Do not fret, my lamb. I come to you alone."*

A harrowing chorus of giggles erupted behind the door, and she heard Claudia shush them.

"The Reverend Mother is very upset with you," the mad nun continued. *"You stole her key. She demands you be punished."*

What do we do, mouthed Lucia.

Ursula had no answer.

"I know you're in there, Sister Ursula. And your little friend

too. Save us all some time and give her to us. Do me this kindness, and I promise your death shall be so exquisite that centuries from now, poets will compose elegies in your honour."

"Leave us alone," Ursula said. She staggered to Lucia on legs that trembled with unease. "She's no one's to take."

"They're going to kill us," said Lucia.

"No. We're safe in here. They'll give up and go away soon enough." She pretended to smile, and wished she could believe her own lies.

At once, dozens of fists hammered on the door.

"Let us be!" shouted Ursula. "She's just a child!"

"A child? She is God's test!" The pounding rose to a crescendo. Then, all at once, it abruptly ceased.

Ursula took Lucia's hand. "You see? They—"

Thud!

A heavy object slammed against the door.

Ursula turned. "Lord have mercy," she breathed.

"What's that sound?" asked Lucia. "Is that—"

An axe head smashed through the door, and both women screamed. Splintered wood rained down on the stone. The gap was slender, but through it, sneering faces jostled to peer through. One cold, calculating eye muscled its way to the front.

"I see you," said Claudia. *"Unlock the door and help us purge this holy place of her evil."*

"Go away!"

Claudia glared at her. *"Very well. Have it your way."*

A moment's respite, and then the axe resumed battering the door. Ursula looked around for a weapon in desperation.

Crash!

The blade broke through once more, creating a hole almost wide enough for an arm.

"Keep going!" roared Claudia. *"I grant you God's holy power!"*

"We have to do something!" cried Lucia.

"I know!" Ursula paced. "I'm trying to think!"

The window drew her gaze, and she banished the thought. Lucia was too weak. She would never make it. Neither of them would, not with the storm. No, their only chance — *smash!* — was to defend themselves.

A nun prised the blade free. The scarred, nightmarish face gazed at Ursula through the breach. Despite the spoilt skin, she recognised Sister Giulia. No one else in the convent could wield an axe like her, which was why her main task in the run-up to winter had been chopping the firewood. She wrested the blade loose and swung again. The door shuddered from the onslaught. Lock or no lock, it wouldn't hold forever.

Lucia clasped her hands together and bowed her head. She started to pray, her words harsh and sibilant to Ursula's ears.

What to do, what to do, what to do?

She thought of Henrik.

You can't save everyone.

But she had to save *someone*. She had to at least *try*.

Henrik's hip flask lay at the foot of the bed. She picked it up and shook it, listening to the liquid inside.

"Maybe," she muttered, rousing Lucia from her strange prayer and handing her the flask. "Hold this," she said, then gripped the backrest of her chair in both hands. The wooden seat, which was older than Ursula, and older, mayhap, than the Mother Superior herself, bore two wide grooves from the pressure of centuries of buttocks. It had served her well over the years, and she was almost sorry to see it go.

Almost.

She raised the chair high and brought it down against the stone floor. The sturdy wood cracked, but did not break.

Whack!

The axe head burst through the door with stunning ferocity.

"Your death will be legendary!" shrieked Claudia. She was working herself, and her flock, into a frenzy. *"The devil himself shall avert his eyes from your destruction!"*

"Not today he won't," said Ursula, and she brought the chair crashing down with all her might. It broke apart, and she stooped and grabbed one of the legs.

"Ursula," whimpered Lucia. "Something's coming back to me."

"Not now," she snapped, ripping the sheets from the bed and wrapping them around the chair leg.

Thud!

A chunk of door smacked onto the floor.

Ursula opened the flask of brandy and tipped the contents over the fabric, drenching it.

Lucia was trying to sit up. "But I think—"

"Please," she interrupted. "I'm trying to protect us."

Crack!

The door wouldn't hold much longer.

Ursula tossed the empty flask aside and hurried around the bed to the candle. Holding the chair leg over the flame, the sodden fabric lit with a quiet fury. Would it be enough?

A metal hinge clunked to the ground. The door leaned awkwardly, the nuns throwing themselves at the weakening barrier with reckless abandon. Like rats deserting a sinking ship, they scrambled through the gap, the weight of their bodies causing the door to groan wider.

With the flaming torch held aloft, Ursula stormed

towards them. One nun — Sister Elisabeth, she thought — was almost through.

"Stay back!" she shouted, brandishing her fiery weapon. Elisabeth hissed and recoiled, tumbling backwards into the hallway, only to be replaced by another of her sisters, a nun whose face was so twisted and aberrant that Ursula could not recognise her. The abomination reached for the torch, attempting to snatch it, and Ursula obliged. She rammed the chair leg at the nun's arm, holding it to her tunic. Smoke rose, the fabric sparking and then burning. With a blood-curdling wail, the woman went up in flames. She slid back down the door, shrieking.

"I'm sorry!" cried Ursula. "I don't want to hurt anyone. *Just go away!*"

But the blazing nun would not give up. While the others kept their distance, she clambered up the sagging door, hooking her fingers over the top. The smell of burning wood and bubbling flesh co-mingled in an acrid stink.

"Stay back!" She used the torch to batter the woman's hands. "Leave us be!"

But she was too late.

The door itself was ablaze.

Behind the rippling flames, the other nuns stood by the wall, waiting. It was a matter of time now. A matter of patience.

For Ursula, both were in short supply.

She turned to Lucia. The girl was praying again.

"I don't know what to do," she wept.

The door burned brightly, hanging off its final hinge. In a few moments, it would fall and grant the nuns entry.

"You did all you could," Lucia whispered, her hands clasped so tightly that her knuckles turned white. She opened her eyes and stared at her. "Go now. Save yourself."

"Go where? There's nowhere for us to go!"

The door hit the ground with a tumultuous crash, the hideous nuns hesitating in the doorway, waiting for the flames to die down. Some stripped their robes off and threw them atop the pyre to quell the blaze.

"She's innocent!" cried Ursula. "I won't let you murder her!"

"The dying has begun," said Claudia from behind the wall of fire. "The great winter of suffering has arrived. What price one peasant girl's soul against God's daughters? What price her soul against your own?"

"I care not for my soul!" She gripped her torch. Already, the flaming rags were withering to nothing.

A nun leapt over the door and landed in the room.

"Sister Virginia, no," said Ursula. She hadn't seen the woman since the day she had choked on a nipple, and by God, how she had changed. Her clothes were ragged and hung off her body, exposing the boils and warts that populated her face and neck, some throbbing, others already having burst, the weeping skin unleashing waves of infected debris.

"Join us," croaked Virginia. "And together we shall end this. The Mother Superior demands it."

Ursula wielded the torch, wisps of ash swirling through the air. "The Mother Superior is dead!"

More of them were coming. They advanced, and only the dimming heat from the torch kept them at bay. Ursula backed away until she hit the wall. The flames sputtered on the end of the chair leg.

It would not last much longer.

"Keep away from me!" She sidled to the window. "Stay back, you foul things!" The torch extinguished itself, the glowing embers of the burning bedsheets fading like dying stars. Ursula hurled the useless stick at the nuns and turned to the window.

She shouldn't do it.

She would surely die.

But if nothing else, at least it offered her, and Lucia, one last chance at survival.

"I'll come back for you," she shouted, and as the flock of nuns crowded Lucia and dragged her from the bed, and more staggered into the room with outstretched, groping fingers, Ursula threw open the window and clambered out into the raging storm.

"I swear on all that is holy... I shall return for you!"

33

───────

Ursula gasped as the freezing air swept her breath away.

Gripping onto the window frame, she swung her body out of the room, planting her feet on the narrow ledge. It was four-inches at most. Her heels hung over the edge, and she refused to relinquish her grip on the frame. Only when obscene fingers grazed her flesh did she dare release it, and with that motion, she fully committed to her insane escape. Bitterly cold air whirled up her tunic, billowing the garment around her waist, and in raw, desperate hysteria, she flattened her palms against the wall and shuffled along the ledge.

Right, left. Right, left.

She didn't look down, for she knew all-too-well the enormous, fatal drop below her window. Instead, she dug her fingers into shallow furrows in the stone and moved an inch at a time.

Right, left. Right, left.

She heard laughter, and glanced over her shoulder.

Her beloved sisters, with whom she had grown up in the

convent, hung half out of the window, their cracked faces wraith-like in the midnight gloom.

"Come back, Sister Ursula," said one. "We're waiting for you."

"You belong with us," cackled another.

"You belong in hell!" she cried, her cheek pressed to the wall. The wind battered her, carrying her words across the valley and towards the distant mountain peaks.

Don't look down.

Her limbs trembled from the cold, her hands turning a mottled pink.

Do not *look down.*

The nuns retreated inside. Even with their rotten, diseased minds, they would not risk venturing onto the ledge. The window closed, the latch snapping shut with a muffled *thunk.*

She closed her eyes, clinging to the wall as the wind buffeted her, afraid to move, afraid even to breathe. Her ankles began to hurt, and she adjusted the angle of her feet, bringing her heels to rest on the ledge. To turn her head, she had to push back from the outer wall, then flatten herself once more so she could see where she was going.

And where are *you going?*

The only place she *could* go. The ledge ran the entire length of the building, so she would follow it to the corner, and then, somehow, make her way around.

It's not far, she lied to herself, blinking snow from her eyelashes. *You can do it.*

The wind had died down. But for how long? She couldn't wait indefinitely. She had neither the physical strength nor the mettle.

It was now or never.

Right, left. Right, left.

She slid her feet along, the flat soles of her sandals struggling to gain purchase on the icy ledge. Still, she had to hurry. She was getting colder, her fingers tightening, joints stiffening. The plummeting temperature would take a brutal toll on her body.

She looked for a handhold. One stone jutted out further than the others, and she reached it.

She felt sick.

Holding onto the rock, Ursula half-slid, half-dragged herself along the ledge. She chanced a look back at where she'd come from. The window was still so close. How long had she been going? She wanted to cry, but the temperature would not permit it.

Keep onwards.

Her progress was slow but steady, and it emboldened her. She sped up, fearful of Lucia's safety. Where would they have taken the girl? One of the chapels? Or was she already dead? Ursula's hands moved from rock to rock, her feet—

"No!" she screamed, as a violent gust of chill wind struck her. It smacked her face against the stone, and she slipped, one foot sweeping out across the vast emptiness. The wind lifted her tunic and stroked her legs, and she dug her nails into the rock until the force lessened, before swinging her leg back onto the ledge.

Out of pure instinct, she looked down.

The seething snowfall had calmed enough for her to see all the way to the moonlit treetops that punctured the swirling mountain mists hundreds of feet below. Her gaze travelled along the cliff-face with its angry, savage rocks that would massacre any poor soul who tumbled headlong into the deadly abyss. Death would come long before she hit the ground, she knew, but in those agonising moments—

She tore her gaze away and closed her eyes.

That had been a terrible mistake.

She considered trying to kick the glass on a window to break through, but to do so would mean standing on one foot and holding her leg out, at which point the wind might easily catch her flowing robes.

No, she would carry on. Her nerves were too shattered, and the corner was not far now.

She shuffled her feet. The drop shortened as the mountain rose to meet the convent, each tentative step carrying her closer to safety. She reached the corner and wrapped her arm around, searching for a handhold and finding an irregular rock. She gripped it tightly and slid on tiptoes around the wind-blasted edge. Her foot nudged something, and a creature slammed against her leg. She almost lost her grip, teetering backwards and whirling her arms as an alpine chough flew from its perch on the ledge, flapping its wings with an angry chirrup.

Ursula hooked her fingers into the wall, and she jerked her hips forward, her torso following and smacking the stone. Her heart pounded, and she waited until she had calmed before resuming her painstaking journey. The east wing of the building was more protected from the wind, and presently, she found herself barely twenty feet off the ground. The snow drifts made it appear even less, and she was grateful for them, as they allowed her to get down the easy way.

By jumping.

She took a breath and leapt from the ledge. The snow broke her fall, and she fought free of the white powder before it caved in on top of her.

"I made it," she panted, and gazed up at the convent. The ground felt solid beneath her feet, and she had never been more grateful to stand upon it. She pressed her hands into the snow, gripping blades of grass and ripping them from the earth to convince her tortured mind that she was, indeed, safe.

Shivering from the cold, she looked over to the cottage. The fire was burning inside, casting its soothing glow across the walls, and Ursula burst into exhausted tears as she trudged towards the old building.

In a few moments, she would be reunited with Gertrude and Henrik.

She almost smiled.

With dear friends by her side, there was no horror she could not face.

34

———

IT WAS THE FOOTPRINTS THAT FIRST ALERTED URSULA TO potential danger.

Through the deep snow, a path had been ploughed from the convent entrance to the cottage by the trampling of many feet. Small footprints, bearing the same flat sole as her own sandals, riddled the ground.

The nuns.

They had been here, and paid Henrik and Gertrude a visit. Worst of all, the prints all headed in a single direction. If the nuns had gone into the cottage... then they had never come out.

Ursula hesitated.

Either Henrik had killed them, or...

The alternative did not bear thinking about.

Keeping low, she crept to the building on aching legs and peered through the window. Frost coated the glass, yet she could make out figures lying on the floor. She looked away, horrified to imagine she was spying on her friends making love. But whilst she knew very little about s-e-x, something did not seem right. There was too much movement, too many limbs. She returned her gaze to the window and carefully wiped her sleeve across the frosty glass.

Her heart sank.

The nuns were there, crowded together on the floor in a berserk frenzy of flesh, doing things to each other that Ursula did not know could be done. In horrified fascination, she watched as their bodies intertwined, their faces and hands stained red with blood. The rot besmirched them, and through occasional gaps in their tangled limbs she caught sight of Henrik.

Or what was left of him.

Bile rose in her throat, and she forced herself to swallow it. "No," she whispered, and looked to the skies as if expecting God to be smiling benevolently down on her. He was conspicuous by his absence, although a golden star shot through the night sky before blinking out of existence.

A sign? Or another shallow mockery of her faith?

She turned back to the window. A body lay on the bed.

Sister Gertrude.

The dead woman's eyes stared accusingly, the sheets around her soaked in blood.

Ursula pressed her nose to the glass.

Henrik's pistol was in Gertrude's hand. Why? Had she shot herself? Was there no hope left for any of them? Ursula didn't believe that. Lucia lived, she was certain of it, and rescue was still an option... but only if she could get her hands on that gun. Then, no one could stop her.

And what if you have to use it?

Then she would.

You're a nun.

Not anymore. Now she was simply a woman who believed in the inherently good nature of humankind. These women — her sisters, her friends — had been corrupted by a disease that had systematically dismantled everything she held dear. And yet, the unknown malady had also shown her the way. God had placed her upon this earth to heal... and to protect.

The bell tolled.

The nuns raised their heads, and she ducked out of sight. Who was ringing the bell *now?* Was it some sort of signal? Ursula threw herself behind a snowdrift and watched as four naked, blood-drenched women wandered in single file through the snow as if drawn by a clarion call.

They killed them. They killed Henrik and Gertrude.

Well, maybe not Gertrude. She had killed herself. Would she go to hell for that? Ursula didn't know, and this was not the time to think about it. She plodded around the building, thinking about how, with Henrik and Gertrude's passing, everyone in Sant'Arcangel was now dead or insane.

Except Lucia.

True. And it was up to her to mount a rescue. But how? With one gun? She didn't even know how to use it. She inhaled deeply. Beyond the door lay unimaginable terror; her friends, dead and torn to shreds. More than anything, she wished not to enter. But if she was to stand a chance of saving Lucia, she needed that gun.

She let her breath out, placed her hand on the door, and pushed it open.

A nun stared up at her.

Isabelle's lover, Sister Maria.

"Ursula," she slurred, and broke into a wide, wicked smile.

35

Sɪsᴛᴇʀ Mᴀʀɪᴀ ᴡᴀs ᴀ ᴠɪsɪᴏɴ ᴏғ ᴘᴜʀᴇ ʜᴏʀʀᴏʀ.

Kneeling in a lurid puddle of crimson gore, and with half-chewed entrails draped over her shoulders, she nibbled on a stubby chunk of meat, the blood staining her teeth. Her face was relatively unmarred by the rot, for unlike the nuns Ursula had seen through the window, where the nexus of the disease centred around the heart or the neck, the foul darkness in Maria spread from between her legs. It was dark and crusted and appalling, vile liquid weeping from bulging, quivering lesions. From this nucleus, the rot scattered into thousands of thin lines that spider-webbed across her torso.

Henrik, on the other hand, was in pieces. His limbs had been hacked off, and his severed head lay on its side with the spinal column jutting from the stump. Deep slashes scored his upper chest, while his nipples appeared to have been bitten off. And as for his genitals...

Ursula suddenly realised what Maria was nibbling on.

Despite all the grotesquerie she had thus far witnessed, the sight of Sister Maria sinking her teeth into Henrik's fleshy manhood shocked Ursula to her very soul. She dropped to her knees and emptied her stomach as, in her periphery, Maria rose, letting the half-eaten meat drop to the floor. She sniffed the air and stepped closer. "You're still pure. I can smell it."

"Let me pass," said Ursula. Nervously, she rubbed the cross that hung around her neck. "I... I don't wish to hurt you."

Maria choked a wheezing laugh. "Hurt me? You wouldn't hurt me. Not sweet, *innocent* Sister Ursula."

Behind the woman, sprawled across the bed, lay Gertrude. Ursula stared at the gun in her lifeless hand and wondered if any trace of Sister Maria remained in her damaged brain. And if so, could she somehow reason with her?

"Please," she said, softening her voice. "We've known each other for years. We're *friends.*"

Maria tilted her head. "Friends?"

"Yes! You, and me, and Isabelle. You remember Isabelle, don't you?"

"Isabelle," said Maria. Saliva trickled down her chin. *"She* did this. Then she abandoned me. Left me to rot. To die." Her jaw slackened. "But *you* could help me."

"Of course," said Ursula. She was making definite progress. Perhaps Maria was not as far gone as she appeared? "I'll help you any way I can. Just tell me what you require."

"Kiss me." Maria gestured at her septic vagina. It seemed to pulsate. "Right... *here*. Bite me. Make the pain go away."

Ursula tried not to let the revulsion show on her face. "I can't do that, Maria. You're unwell. You need a doctor."

"I've already seen a doctor." She glanced at Henrik's

disembodied head. "He couldn't help me. Nobody can, except *you*, little virgin."

Maria moved closer, raising her arms in a hopeful embrace, and Ursula made her move. She bolted like a startled mare, dodging past Maria towards the bed. The naked nun shrieked in surprise and lunged at her. Ursula skipped out of the way, but her feet slid on the blood. She hit the floor, jolting her side and coming face-to-face with Henrik's shrieking visage. Maria groped for her legs.

"Come back, little virgin! Eat my flesh... *taste me!*"

Ursula kicked free and crawled towards Gertrude, her hands and feet slipping in the bloody puddle that spread to all four corners of the room.

The bed was almost within reach.

She heard Maria slopping through Henrik's remains in pursuit. A hand snatched at her ankle, yanking her tunic and tugging her backwards. She squirmed onto her back. Her sandalled feet struck her attacker's arms, but Maria's firm grip could not be loosened. Like a withered insect, she crawled over Ursula's legs, leering spitefully. Ursula waited for the right moment, then brought her knee up sharply against Maria's chin. The nun's jaws snapped shut with such force that several of her teeth shattered from the impact.

"Stop!" screamed Ursula. "In the name of God, stop!"

Maria grinned crookedly atop her. "God?" She spat a thick glob onto Ursula's cross. "There's no God here, little virgin. Only *you*, and *me*." She lifted the hem of Ursula's robes, her rotten hands seeking entry.

Ursula gazed at her wooden cross, coated in a mixture of dark blood and broken, powdery enamel. She had received that cross on the day she passed the novitiate and became a true nun, and since then, it had never left her person, even when she slept and bathed. To see it defiled thusly horrified her. And so, as Maria's stubby fingers forced their way up her thighs, Ursula reached for the cross, *gripped* it, and snapped the cord from around her neck. She clutched the holy symbol in both hands.

"He can't save you now," sneered Maria. She leaned in, their faces inches apart. *"God is dead."*

Ursula drew her arm back. "Tell that to *him*," she snarled, and plunged the cross into Maria's eye-socket. The decaying nun roared in agony as her eyeball popped, the carved talisman protruding from her face like a lone tombstone in a barren churchyard.

Ursula scrambled out from under her, clawing her way towards the bed.

Towards the gun.

She tried to snatch it from Gertrude's cold hand, but the dead woman would not relinquish the weapon, her rigid fingers fixed around the handle in a death grip.

Maria sat screaming on the floor, grasping for the cross. With a slimy hiss, she plucked it free. The burst eyeball gushed down her cheek in a cascade of oily sludge.

Ursula returned her attention to the gun. She pinched Gertrude's index finger and snapped it at the knuckle. The bone cracked, the skin splitting. Her middle finger was next. That one snapped like a dry twig.

Maria's bare feet plodded across the blood-soaked floor. The fire danced her looming shadow against the wall, and as Ursula broke the last of Gertrude's fingers, a wet hand flopped onto her shoulder. She snatched the gun and spun, aiming at Maria's face. The woman glared through her one remaining eyeball.

You can't do this. You can't kill. You're a——

She closed her eyes and pulled the trigger.

For someone who had never even held a gun, let alone

fired one, it was a miracle shot. For the bullet flew true, as if God himself had guided the projectile directly into Maria's good eye.

The socket exploded.

Maria teetered on the spot, screaming and clawing at her face, her ragged nails raking her skin and peeling up troughs of flesh. Her feet skimmed across Henrik's blood, and she toppled sideways towards the fire. With a savage *crack,* her temple struck the stone mantelpiece, and she slumped limply to the floor. Her leg twitched, kicking out at nothing, as blood oozed from both ruptured eye-sockets.

A single ragged sigh escaped her lips... and then Sister Maria moved no more.

36

———

The gun smoked in Ursula's hand.

Sister Maria was dead... and she had killed her. Horrified, she turned away from the corpse, but in the melee, Henrik's limbs had been knocked across the room, and everywhere she looked, she saw a different part of him.

She closed her eyes and stood by the fire. Like everything else around her, the flames were dying. Had she doomed herself to hell through the act of murder? Perhaps. Killing was a sin, arguably the greatest of *all* sins. Her only hope for a peaceful afterlife lay in the fact she hadn't killed Maria for herself; she had done it for Lucia.

Lucia.

She started to cry at the thought of her guiding light. What horrors must she be enduring? Ursula opened her eyes and drew in several long, aching breaths. It was up to her now. Gertrude was dead. Henrik was dead. They were all dead. Every single one of them.

And you're next.

She stared at the gun. How many more times would it shoot? She did not know the answer, nor how to check.

Leave. Take the blankets and ride the horse down the mountain.

"No," she said, and watched the dying embers of the fire spark and crackle. The gun felt surprisingly light in her hand. "Not without my friend."

~

Ursula — she could not call herself Sister Ursula anymore, not after what she'd done — knelt before the bed and said a final prayer.

It felt odd to be praying when she was no longer a nun.

Not bad, but... different.

She removed her wimple and tossed it on the fire, though she kept her head covering on. It was, after all, freezing out there. Then she bundled up an armful of blankets, took a small wooden cross from the wall, and trekked through the snow to the stables.

The horse snorted when she entered. Two blankets already lay over the powerful beast, but she added another and placed one on a bale of hay.

"Keep these safe, please." She patted the horse's snout. "And get some rest. We have a tiring journey ahead of us."

The horse neighed in response, and her limited preparations were complete. All that remained was to venture back into the convent and rescue Lucia. She hoped she wouldn't have to kill again.

But she would, if she had to.

She would kill them all to save Lucia.

For like her, they were no longer women of the cloth. In Ursula's mind, they weren't even women anymore.

They were devils... and devils had no business in a house of God.

37

———

THE MOON COWERED BEHIND A VEIL OF STORM CLOUDS AS Ursula entered Sant'Arcangel for the very last time. Most of her life had been spent within these hallowed walls, and the thought she would never return frightened her almost as much as her impending confrontation with Sister Claudia. These women were her sisters. Sant'Arcangel was her *home*.

Only now, everything had changed.

She gently closed the door and stood in the thunderous silence of the entrance hall, clutching the pistol. So much deadly power contained within such a small, insignificant-looking contraption. She hoped the sight of the weapon would act as a deterrent, and that she would not have to use it again. The stain of Maria's blood on her hands — and on her soul — would never fully leave her.

In the corridor, candles had been lit in the wall sconces. She lifted the nearest one down and listened.

The bell no longer rang. Silence reigned supreme.

Where could everybody be? The ruined chapel? That didn't seem likely. It was too cold. Other than that, the largest area for the sisters to gather would be the refectory, as the new chapel struggled to comfortably fit the full flock. Then there was the kitchen, which could—

What are you doing?

Occupying her mind. If she thought about what awaited her, or what she might see, and what she might have to do... well, then, she would surely go mad.

"The refectory is closest," she whispered to quieten the voice in her head, and with the candle in one hand and the pistol in the other, down the corridor she walked. She feared not the shadows, for although anyone could be lying in wait, a feeling in her gut told her the nuns were huddled together somewhere.

Upon arrival, the refectory was quiet. The unlit room suffered in darkness, and Ursula's candle felt like a single dying star amongst the vastness of the cosmos. Encircled by its protective light, she passed through to the kitchen, where cold ash lay undisturbed in the fireplace and loose potatoes festered beneath fungal mould as if they had sat there for months.

Nothing, it seemed, was safe from the rot.

She left the kitchen and the refectory and stepped back into the corridor's mournful embrace. Who had lit the candles, and why? Did they lead somewhere? She decided to follow them in the opposite direction.

Audentes Fortuna iuvat, she thought.

Fortune favours the bold.

Past the library and the entrance hall she crept, her sandals slapping off the stone floor. Ahead, the final candle shimmered outside the door to the new chapel.

Strange... she heard nothing from inside.

Approaching cautiously, she tucked her candle behind

her back and peered around the doorframe. The room was well-lit and uninhabited, and smelled strongly of burning. Not like a crackling fire, though. That was a pleasant scent, whereas this pungent odour was more like scorched fabric... and overcooked meat.

Apprehensively, Ursula entered. Something was different. The Last Supper tapestry, which had hung proudly since long before her arrival, was gone. The beautiful design was now a mass of cinders draped over a charred skeleton. From the figure's posture, and the way the hooked fingers clawed at thin air, she could tell the person had been burnt alive.

More alarmingly, the fallen tapestry revealed a passageway carved into the wall. Had it always been here, hidden away from prying eyes? And was that... was that *singing* she heard?

It was.

A massed chorus of *Ave Maria,* as if someone knew she had murdered Sister Maria and was cruelly taunting her.

"What fresh hell is this?" she muttered, and entered the passage. Inside, stairs led down into a dark void. Her candle flickered as she took each step carefully. A fall now, and the consequences would be disastrous. Down she walked, down and down and down, deeper into the belly of Sant'Arcangel until the light from the chapel no longer touched her. A rank stench permeated the air, the damp stone slippery underfoot. The last step led into a flooded pool that soaked her heavy tunic. Lowering her candle, she saw the water was a murky green, and on either side were low, shallow caves in the walls, two, sometimes three berths high. Interred within each hollow were the ancient remains of the long-deceased. Skulls, decomposing bones, even full skeletons wrapped in tattered cloth, their arms crossed over decaying ribcages.

Ursula nodded in understanding.

She was standing in Sant'Arcangel's hidden catacombs.

Heart pounding, she swept through the ankle-deep water, pausing at a larger cave between the berths, in which skulls, piled from floor to ceiling, lined the walls. Three wooden crosses protruded from the filthy water in front of posed skeletons wearing ragged robes and wimples, each holding a tarnished metal cross, and framed by archways constructed from human pelvises.

She turned away and continued on. So as not to announce her presence, she laid her candle in a berth and proceeded onwards, trailing her hand along the slimy wall.

So many corpses.

To think, all this time they had been living their quiet, repentant lives, walking and eating and sleeping and praying above the bones of centuries of women who had come and gone before them. Ursula found it achingly sad. All those dedicated servants of God now rotting in a crypt, neglected and forgotten. What good had their worship done for anyone up here, far from civilisation? Or did they not care? How many of God's faithful, she wondered, sought only to save their *own* souls?

An agonised scream cut through the massed voices and reverberated off the tunnel walls.

Ursula's heart raced, for she recognised the voice instantly.

Lucia.

The girl was alive. Somehow, she was *still alive.*

With the gun in her hand, she advanced through the ossuary as the choir reached a feverish dissonance. Their song was anything but beautiful; the singers were off-key, some bellowing the words, others weeping. It was the dread shriek of the damned.

She turned the corner and there they were.

Her head swooned, and she couldn't seem to stop her limbs from shaking. For beneath a domed ceiling decorated with a faded fresco, a gathering of naked, rotting nuns formed a circle around a tall pile of wood.

A funeral pyre.

Lucia stood atop it, bound by her wrists to a wooden stake. She screamed as Sister Claudia lashed the cat o' nine tails across her bare, bleeding stomach. The damage Claudia had wrought on Lucia's young body was shocking in its sadism. Only her face had been spared, while her breasts and thighs hung in blood-soaked ribbons, ripped and shredded by the nine vicious cords.

Ursula cried as the last remnants of her hope evaporated. They would *never* make it down the mountain. How the girl was even still alive and screaming was a mystery.

Claudia whirled the cat o' nine tails overhead, and with a fierce cry, cracked the whip against Lucia's side. Chunks of flesh tore free, blood spraying from between broken ribs.

Ursula stepped forward and raised the gun in her trembling hands.

"Stop!" she roared, struggling to be heard over the satanic choir. She considered shooting into the ceiling, but did not wish to waste a bullet. Instead, she ran at the nearest nun and shoved her. The woman fell into the circle, and Ursula retreated several steps.

The choir died away. Sister Claudia turned towards her, and one-by-one the others followed.

She glanced at their faces. The rot made identification of most of her sisters difficult, but one thing was certain.

There were an awful lot of them.

Claudia smiled. "Sister Ursula... I believed you to be dead."

"Please, stop what you're doing," she said. She waved the gun back and forth. "You're *killing* her."

Out of the corner of her eye, she saw movement. Sister Augusta teetered towards her on viscid, withered legs. Ursula did not hesitate.

She aimed and fired.

The bullet pierced Augusta's throat with a soft pop. The woman stumbled, then dropped like a felled tree, smacking violently onto the floor. Dark blood pumped in steady waves from the dead woman's jugular, and as the shot resounded percussively throughout the catacombs, dust and dirt and small pebbles rained from the ceiling. Ursula stared at the downed body. She had killed for the second time. So why did she feel nothing? Why was she numb to the carnage?

Was sinning so easy after all?

"I mean it!" she shouted, turning the gun on the nuns. "I do not wish to harm anyone, but I'll... I'll kill you *all* if I must. You are no longer my sisters. None of you!"

She locked eyes with Claudia. Beside the mad nun sat the Mother Superior in her wheelchair. The woman looked like she had recently been dug up from the grave.

"Who are you to question God's design?" Claudia asked with a disappointed shake of her head.

"And who are *you* to take an innocent's life?"

Aware of the looming presence of the sisters closing in, Ursula took another step back. She glanced over her shoulder to ensure there was no one behind her.

"Innocent?" spat Claudia. "This fiend is the progeny of Satan himself! The devil's offspring, in the flesh. And you dare to *protect* her?"

"She's no more a devil than I am," said Ursula.

The nuns murmured in agreement. She had said the wrong thing.

"No, no, you misunderstand. I'm no devil. What I mean to say is, she's nothing but the daughter of a peasant. And even if she *were* a devil, it's not our place to judge. We worship God, Claudia. We are his servants, not his assassins."

"You can't kill a devil," said Claudia. "You can only send them back to hell."

A nun shifted restlessly nearby. Startled, Ursula spun and shot her. This time, her aim was off, and the bullet buried itself in the belly of old Sister Carmela.

"Stay back, all of you!" Spinning slowly, she walked towards the pyre. "I'll shoot anyone who comes near."

"You can't stop us all," said Claudia.

Ursula said nothing. She passed in a wide arc and looked up at Lucia. The tortured girl struggled to raise her head. Her legs, shorn of their skin, had given up, and she hung limply from the pole by her wrist bindings, which cut into her flesh.

Ursula turned to Claudia with tears in her eyes. "Why? Why did you do this?"

"Because of God." She gestured at the abbess. "Through her, he told me that the devil must perish to restore order to his house."

"God didn't speak to you! The Mother Superior is dead... can't you see that? It's all in your—"

"*I am the Mother Superior now!*" screamed Claudia. She cracked her whip against the floor as a punctuation mark. "That husk in the chair is but a vessel through which I commune!"

Ursula just stared at her. This was an argument she could not win. "You're insane," she said.

"Perhaps," said Claudia. "Perhaps we *all* are. But that changes nothing. "

She turned to her flock.

"Burn her," she screamed, and pointed a wizened finger at Lucia. "The heretic must not live!"

38

———

Ursula scrambled up the pyre, the firewood shifting beneath her feet.

Could she save her? Was there still a chance, however slim?

The nuns advanced, the circle drawing ever-tighter as she reached Lucia and stood before her. Up close, her young friend looked no healthier than the ancient skeletons in the ossuary. Claudia's cat o' nine tails had ripped the skin from her bones, the damage so severe that, through splintered ribs and torn muscle, Ursula saw Lucia's exposed heart beating with all the force of a butterfly's wing.

"You came back for me," Lucia rasped.

She stroked the girl's blood-flecked hair. "I promised I would."

At the sound of footsteps, she turned. A nun, her spoiled skin dripping from her face, approached with a flaming torch. Without thinking, Ursula aimed the pistol and fired. The woman fell, the torch rolling from her spasming hand.

"My memory is returning," said Lucia. "If I only had more time, I think—"

"There *is* no more time."

"No... more... time?"

Ursula pressed her forehead against Lucia's and placed the barrel of the gun against the girl's temple.

"No, my friend. We're all out of time. But I *can* make sure they don't hurt you anymore." Her finger wrapped around the trigger, and she wept. What else could she do but give the girl the dignified death she deserved? They had battled the devil, and the devil had won.

"I'm so sorry," said Ursula.

"Don't be," wheezed Lucia. "You tried your best."

Bracing herself, Ursula smiled through the tears.

"I love you," she said, and squeezed the trigger.

Click.

Nothing happened.

She tried again, pulling harder this time.

Another empty click.

Behind her, Claudia laughed.

Ursula stared uncomprehendingly at the pistol. Was it broken? Or had she run out of ammunition? She shook it, hit it, pulled the trigger over and over.

It would not work.

The weapon slipped through her petrified fingers and rattled down through the stacked firewood. She looked at the nuns, at their putrid faces and diseased, blighted bodies. One of the withered sisters lifted the fallen torch and swayed towards the pyre.

In a state of sheer dread, Ursula glanced around the dimly lit cavern, searching for a weapon. Some of the sisters carried knives. One held a scythe, and Sister Giulia skulked in the shadows with her woodchopping axe. The nun with the flaming torch was almost upon them. Out of ideas, she reached for Lucia's wrist bindings.

"Burn them!" shrieked Claudia. "Burn Satan's daughter and her infidel protector! Both must perish within the cleansing fire!"

The light grew brighter as the flame neared.

Lucia squinted at Claudia through half-closed eyes. "I think I *know* her," she whispered. "But she was younger. Much younger."

Ursula barely heard her. She worked the knot, but her fingers were tired and sore. Her entire body throbbed with fear and agony. Behind her, the nun stabbed the torch at the logs. The dry kindling caught fire, singeing the soles of Ursula's sandals.

"Stop!" she screamed, as grey tendrils of smoke rose around her. "Please stop!" She picked up a burning log and hurled it at Sister Claudia. The throw fell short, though Claudia took several precautionary steps back.

"Sister Giulia," she said. "Take care of Sister Ursula before she ruins everything."

Hefting her trusty axe onto her shoulder, Giulia strode towards the smouldering fire with an unseemly grin on her wasted face.

"That axe," said Lucia, her eyes widening. *"That axe."*

Ursula kicked blocks of sizzling wood at the woman, but more kept sparking beneath her. "Don't worry!" she said, as she resumed uselessly fumbling with the firm knot that bound Lucia to the stake. "I'll get us out of here!"

"No, I remember now." Lucia stared past Ursula, her breathing intensifying. She drew in lungfuls of air, her mutilated chest rising and falling, her exposed heart pumping wild jets of blood from her body. "I remember what they did with *that axe.*"

Ursula looked back. Giulia was right there by the fire, her weapon raised high as she prepared to swing.

"I remember it all," growled Lucia. Her body shook, eyes narrowing. Blood sprayed all around, dousing the flames in a macabre fountain. *"I remember everything!"*

A sickening thud sounded behind Ursula. She flinched, waiting for the pain of Giulia's axe cleaving into her body.

It never came.

Instead, the nuns started screaming, and only then did she turn.

Ursula's jaw dropped. "God help us," she breathed.

Sister Giulia held the axe with both hands, but the blade was embedded in her own face. The blow had bisected her head. The two sides slowly peeled apart like petals blooming in the summer sun, her skull cracking as it split and unleashed a flood of chunky black blood and smashed brain matter over the floor.

Ursula did not understand, but she couldn't waste this opportunity. As the nuns screamed and gasped, she returned her attention to Lucia's bindings. The knot sizzled in her hand, scalding her palm before bursting into flame.

"I remember," said Lucia in a placid voice utterly at odds with the havoc surrounding her.

"We have to leave," said Ursula. "We have to go, now!"

Lucia calmly lowered her arms. "I cannot leave. I am here for a purpose."

"What do you mean?" She tugged on her friend's arm. "We must—"

"I am where I need to be!" yelled Lucia. She gripped Ursula's face with both hands. *"You...* you showed me kindness. You treated me as a friend." She shook her head. "This is not for your eyes."

"I don't understand," said Ursula. The pyre was fully ablaze, the burning wood cloaking them in dark smoke.

"I remember what they did to me," Lucia smiled. "Let me show you. Through my eyes... and those of my father."

She brought their lips together, and a tingling sensation flooded Ursula's brain. Her vision blurred, and when she tried to open her mouth to scream, she found she had no mouth, as if she no longer existed other than as an incorporeal form floating through space as stars spun around her.

Was this heaven?

Was this hell?

A blinding flash of light, the crack of a whip, and then—

Crack!

She stands before an open door, conversing with a nun. The sun is high and bright, the nun young and beautiful, and it takes Ursula a moment to realise she is talking to the Mother Superior, and that the doorway is the entrance to Sant'Arcangel. She places her hand on the woman's shoulder, but it does not belong to her. It's the rugged hand of a working man, the nails untrimmed and filthy, the coat sleeve torn. The Mother Superior smiles, and—

Crack!

They're inside the convent. Ursula, or whoever's body she presently inhabits, watches as the abbess locks the door and sheepishly fondles the cross around her neck.

Crack!

A candlelit dinner. The soft glow accentuates the Mother Superior's coy glances and flirtatious smiles. In bed, coarse hands seek warmth and softness. Lips smack, and groping fingers brush forbidden places as the abbess cries out in pleasure, one hand clutching a crucifix that hangs from the headboard on rosary beads.

Ursula wants to look away. She has no desire to witness the abbess in the throes of passion, yet these are not her eyes she sees through. She's a passenger in someone's else's body, in someone else's mind, and with no way to avert her gaze, she can only watch helplessly as the woman struggles beneath her, gripping her long hair and pulling out clumps as the monstrous phallus — god, it's red, so very red — thrusts in and out while cloven hooves scratch at bare breasts and—

Crack!

A scream, and then darkness blacker than night itself.

Push, a woman shouts. Push!

A rush of light. The darkness splits as huge hands reach for her. She's upside down, crying, surrounded by nuns while the Mother Superior lies naked on the bed, her hair plastered to her sweating face, a wooden block clenched between her teeth.

It's an abomination, someone yells. An affront to God!

Crack!

Time breaks apart before Ursula's eyes. Days pass. Months, years, all in the blink of an eye. She's a child learning to walk, toddling towards the Reverend Mother with arms outstretched. The woman kicks her in the face.

Crack!

She awakens as a teenager, pounding on the locked doors of a closet with weak fists, sobbing and weeping and begging to be released.

She's been there for days.

Crack!

The old chapel in all its lustrous former glory. She's naked, and tries to cover herself as the Mother Superior parades her before the congregation, using her as an example in some twisted sermon about the sins of the flesh while an impossibly young Sister Claudia watches from the front row with the cat o' nine tails cradled in her lap.

Crack!

Bent over a pew on the Mother Superior's instruction, the sisters take turns with the whip, beating the evil out of her. Someone laughs. She begs for mercy.
They show her none.

Crack! Crack!

More screams. Her own this time, as she dresses in front of a mirror. She stares into the broken glass, and Lucia stares back at her, sobbing. Blood trickles down her reflection, and the door behind her opens to reveal the Mother Superior's stern, disapproving face.

Crack!

It's snowing outside as she walks the path from the convent. Cast out in nothing but a thin tunic, her bare feet turn blue in the snow. The apple, all they had allowed her to take, drops from her frozen hand. Ahead of her stands a man shrouded in shadow.

Whack!

The axe strikes her in the back. She screams and spins, her spurting blood staining the sparkling white snow. The effect is strangely beautiful. She collapses, and the abbess brings the axe down again. The blade thuds into her thigh, striking bone. She holds up her hands and, through splayed, bloody fingers, sees the axe roar down one final time.

And then—

Thud!

—the kiss ended.

Ursula staggered from the pyre, unable to comprehend the horrors she had witnessed. The beatings, the cruelty... Lucia's *murder* at the hands of the Mother Superior. Her *birth* mother? It was all too much. She tried to close her mind, but the sight of those hooves, red and hairy and pawing at the Mother Superior, would not leave her.

Lucia smiled. "Now you see. Now you understand."

Understand? She was even more confused! How long had passed? She had lived a whole lifetime during that kiss, yet the nuns had not moved an inch. It was as if time itself had stood still, but then... time had always held little meaning in Sant'Arcangel.

"Go," said Lucia. The flames blazed around her, charring the logs. "Leave now, or I shan't be responsible for my actions."

An invisible force struck Ursula, sending her stumbling backwards.

"*Kill them!*" shouted Claudia. "*Kill them both! The prophecy is coming true!*"

Lucia raised her raw, bloody arms in a Christ-like pose. The flames caressed her legs. She tilted her head back.

"*I bring sickness!*" she cried, and started to rise. "*I bring plague!*" The assembled nuns screamed, backing away in disbelief and utter, total horror. Only Claudia and Ursula remained still, for only they could believe their eyes.

Lucia was levitating.

She hovered above the fire, violent spurts of crimson blood gushing from her torn, devastated body. The cavern rumbled. Stones and debris crashed to the ground, the flames reaching the stake and burning it black. Lucia gazed out over the nuns of Sant'Arcangel. She stared at them, one-by-one, and smiled.

"To you, my dear sisters... *I bring death!*"

39

———

At Lucia's word, hell descended upon Sant'Arcangel.

A change in the atmosphere brought the screaming nuns to their knees, clutching their heads as the catacombs shook mightily. A huge rock dislodged itself from the ceiling and crashed down atop one poor sister, obliterating her in a pool of blood and shattered bone.

Another nun — Sister Virginia, Ursula thought — gripped her own ears, pulling and twisting them with all her might. The lobes tore, allowing Virginia to bunch the organs in her fists and wrench them from her head, leaving two gaping bloody holes. Ursula could not tell whether the woman was crying or laughing.

Turning away from the atrocious display, she stumbled towards the passageway.

Shrieking, weeping bodies blocked her path. There was Sister Beatrice, her naked body bursting with pus that seeped from cracks in her decomposing flesh. She dug her fingernails into her own neck, clawing at her throat and inserting her fingers. Beside her sat a cross-legged nun, who battered her own face with a sharp stone, clubbing at her skull until it shattered. Even then, she did not stop.

A hand grabbed Ursula's sleeve. She turned to find Sister Elisabeth, her eyes wet and pleading. Her jaw was missing, and her fuzzy tongue drooped down her chest. Ursula shook free and ran, dodging and leaping over the sisters of Sant'Arcangel, who writhed and screamed and tore themselves apart in a frantic bacchanal of self-annihilation.

The ground was awash with blood and entrails and ragged, torn limbs. As Ursula reached the flooded tunnel, she glanced back at the chaos. Two nuns were dragging Sister Claudia across the floor by her legs as she repeatedly struck herself with the cat o' nine tails. The sisters took a limb each and pulled in opposite directions. Somehow, over the screams and the wails and the tumultuous crash of rocks tumbling from the ceiling, Ursula heard the woman split. She tore open, her pelvis shattering as her legs reached impossible angles, her stomach disgorging an oozing swamp of fetid guts.

The carnage was absolute.

Ursula knew she should flee, but she couldn't help herself.

She had to see Lucia one last time.

"My god," she said as she turned back.

But Lucia was quite the opposite.

The young girl floated above the Mother Superior's wheelchair with arms open wide. The abbess raised her blood-caked face and gazed up at the seemingly angelic figure.

Lucia smiled down upon her.

"Mother," she said serenely. "I finally came home."

Suddenly the wheelchair moved of its own accord. It shot towards the burning pyre, the wooden wheels clattering off the stone. The Mother Superior opened her mouth in a silent scream, the wheelchair picking up speed until it rammed directly into the flames and erupted out the other side as a blazing inferno. The chair carried on until it hit the wall, then rebounded and rolled backwards through the mass of mangled, dismembered bodies.

"Gaze upon your flock!" laughed Lucia, her face melting into a grim parody of innocence as she watched her mother burn. *"Where's your god now?"*

That was as much as Ursula could stand. She splashed into the water, wading towards the stairs through hundreds of skulls dislodged by the tremors. The awful cries of her sisters faded, and a chill wind whipped through the tunnel. The route was straight, so Ursula shielded her head from the falling rocks and hurried onwards, death nipping at her heels like a ravenous predator.

She tripped on the first step, righted herself, and began her ascent, bundling the hem of her sodden tunic in her fist. Ahead, dim light shone through the passageway entrance. The rock shifted, the gap narrowing.

Ursula turned sideways and slipped through as the ceiling caved in behind her, sealing the tunnel. She stumbled over the burnt corpse and went sprawling. A thin crack in the stone opened beneath her hand. She felt the ground tremble, and got to her feet as the crack widened, shooting out to the walls. With a colossal groan, the floor split wide open.

The chapel was coming down, and with it, the entire convent.

A metal candelabra clanged onto the ground next to her. The fissure stretched, the stone grinding apart and swallowing the fixture whole. Ursula gazed down into the catacombs and knew the screams she heard would haunt her for the rest of her days. Above her, the ceiling fractured, a cloud of dust particles eddying through the air. She ran into the corridor, where statues toppled and smashed.

The floor was sinking.

She scrambled up a slope as an enormous crevice opened, thunderous flames leaping and spitting from the immense heat boiling beneath the convent.

A welcome blast of freezing air swept by. The entrance hall was close. She sped up, and was almost at the door when a bedraggled figure lumbered through the archway with arms outstretched, groping through the darkness.

Sister Maria.

Ursula was going too fast to stop. She clattered into the eyeless nun at full speed, their heads colliding, the pair crashing to the ground.

"Who's there?" asked Maria. Blood trickled from her empty eye sockets. "Is that you, little virgin?"

Dazed, Ursula rubbed her forehead. Through blurred vision, she saw two Marias crawling towards her.

"It is you!" snarled the nun. "I can smell your unspoilt cunt!"

Further down the hall, the ceiling collapsed, taking much of the east wing sleeping quarters with it. Ursula had only seconds to get out. She tried to stand, but the floor sagged beneath her. The entire building groaned, stones crumbling, wood cracking and splintering.

"I'll kill you for what you did!" slurred Maria. Her gruesome hands pawed at Ursula's tunic. "You took my eyes!"

Fire burst through a crack in the floor mere inches away. Ursula felt herself sliding towards it. She dug her fingers into the stone, halting her progress as Maria clambered on top of her. More flames erupted, close enough to reach out and touch, but Maria didn't seem to care.

"Give them to me!" she kept shouting. "Give me your eyes!"

Ursula's fingers could not sustain the weight of both women. Three nails snapped off, and she slid further towards the fissure. A chunk of stone gave way beneath her head, leaving it hanging over the vast, flaming chasm. The heat prickled her neck, and the stench of burning corpses filled the air.

"Your eyes!" cried Maria. "Give them to me!"

Ursula was losing her grip. Using both hands, she clung on in desperation, allowing Maria unimpeded access to her face as she grasped and clawed. Maria's withered fingers settled on Ursula's cheeks. The tips scraped her eyeballs.

"Your eyes," she smiled. "Give me—"

Two blackened, charred hands emerged from the chasm, clamping down on Maria's arm. The mad nun screamed as smoke rose from her bubbling flesh. A head appeared, and Ursula closed her eyes. She knew who it was, and she did not wish to see, up close, the demon that had once answered to the name of Lucia.

That had once, briefly, been her friend.

"Sister Maria," it snarled in a voice Ursula scarcely recognised as human. *"You belong to me now."*

A weight lifted, and Ursula opened her eyes to find Maria gone, the woman's scream reverberating off the chasm walls. She was still screaming as Ursula dragged herself up the slope and onto to her feet. Through the entrance hall she hurtled, leaping into the snow and heading for the stables.

Inside, the horse stepped from hoof to hoof, expelling steam through his nostrils. Ursula wrapped herself in the remaining blankets, then, using a hay bale as a step, clambered onto the horse. With a kick, the muscular beast galloped from the stables, and as they took off down the trail through the vegetable gardens, Ursula looked back at the convent.

Sant'Arcangel had stood for two-hundred-and-ninety-nine years... but it stood no more. Stone-by-stone it disintegrated, tall flames roaring through windows that shattered as the roof caved in and the building slumped wearily into the ravenous jaws of the mountain. The rear wall was the last to go, remaining upright a few seconds longer than the rest, before keeling backwards down the cliff face. By the time the wall hit the rocks at the bottom of the valley with a resounding crash that echoed for miles around, Ursula was already deep within the forest. The trees blurred by, and she wrapped her arms around the horse's neck and clung on.

Funny, though.

She could have sworn she heard the old chapel bell tolling in the wind...

one...

last...

time.

40

────

She couldn't tell.

At first, the trees provided shelter. They blocked the wind, and their broad canopies protected her from the unimaginable strength of the blizzard. At length, however, she ran out of trees, and once out of the sanctity of the forest, she and her horse were exposed to the worst of the elements.

She hugged the blankets around her torso and pressed herself to the steed for warmth, but the frigid chill took a heavy toll.

"Please," she shivered, rubbing the horse through the blankets as it slowed to a befuddled canter. "Just a little further."

Her pleas were fruitless. The canter became a lethargic trot, and by the time they arrived at the large boulder that designated the halfway point between Cerbesca and Sant'Arcangel, the horse was spent. He knelt slowly, dipped his head, and lay still.

Ursula was too tired and too cold to cry. She slid off the

dead animal. The snow was shallower here, but still reached her ankles. She swaddled herself in blankets, then began the long solo trek to Cerbesca.

The going was hard. Several times she fell and struggled to stand, but each time she managed.

It all felt like a dream.

Had she gone insane? Possibly. She had witnessed enough horror and bloodshed to last a dozen lifetimes, but that wasn't what bothered her. No, the thing that truly frightened her, and kept her walking onwards, away from Sant'Arcangel, was the ghastly vision she had seen through Lucia's eyes.

Through Lucia's *father's* eyes.

Her father.

That word was blasphemous, for he was no *man*. He was—

A vicious gust hit her, striking with such force that it knocked her off her feet. She landed on her backside and lost her grip on the blankets. The wind carried them across the open fields, and, unable to give chase, she sat there, watching her only protection from the cold sail high over the valley like exotic birds.

Her teeth chattered so violently it hurt. She rolled onto her front and forced herself up, trudging stiffly through the snow on numb feet.

Where was she? And why was she here?

Her brain wasn't functioning properly, and when her legs gave out, she slid to the ground and didn't even try to stand. Her strength, and her determination, were gone.

So there Ursula lay, the last survivor of Sant'Arcangel, weeping until the tears froze in her eyes and she could no longer blink. In the distance, she heard the cries of a coachman, and the stamp of hooves against the track. Weakly, she raised her head.

A faint light drew closer.

A lantern, swaying in the night, the snow flurrying around the beautiful golden beacon.

Ursula lifted one hand, cried out, and then closed her eyes.

This time, they stayed shut.

41

———

CRACK!

When Ursula awoke from her dreamless sleep, she found herself swathed in heavy blankets in the seat of a coach. Horses' hooves pounded the track as the wheels juddered over rocky terrain. To her right sat the coachman, clad in a long coat with a woollen scarf below his eyes and a hat pulled low to protect from the snow. When he snapped the reins, the sharp sound made her jump.

Crack!

"Rest now," he said. The scarf muffled his voice, but she recognised the brusque tones of Dr Franco. "We shall arrive in Cerbesca shortly."

She shivered in her manmade cocoon. Was this a dream? It didn't feel like one.

"Dead," she whispered.

"What's that?"

"My sisters are dead. Every one of them."

Dr Franco nodded. "I suspected as much. When I heard the toll of the bell all the way down in Cerbesca, I feared something was amiss." He placed a gloved hand on her shoulder. "I thought I'd better investigate, but when I came across you, near death... well, I had a strong inclination I would find no more survivors. Call it doctor's intuition."

"The Mother Superior... the devil..."

"Hush, child. We'll get some food in your belly soon, and a cosy bed to lie in. Cerbesca is just around this bend."

"But the *devil,*" she said urgently. "The devil's daughter..."

"Don't exert yourself. You're safe now." He cracked the reins once more and stared ahead. "Everything is going to be alright."

When next she opened her eyes, the coach had come to a stop outside a large building. The painted sign read *La Locanda Cerbesca,* and shadows roamed back and forth through the fire-lit, frosted windows. At last, she allowed herself to cry. Peering out over the quiet street, she vaguely recalled the thatched houses and serene glow of the gas lamps from her childhood. It was far from the candles and solitude of Sant'Arcangel, and the sight made her nervous.

"Come now, there'll be plenty of time for tears," said Dr Franco as he alighted from the coach. "Can you stand?"

She shook her head.

"Very well. Then I shall carry you." He lifted her fatigued body into his arms and brought her past the Locanda to a neighbouring building with a conical roof. "My home is next to the inn. It's noisy, but I sleep little and spend much time in my practice, so the sound of revelry rarely provokes me."

She nodded, too exhausted to speak.

The doctor unlocked his front door and carried her

through the hallway to a small bedroom. There, he trans-ferred her to the bed, and Ursula sank into a mattress softer than any she had ever known. She felt quite at home, for the only other furniture was a closet and a bedside cabinet, and it reminded her of her cell back in Sant'Arcangel. The biggest difference, she noted, was the addition of an opulent fireplace, above which hung an oil painting of a woman in her finery holding a squat dog with a black face and a curly tail. The dog's tongue lolled out of his mouth, and he wore a red bowtie.

"My mother," said Dr Franco, "and her faithful hound Boingo. They watch over me as I sleep." He chuckled through his scarf. "My goodness, it's chilly, isn't it? I'll get a fire going." Crouching by the hearth, he loaded coal from a brass scuttle and lit it with a match.

"Ursula," he said as he used a poker to stoke the flames. "I understand you may not wish to speak of such matters right now, but I must enquire about my dear friend Henrik. Is he...?"

"Dead," she mumbled. She tried to sit up. "I'm very sorry."

"Most regrettable. He was a fine fellow. Tonight, I shall toast his memory, and when the weather calms, I'll take the coach up the mountain to retrieve his—"

"No!" she cried.

He looked over his shoulder at her. "I can't very well leave him up there. The man deserves a proper burial."

"No one can ever go back there again. They carried a disease. A plague."

"Who did?"

"The *nuns.*" She sighed. It was too complicated to explain. "They killed Henrik... and then Lucia killed *them.*"

"Lucia? I'm not familiar with the name." She started to

answer, and he interrupted. "I say, would you care for some brandy?"

She nodded weakly.

He left the room and promptly returned with a half-full bottle and two glasses. "So tell me," he asked, as he decanted the liquid into the receptacles. "Who is this Lucia you speak of? One of your sisters?"

"No. The girl we found."

"Ah, I see. And you're telling me *she* murdered the nuns of Sant'Arcangel? That frail child?"

"Yes, but... oh, you'll never believe me." She closed her eyes. All she wanted was to sleep. "It's so fantastical, I question whether I believe it myself."

He helped her sit, fluffing the pillow for her to lean against, and handed her the brandy. "Here, drink up, then warm yourself by the fire."

She sipped, looked deep into the glass... and downed the rest.

"Tell me more about this Lucia," he said, taking the empty container from her. "How could such a fragile creature be responsible for the death of so many?"

Ursula considered what to say. If she told him the truth — or what she believed to be the truth — he might have her locked away in an asylum. She needed time to think, and decided to offer only the vaguest explanation for now. "At first, the girl remembered nothing of her life. I tended to her, and named her Lucia."

"You always did have a good heart, Sister Ursula."

"Please," she said, as he offered his arm and helped her out of bed. "Do not refer to me as Sister. After the things I've done, I am no more a nun than you are."

"A bold claim," said the doctor. She could tell he was smiling beneath his scarf. "But duly noted."

With his assistance, she hobbled to the fireplace and stood, basking in the heat.

"Conditions deteriorated shortly after you left," she continued. "Disease ravaged the convent, a sickness that destroyed the body and the mind. It turned the sisters into..." She struggled to find the words. "...into *degenerates*. They did terrible things to themselves, and to each other. For a long time, only myself, Henrik, Gertrude, and Lucia were unaffected. Then Gertrude shot herself, and... and..."

Franco stood behind her. "Go on."

But she did not wish to discuss it. Not yet. Not until she trusted herself to discern fantasy from reality. "I'm sorry," she said. "I feel a fit of the vapours coming on, and would very much like to lie down again."

"Of course. But first, pray tell, who *was* this Lucia? Did you ever ascertain her background?"

Ursula swallowed. Her legs were weak. "I... I know this sounds silly, but I believe she may have been—" she involuntarily crossed herself "—the Mother Superior's daughter."

Franco sighed. "Yes, I thought as much."

"You did?"

"Indeed. It was the placement of her wounds that jogged my memory. Three axe blows; one to the thigh, one to the stomach, and one to the back. I would have liked to have questioned her, but it was imperative I left that accursed place before the storm hit." He paused. "Literally *and* figuratively."

"I don't understand. How—"

"Your beloved Reverend Mother *murdered* that girl with an axe, and buried her corpse deep within the forest. She believed the child to be the offspring of an unholy union between herself and Satan, of all people."

Ursula thought of the cloven hoof in her vision, so red and inhuman. Her heart beat erratically. "Please, I must lie down."

Dr Franco placed his hands on her shoulders. "In a minute. First, you need to remove your clothes. Those wet garments will do your constitution no good at all."

"But—"

"I'm a doctor, Ursula. You won't be the first naked woman I've seen, nor will you be the last. Now strip, or risk exasperating your already subnormal temperature."

He was right, of course. And so, with Dr Franco's hands steadying her, Ursula removed her head covering. Her wet hair fell in front of her face. She reached for her cross, remembered she had stabbed it into Maria's eye-socket, then undid her cincture belt. Remaining respectfully behind her, the doctor helped lift her damp robes over her head, and with frozen fingers, she pulled down her under-skirt and long socks.

"May I have a nightgown?" she asked, hideously aware of her nakedness.

"Of course," said the doctor. "We need to keep you warm, after all. Bring back that rosy glow in those—" he smacked her bare bottom "—plump cheeks of yours."

"Dr Franco!" Why had he done that? Appalled at his behaviour, she half-turned to him, covering her breasts with one arm and her pubic region with the other. "The night-gown, if you please."

"All in good time, Ursula. Don't you wish for me to finish my tale?"

She saw the way he leered at her, and turned her back on him. "Actually, I... I think I should like to leave now."

"And go where?" he asked cheerily. "Outside, into the cold and the snow? You're safest here with me."

"Then fetch me something to wear, I beg of you." Humiliated, she bowed her head. "I'm not used to being seen... like *this*."

"Nuns," he chuckled, ignoring her request. "So delightfully chaste." The fire crackled, and he continued. "I was there, you understand, when the Mother Superior murdered her daughter. She wasn't called Lucia then. I can't actually recall her name."

His fingers played across her shoulders. It felt like a violation.

"I even helped the Reverend Mother bury the poor girl. At the time, I was new to the area, and did not know any better. When she told me she had made love to the devil, I'm not ashamed to tell you, I *laughed*." He ran his hands over her shoulder blades, then down, lower. He must have removed his gloves, for she felt his coarse skin rasp against her own. "But it seems she was telling the truth," he whispered in her ear. "Because the devil's daughter returned, didn't she, seeking vengeance on those she believes wronged her."

"Please," said Ursula. Tears flooded her eyes. "Furnish me with clothing and let me leave in peace. I'll tell no one about this. Not ever."

"But you have nowhere else to go," he said, giggling as his hand slid over the rounded flesh of her buttocks, his fingers—

"No!" she screamed, and wriggled free of his grasp. She ran for the door and backed into the hallway as his hands — those *rotting, shrivelled* hands — unwrapped his scarf, revealing his nightmarish face.

He looked her over. "You don't carry the mark. Why, if the progeny of Satan set out to destroy Sant'Arcangel and everyone in it, did she let you live?"

"I was kind to her," Ursula sobbed. She bumped into the front door, her fingers closing around the handle.

"Kindness!" he laughed. "How novel. And so disgustingly *you,* Sister Ursula." He came for her then, and she threw open the door and ran onto the street, his mocking laughter following as she staggered outside on aching legs. Stark naked, she glanced up and down the unfamiliar thoroughfare. Where to go?

Of course!

The inn. There were people there. People who could help her, and save her from the deranged clutches of the diseased Dr Franco. She heard his footsteps crunching through the snow.

"Go away!" She stumbled towards the inn. "Leave me be!"

Her feet slid on the ice, but she kept her balance through sheer terror. No longer caring about her state of undress, she reached the inn and barged through the doorway.

"Help me!" she cried. "Somebody..."

Her voice trailed off, and her miserable heart froze in her chest.

"My God," she said, for what she was looking at was a scene beyond even her most feverish, torrid night terrors. Her body trembled with fear and awe. "Dear God, it cannot be!"

In the centre of the room sat a head.

A huge, grotesque head, so enormous that its cranium broke through the ceiling. The mouth and nose and eyes squirmed in the flickering firelight. Part of the cheek slopped to the floor, and only then did Ursula realise the leering face of the devil was made up of dozens of nude bodies engaged in repulsive acts of carnal violence.

She felt sick, yet could not tear her gaze from the foul monstrosity.

The eye sockets had been created by humans bent at such severe angles that their spines had broken, while the nose was two women, their gaping posteriors forming the nostrils. The cheeks and forehead comprised interwoven men and women inserting their fists into each other's blood-smeared anuses, as they crawled over one another in a seething mass of rotting limbs, their flaking skin slick with rancid, bloody pus.

It was an unspeakable orgy of total bodily destruction.

The mouth opened, and a woman with spoiled appendages squirmed out like a ravenous tongue. She reached for the man who had fallen to the floor, grabbing and pulling him into the waiting, hungry mouth. Shrieking skinless skulls formed rows of teeth, and they bit down, bursting his belly.

The man screamed.

Everyone was screaming, it seemed, apart from Ursula, for she could find neither the voice nor the words to express her utter revulsion at the spectacle.

Beneath the head, bones splintered and cracked as writhing limbs thrashed like snakes, the immense weight of the sexual carnage crushing those poor souls who formed the jaw and neck. Broken arms and legs skewed lifelessly from under the throbbing, living organism, guts and skin and blood and pus intermingling into a soupy paste that flooded over Ursula's bare feet.

She took a dazed step backwards. The icy wind from the open door caressed her back.

The coach. Get to the coach and ride to—

A hand pressed down on her shoulder.

She turned to face Dr Franco. His shirt was unbuttoned, the fungal mould on his chest undulating with excitement.

"Where are you going, Sister?" he asked, and roughly shoved her forwards.

She skidded on the pus-soaked floor and fell awkwardly to her knees before the dreadful head. The mouth yawned open, the mangled lovers parting to allow the tongue to slither towards her. Decomposing hands grabbed her wrists, dragging her through the blood and the slime and the entrails. She kicked and fought and prayed for salvation, but more hands reached for her, pulling her by her hair and ankles. Foul digits invaded her mouth, and she bit down on them, releasing a flood of juices down her throat. She vomited as the damned creatures hauled her into the devil's maw amidst the swarm of diseased, copulating bodies.

Through the ungodly lips, she saw Dr Franco slam the front door and turn the key in the lock. And when the enormous jaws groaned closed, and the broken skulls slotted into place, sealing the mouth shut, Ursula finally found the strength to scream. By then, however, it was too late, for there was no one sane left in Cerbesca to hear her cries.

All that remained for kindly Sister Ursula was the darkness, the terror... and eternal, godforsaken suffering.

AFTERWORD

Thank you for reading The Suffering. I hope you enjoyed it, as much as one *can* enjoy such a relentlessly downbeat tale!

Ironically, it was a fun one to write, because I got to go to Italy for research and wander around 16th Century convents. The story was conceived as an homage to the Italian nunsploitation films of the 1970s, a short but productive cycle of movies with lurid titles such as *Diary of a Closeted Nun* and *Cristiana, Devil Nun*. I've gotta be honest with you, none of them are particularly amazing, but I adore the iconography, the clothing, and the architecture of nuns and convents, so I was determined to write the great nunsploitation story that never was. If you *are* looking for a genuinely good nun film, I'd recommend 1947's staggeringly beautiful *Black Narcissus* by Emeric Pressburger and Michael Powell, and the insanely blasphemous Ken Russell flagellation-fest *The Devils*.

Partway through writing, I realised I was also drawing a lot of inspiration from the classic Hammer Horror gothics. I never, ever write with real people in mind as my characters... except here, where Dr Franco is *very* clearly meant to be Sir Christopher Lee.

Anyway, if you enjoyed reading this one half as much as I enjoyed writing it, then I'd consider that a win. There's little I love more than being able to indulge my fondness of archaic language, and I tried my best to ensure every word in the book was era-appropriate. But at the end of the day, this is pulp horror, not historical literary fiction, so a few deviations from reality in this story about rotting sex-mad cannibal nuns doesn't bother me.

Thank you, as ever, to my lovely wife Heather, who got to enjoy some rare peace when I went off to Italy on my research trip.

Belly rubs for Boris the pug, who was no help at all during the writing of this story, but who does have a very funny face.

Thanks to Maciej for his amazing cover.

Cheers to Steve, Connor, and Elli for being cool. You are real ones.

And that's it. No more thanks for anyone.

Nah, I'm kiddin' on! Thanks to you, dear reader, for continuing to follow me and read my weird, twisted stories. There's a lot of fun stuff coming up, I promise you. Monsters, aliens, slashers, high fantasy, medieval folk horror, deadly conspiracies... stick around, and I'll try my best to make sure you don't regret it.

MUSIC

This book was written to the soundtracks of a bunch of 1960s Italian gothics. You can my find my complete writing playlist on Spotify, under "Italian Gothic Horror" if you want seven hours of spooky listening fun. And yes, it's designed to be listened to as is, not on shuffle, as I've organised all 139 tracks into a specific order. Otherwise, here are most of the albums I picked tracks from; I'll use their Italian titles where appropriate, as that's how they're listed on streaming platforms.

Aldo Piga — *5 Tombe Per Un Medium*

Aldo Piga — *Il Mostro Dell'opera*

Alessandro Alessandroni — *Lady Frankenstein*

Armando Trovajoli — *Lycanthropus*

Angelo Francesco Lavagnino, Carlo Savina — *Il Castello Dei Morti Vivi*

Carlo Innocenzi — *The Mill of the Stone Women*

Carlo Rustichelli — *I Lunghi Capelli Della Morte*

Carlo Savina — *La Cripta e L'incubo*

Ennio Morricone — *Nightmare Castle*

Les Baxter — *Baron Blood*
Les Baxter — *Black Sunday*
Piero Umiliani — *La Vendetta di Lady Morgan*
Riz Ortolani — *La Danza Macabra*
Riz Ortolani — *La Vergine di Norimberga*
Roberto Nicolosi — *La Maschera Del Demonio*
Roman Vlad — *The Horrible Dr Hitchcock*

ABOUT THE AUTHOR

David Sodergren lives in Scotland with his wife Heather.

Growing up, he was the kind of kid who collected rubber skeletons and lived for horror movies. Not much has changed since then.

His best known books include the gory and romantic fairy tale The Haar, the blood-drenched folk-horror Maggie's Grave, and the analog-horror fever dream Rotten Tommy.

instagram.com/paperbacksandpugs

9 781917 910095